WAIFS OF THE WASTELAND

WAIFS OF THE WASTELAND

by
Wayne Beauvais

Oak Tree Press   Taylorville, IL

Oak Tree Press

Oak Tree Press books may be purchased for educational, business or sales promotional purposes. Contact Publisher for quantity discounts.

Trade Paperback Edition, January 2012
Cover by Reese-Winsow Designs
Text Design by Linda Rigsbee

ISBN 978-1-61009-028-5
LCCN 2011936100

DEDICATION

For Maddy, I couldn't have done it without her eyes—

ACKNOWLEDGEMENT

I got lucky when this book found a home at Oak Tree Press. Sunny, Dawn, Jeana, and Billie, you ladies are the cat's meow, and you run a swank operation; and that ain't no baloney.

CHAPTER 1

"**G**uys like us can't fall in love. We cons ain't got the heart for it. That's scientific fact."

Big Larry Fornelli, a small-time bootlegger what ran afoul of the law when his twist sold him out to the coppers, talked like this pretty regular while we was cellmates in Joliet. Back then I didn't know no better and figured his words as true enough, not being much versed in science and other kinds of hoo-doo. Hell, I didn't think much of love myself, my experience being as bleak. Back then—this was in '19, it must have been—I didn't much get the world or its workings, knowing the country had just finished the Big One, remember? The war to end all wars? Ain't that a hoot, seeing as how the world took it on the kisser and keeps taking it all these years since? Seems to me, back then the world wore rose-tinted cheaters it didn't know it was wearing. But that's how things was. Ain't no science to it, just a cheap trick so the world could fool itself. Always figured the world could have used a jolt in Joliet, just so it could lose the cheaters and see things proper.

But this ain't Big Larry's story, and it ain't mine, neither; and it sure ain't no sorry rumination on the nasty cruelties a blind world commits in the name of justice and such. Nope, this story belongs to Joe Holder, my next cellmate, and the egg what could have crammed Big Larry's words right down his throat, he was that tough. I mean it. A genuine tough guy, a roughneck rougher than any other yahoo behind bars, a goon what could have digested glass and busted a fist through concrete. Course he wasn't so old as the rest of us, being in his early twenties; and maybe that explains it some, why he could hold on to love so tight, even when the rest of us long ago had become like Big Larry and bitter about its shortcomings. Which was curious, cause young as he was, he didn't wear no rose-tinted cheaters, and he was square on how things worked, but he had him that one peculiarity—he carried around love like it couldn't get snuffed; like it was a fire in his hands, a fire what couldn't burn him. But, in the end, it did; it blistered him bad. It scarred him. Which proves science and all its facts is a lot of hooey. Truth was, he was one of them oddballs you hear about, like the lost unicorn wandering the desert. Hell, Joe could have sung to that unicorn, for all I know about love and its deviances, the both of them there in that desert defying the laws of the heart. And that's the pity of it, that he couldn't stop loving, because in the end he had nobody to love, not even Rose Allen Frazier who the world called Symphony.

I first seen Symphony in person about ten years ago, around May of '25, at a premiere for a flicker called *CHILDREN OF THE STORM*. She was one of the stars in it.

It was one of them Hollywood nights where the searchlights stab the sky. I know you've seen them. Ain't we all seen those nights on the screen, right there in them fancy picture palaces we got in this country? Seems like there is more of them palaces than there is churches, or so I could swear from what I've seen—with us sitting in the dark of them and watching them kings and queens of Hollywood flicker across the screen like gods of light and shadow, and us sitting there with our mouths agape, breathing the same as everybody around us, breathing like in a chorus; and our eyes dancing from the wonder of it, the other world magic of it. And the funny thing is, after a minute or two, we forget it's just lights and shadows jumping on a white screen, and we come to take it for the Real McCoy. As if we're in the middle of its realness, and not gaping at a Movietone news short of a Hollywood premiere.

Anyway, on this night, the night I first seen Symphony for real, Joe and me pushed our way through the crowd. Don't nobody stand for long in Joe's way, and he cleared a path, even as some bitched and moaned till they seen who he was, till we claimed us a spot on the rope strung from the street to the steps leading into the theater. Damn, it was tight, that spot closer to the steps than the street, with bodies jabbing elbows and dancing on tiny feet, as if they was ready to climb atop us to get closer to the rope meant to hold us all back. But Joe, he wasn't none perturbed; he just give them all a look—a grand look it was, full of threat and righteousness—so they backed off, the lot of them, too cowed to face the tough guy Joe surely was.

Cept for this one slip of a girl—she being near to fifteen, or so I'd guess—she wasn't cowed none. From beneath her cloche hat, red bangs clamped to her forehead, with spit curls near her ears, was these raccoon eyes made up to be big and bruised with chalk or whatever you call that stuff women used to blacken their eyes like they did back then. Them eyes glistened as if she was about to step pure and certain into the arms of Jesus. Which explained why she wasn't cowed none, you see. And her lips was painted like a cherry version of Cupid's bow, or near about that small. She had a autograph book in her fist close to her breast. She looked to Joe and me and bounced some, saying to me, a stranger but that didn't seem no never mind to her, saying, "I know her. I know Symphony better 'n anybody."

Joe perked up, hearing this, for Symphony, though she didn't know it yet, had a rendezvous of sorts with us; and I could tell any word of her, even from this slip of a girl, would snag his notice. He said, "Where'd you get to know her?"

"Down in Anaheim. At the Arcadian."

"The Arcadian?" Joe looked at me, confused, so I told him she means a theater.

"I've seen every one of her pictures. That's how I know her. She's the bee's knees. My favorite was *A FORTUNATE LADY*. Did you see it?"

I shook my head. Joe didn't even do that. Neither of us went to the flickers except once about a month before, a couple days after he got of Joliet, but I'll tell you more about that later. He was probably as flummoxed as I was by this girl, by how she knew Symphony without ever meeting her.

"Yancey Dix was in that one, too," she went on. "He was this prince who was pretending to be a waiter so he can prove to his father he can work like a common person. He meets Symphony while working at this big party. You know the kind of party—with hooch and that kind of dancing?"

She shimmied her rounded shoulders and spun her hips and I knew the kind of dancing she meant—the kind what gives a man a stiff one.

"At first she thinks he's just a nobody, but then he woos her one night in New York—they go just everywhere—and she falls in love with him, even if he isn't rich like she wanted a man to be. Of course it all comes out swell in the end, because he's prince, isn't he? Everything she really wanted and more.

"Yikes, Yancey Dix is so dreamy. A regular sheik, if you ask me, and handsomer than Ronald Coleman or even Valentino."

By now I'd had enough of this girl, but I could see Joe hanging on every word, his eyes glittering as bright as her eyes. I figured he was looking for clues on what to say to Symphony. Hell, he'd been spending the past few weeks, ever since we was back in Missouri, practicing what he was going to say first. He worried over it plenty, asking my advice a dozen times a day, till I near tore out his tongue by the roots. But I never did that, cause those first words mattered too much and they had to be right. Funny though, couldn't neither of us find them words, not even now, with her close and getting closer.

The girl held up her autograph book, saying, "See, I already got Yancey Dix." She showed me and Joe a BEST WISHES scrawl with a Big Y followed by a flat line and a big D followed by a shorter flat line. "I got it down in San Diego a year ago, at the premiere for his pirate movie. And see right here—" she pointed to the bottom half the page— "That's where I'm going to have Symphony sign it. They got to be on the same page. They just got to."

"Why?" Joe asked.

" 'Cause they're a couple, silly. Everybody knows that. *SCREEN ROMANCE* says they'll be getting married after they finish their next movie together. It's a western called *WESTWARD, THE WAGONS*. Neither one of them has done a western before. I can hardly wait to see it."

I could tell what this girl was dishing had knocked Joe for a loop, but he shook it off like a tough guy. Give 'em nothing, that was his motto. Don't never let 'em see how they hurt you, he said often enough, but I could see it hurt, knowing him like I did.

The girl dropped her voice some, sharing a secret with us, "Don't believe what some people say. Don't believe Symphony is a gold digger. They're just jealous because Yancey made her a star."

"She's no gold digger," Joe growled.

"I know," the girl said. "It's so wrong for them to say that. I mean, I know Symphony, and I can tell you she is no gold digger. Not on your life."

Somebody hollered, "Here they come!" and the crowd flowed without moving, like it was the ocean heaving up a tide of people what shifted but stayed put, while a train of automobiles one after the other pulled up to the red carpet, where this swank gent in a red coat and white gloves opened the back doors of each sedan—most of them automobiles I never seen before, each of them sleek and gleaming and long and smooth to the eye; each of them reeking money, with a chauffeur perched in front. Once the door opened, out they came, the kings and queens we been waiting to see. Cameras started flashing. Coppers held up their arms warning us all we was as close as we was going to get. Now each of them kings and queens was smiling, which figured, seeing as how they got plenty of folding green with promise of more to come. Damn, they <u>do</u> have good teeth, I realized, these movie-star folk. Kind of made me wish mine was in better condition, regretting the broken one I got in the front so my smile ain't as pure-on delightful as theirs looked to be.

"Look!" the slip of the girl beside us yelped. "It's them! It's Yancey Dix and Symphony!"

The crowd roared and some was clapping, as first this Dix character stepped out and pulled his coat straight and adjusted a top hat; then he reached into the car and handed out Symphony, and the girl beside me near about shrieked, and she wasn't the only one.

Now right here I ain't going to get sappy like them magazines do when they talk of Symphony, but damn, she was a beauty. Course you know that already. You seen her plenty up there on screen, where they can't hide nothing, the camera being that merciless true. Even today, when the years is starting to wear on her, she's still a beauty. But on that night—she was next to holy, with that wraparound white coat she was wearing, it clinging careful to her hips and nowhere else; and her hair was shorter than now and in what they called finger waves with jewels woven into them. Course she had the same raccoon eyes the girl beside me did, but hers was more exotic somehow—which is to say they was more seductive. Fact was, every inch of her was seductive, as if she was the original woman, the one what God used to mold all other women.

I give Joe a gander, and his eyes danced with the glory of her, so I knew his heart must have been dancing, too. Not that it did him much good, nor any other sap giving her a hungry squint; for that Dix character had her secure in most any way a man can anchor a woman to him. It didn't take no genius to see that. Guys like him, as handsome and man-certain – hell, they got a magnet in them, you ask me, a magnet what draws a woman close. Joe had that magnet, too. He didn't know he had one, but he did, him being every bit as handsome and man-certain and tough to boot—a guy what could stand toe to toe with Dix, and that's just what happened before it was over, both of them drawing on Symphony with their magnets.

Speaking of which, Dix offered his arm and Symphony slipped hers along it, yielding to him, pulled in by that magnet. The horde shouted their names and the flashing cameras near split open my eyes, they was that many. Dix and Symphony glided then on glass wheels, it seemed, along the red carpet, both of them grinning and nodding. Those flashing lights didn't bother them none. Guess movie stars build up a resistance to them over time.

Now the slip of a girl beside me held out her autograph book over the rope, shouting, "Please, Symphony, Please!" so that Symphony veered toward her, reaching to take the book and the pen, when her eyes caught up in the dazzle of lights, finally saw Joe and she staggered a step, backing off, while Joe said nothing but grinned at her. Dix stumbled into her, and they both wobbled, but lords and ladies of the celluloid don't fall on their asses on red carpets—that ain't the way of things in Hollywood. Quick enough they gathered their dignity and glided along till their backs was to us.

Now Joe hollered her other name, "Rose Allen!" She hesitated, and he hollered it again.

Turning, she smiled at him and then she shrugged, her palms open before her, offering this simple question: What did you expect?

Dix checked out Joe and dared to hike a side of his lip a second before folding an arm over her shoulders and guiding her along, away from Joe and me, whispering something at her ear.

By God, Joe wasn't having this rendezvous ruined by any character like Dix; or by her shrug. He ducked under the rope, and that's a definite mistake not to be tolerated in this place called Hollywood. Or so Joe discovered real quick, when trouble landed square on his back.

CHAPTER 2

Trouble in this case was a bull of a copper who tackled Joe with two others right behind, the three of them pinning Joe to the carpet and thumping him a few good ones in the kidneys. Joe shouted out "Rose Allen!" a few more times—he still trying to see her from his new sight line at heel level—but since nobody knew what "Rose Allen!" meant, the words just hung out there. Symphony never turned to see him, disappearing, untouchable, with Dix into the gold of the theater.

Joe stopped his squirming when I nudged one of the coppers from over the ropes, interrupting another thump at Joe's spine, and said, "Don't hurt my pal, there. He ain't right in the head. You know, the War. You know how it is."

Now this copper, thank God, did know, and he took me at my lie—or, more likely, he didn't want the trouble—and he told the other two to stand Joe up. The three of them shoved Joe back under the rope, telling me to get him the hell out of there. Which is just what I done, Joe by then calm enough to know he better play my lie straight.

The slip of a girl shouted out, "Hey! What about my autograph?" but didn't nobody pay her any mind.

It took us some doing to get untangled from that knot of people, but we did, coming out a block away, at a parking lot place where the automobiles what carried the stars into the theater crowded together, one beside the other.

"Damn, I should have said something. Why couldn't I say something to her?"

I didn't have no answer for Joe, thinking he had plenty of time to find them first words, thinking maybe it was some his fault, what had just happened. To be honest, I didn't think this rendezvous business was such a good idea in the first place. That's back when we was in Chicago and fresh from Joliet. I told him so. And I told him again a couple days later when we got to St. Louis, Joe's old stomping grounds, and seen the moving picture I told you we seen. But don't nobody stand in Joe's way, like I said, specially when he gets a wild hair up his ass.

"She could have said something. She should have said something. Why didn't she? I mean, what was that shrug about? And who was that Dix guy? What's his hold on her? Pushing her along like he done. It isn't right, I'll tell you that. It sure isn't right."

I let Joe ramble on some more, figuring he was letting off steam, which is what he did— "It isn't right, what she done, acting like that. Christ! We come across the country to see her. She's got to know that. Am I right, Pooch?"

Pooch is my moniker and I prefer it to what the release papers from Joliet say, which is Luigi Puccinelli. That sounds foreign to me and like I'm a clown or a fat opera singer. I ain't no clown and I ain't no opera singer, and Joe can tell you that. I'm near as tough as him, even if I'm rail thin and barely break five feet while he towers over me at more than six. But that's enough of that.

In time we wandered into the parking lot where them chauffeurs had huddled up and was swapping a couple of flasks. Ciggies hung from their lips, the smoke leaking pearl grey over their heads. An older gent was fixing him a heater, poking a hole in its tip, before firing it up. It smelled of the earth it come from.

"C'mon," Joe said, and he walked up to them wheel jockeys like he belonged there. "Which one of you eggs is Rose Allen's driver?"

Them chauffeurs gave us the once over. I could tell they didn't know what to make of us. A burly one piped up, "Who's Rose Allen?"

"He means Symphony," I told them.

The gent with the cigar spoke up, "Who wants to know?"

"A couple of her friends," Joe said.

A couple wheel jockeys cackled it up, one of them saying, "This guy's got to be ossified."

"Or off his nut," said another.

The gent with the cigar said, "Aw, they ain't drunk nor crazy. They're just a couple of saps."

Now more of them cackled, until the burly one said, "Go chase yourself," to Joe and me.

Joe huffed up. He ain't so quick to rile, but I knew the cackling had got to him, so I took his arm. "C'mon, Joe, this ain't a good idea."

Joe jerked free of my grip.

"There's too many," I let Joe know, and I walked off, figuring he heard me, figuring he knew what I did, that these guys wasn't giving us spit. It took a few moments, but then I heard Joe's feet shuffling after me.

"Where you headed?" he asked me.

"To that diner over there. I need a cup of java."

Once we was seated at the counter, each of us sipping a cup of brew, me downing a sinker along with it, Joe says, "What now?"

"Hell, this was your call, the whole of it. You tell me."

Joe searched my face and seen I was serious, "All right. I guess it wasn't such a good idea, coming out here like we did."

"Aw, I don't blame you none. You had to see it how it was. Now you have. Maybe we ought to light out. Head for Frisco. I always wanted to see Frisco."

"I ain't going nowhere. I come to see Rose Allen, dammit. I gotta talk to her."

"She don't want to talk to you, Joe. It don't take no genius to see that."

"We'll see about that."

We slurped at our java for a bit. The cook fussed around his grill some, asking if we wanted something more. When we told him no, he fired up a radio and listened to a dame singing the blues.

"Pooch, I can't go to Frisco. You know that."

"She's not like us. Not no more."

"That can't be so, what you say."

"She's got money and red carpets and girls what want her autograph."

"That don't matter."

"It does. Believe me."

"We made promises to each other, me and Rose Allen. That matters more."

"It's been, what? Seven years since that promise? You been to prison and she become a moving-picture star. Seems like things have changed in that kind of time."

Joe worried on this some, till he shook his head like he was throwing off a jab to the jaw. I piped up, "And there's that Dix fella."

"Yeah, him."

I remembered how that Dix lifted the side of his lip when he seen Joe. Most might say it don't mean much, but I seen it did—and I know Joe seen that, too. "Could be, she's got feelings for him."

Joe's face crumpled like the coffee was bad. Grabbing my arm, he poured all his hurt and devotion into me, his face saying without words that Rose Allen was his, dammit, and he was ready to die fighting to prove it. Now I know I said he don't show hisself to others – his motto, remember? Don't show 'em how it hurts—but he did to me cause he trusted me. I would not never do him wrong. Hell, I was on his side in this matter. I really did want him to be with his Rose Allen again, even as I knew that probly could never happen. Anyway, I didn't let him see how he was hurting my arm, and he eased his grip some and said, "I just gotta see her, Pooch. I gotta talk to her."

And I said, not rubbing my arm though it needed it sore, "I know, I know—"

"She's got to see me—"

"Well," I told him, "Let's get some shuteye, and maybe tomorrow we'll figure how to make that happen."

Joe clapped me on the shoulder, and left a quarter on the counter before we bungled back out to where them Hollywood lights stabbed the sky. Looking up at them for a moment, I got sad and scared. I can't say why, but I did.

Course now I know why, after what happened in that summer of '25.

CHAPTER 3

Right here and now I'm going to talk some history about me and Joe. I got to do this so you can know the truth about us; I ain't going to pull no punches, neither, but say it for what it was without no apologies. Truth was, Joe was a thug and a hired goon, while me, I was various sorts of a thief, a dipster—which is what you folks call a pickpocket—being my primary talent.

I can hear you gasping, with me saying this, but after you get over the melodrama, you got to hear this, too: we was more complicated than ordinary felons, specially Joe, and that's the truth. Like I said, this ain't no apology, but I'm hoping you ease off on the indignation and hear me out on Joe's story, because he deserves at least that much. Hell, this whole thing, this book, it's his memorial, dammit, and the reading of it requires some deference, if only because Joe was the best man I have ever known, and the most genuine.

That said, here it goes—

Back in the winter of '19, I got me a five-year jolt for dipping the wrong woman's purse, she being the mother of an alderman from Chicago and feisty enough to fight back till I broke her arm and give her a right cross to the jaw. I didn't mean to break her arm, and I only threw the punch so as to get away, but fate jumped up and took the shape of a concerned citizen what tackled and sat on me till I was arrested.

Next thing I know, I landed in Joliet, after a judge called me a scourge to society and a blight on mankind. I didn't mind them words so much, being as how they had some truth, but I'm going to say now what I said then: I ain't no guy what beats on a dame, specially an old one, cept that once to get away, but the judge didn't have him no pity, so I wound up in Joliet sleeping in a cell above Big Larry for near about two years, till he got released. They was slow years, with me scratching the underside of miserable most days.

Funny thing was how lonely I got. There I was, smack dab in a prison full of galoots with nothing to do but play cards and dominos and talk about how the law done screwed them over, which got old fast; or they talked of sex, which only stirred me up, but I wasn't about to do what some of them guys did. I wasn't going to scratch my itch on the sly, if you catch my drift. I ain't no nancy boy; and before you think it, Joe wasn't, neither. We was both straight arrows. But it was a trial hearing all that talk of what a skirt can do for a guy, and I spent much of my time thinking on women, thinking on their breasts and how their backs slide into their butts and the softness of their skin, the smell of them, and of course thinking of their private part and how it feels like it does, till it drove me under a blanket with Mary Five Fingers, which believe me, ain't no kind of meaningful satisfaction.

That kind of disappointment wears a man down, so I avoided such talk mostly by staying to myself. Didn't nobody seem to care none and that was jake by me.

Now wait a minute, I hear you saying, what about Big Larry, my cellmate? Well, I'm telling you, I didn't much care for the man, seeing as how he rarely took the weekly showers we was supposed to have, and his teeth was rotten, and mostly he just lay in his bed, stewing in his own stink. The man disgusted me; the stink of him disgusted me; hell, even his rants about womankind and how they was designed to betray a man disgusted me. Now I don't got no opinions on what women was designed to be, even now I don't, but it was uncharitable, him speaking so downright mean and critical. I remember telling him one night to stop blaming the twist what got him pinched and look to his own sorry ass for what happened. She didn't make him a bootlegger, that's certain, and a piss poor one at that. And I told him about his stink, too, till he threw a punch and I grabbed his jewels and squeezed for what I was worth, which had him writhing soon enough on the floor and clutching himself where I squeezed the manhood from him. An hour later, after he had recovered from the shame of having a short stack like me do him in, he curled up and sulked in his bunk.

In the months what followed that pretty much was what he kept doing; he curled up in his bunk and sulked. We had us a truce, and that's how I liked it fine, even if he never did develop no virtue and wash himself more regular.

Then he was released and Joe got put in with me.

The first time I seen him, Joe scared me. And he scared plenty of other hardcases, too. It was night and we cons was being locked in like they do so we don't get up to any nasty shenanigans in the dark, and this bull led Joe into my cell. After he locked us up, Joe grabbed the bars and squeezed them and pulled at them, till I could see the cords of muscle in his neck and shoulders standing up. Then he commenced to shouting without no words, shouting like a caveman what wants to scare the world, shouting so the sound of it could break open those walls of steel and stone. Other cons shouted back, but none of them was as loud; nor did they have the stamina, with him shouting for a good two then three then four minutes without even taking in a breath, it seemed, and still he was shouting. The guy in the cell across from ours had white eyes and he hollered at me, "That guy's a fucking lunatic. Can't you shut him up?"

I wasn't about to do no such thing. I have a rule. I don't have no truck with cavemen and devils, specially ones which I am convinced are off their nut.

So, I got small in my bunk and waited and was scared like he wanted, till after another minute of shouting he turned and grinned suddenly, and asked, his voice ragged, asking sweet as you please, "What time they let us out in the morning?"

There you have it; that's how we met, and you can believe I didn't sleep much that night, hearing him in the bunk underneath, stirring and sighing every now and then.

After we got to know each other some, a few weeks later I asked him why he shouted like he done, telling him it scared me certain. He guffawed and said that was his plan; he meant to scare us, what with us being nefarious criminals and bad guys to boot. "A fella's got to protect himself, and I figured that was a good way of doing it. If they think you're crazy"—we was in the yard while this happened, and he waved an arm to include everybody wearing prison gray—"even characters like them, as evil as them, can't help but get scared. You better believe it. Ain't nobody bothered me since, have they?"

After chewing on it a bit, I realized Joe was a pretty sharp character, near as sharp as me, and that's saying something. Why, he could walk the yard and corridors, the showers, and didn't no bad guy stand up to him, at least from what I seen. Course it didn't hurt none, how he looked. You ever seen them statues what got made back in ancient times? You know the ones I mean, them statues where a man has got muscles stacked in his stomach and ranging along his arms and shoulders, the kinds of muscle which is ready and quick to move, so that this statue looks near to being a human cat, like a tiger or some such, the whole of it graceful and poised, if only it could move. That's how Joe looked without his shirt on, only he could move for real, the whole of him breathing and complete. Hell, it near took my breath away to see him like that the first time, and in the times since I got to thinking he was a man born out of his time.

And I ain't saying that just because of how he looked. I'm saying it, too, because there was something decent in him. Sure, he'd lost his way and done some wrongs. But, by God, he was the first to pony up and admit he done what he done and deserved his time in Joliet, which I found refreshing after what I heard from the other galoots in this joint. And that ain't all. I been looking in a dictionary to find a word what sums up what he was mostly, and I found this one: courtly. That word about does it. He was courtly and it come to him natural. He was born being courtly, which is curious, given the crimes he committed to get tossed into prison.

And what was they, these crimes? Well, he become a strong-arm man for a Irish gang boss out of Chicago. He was sent to convince local business yokels to buy his boss's protection or he collected money owed in gambling debts, that sort of thing. It bothered him, the violence of it, or so he said. It bothered him to smash up a guy's store as much as it bothered him to break a guy's nose. It felt as if he was shredding his soul, or so he said. Shredding it like it was yesterday's newspaper. But that didn't stop him none. He done it for more than a year before the coppers knuckled down and his Irish boss, feeling the heat, threw him to the wolves. By that, I mean Joe along with a couple other strong-arm thugs was lambs left out in the open, and the coppers didn't waste no time in penning them in. Joe, sounding relieved, said, "I tell you, Pooch, once I get out of here, I ain't never again gonna be a criminal. I just ain't cut out for it."

I believed him then and I believe him to this day. But that didn't make me any less curious, so I asked him, "Why'd you do them crimes, if they bothered you like they do?"

His face went gloomy still for a time till he said, "I did it for Rose Allen."

There you have it—he done his crimes for love. Do you see now why I call him courtly?

In the months to follow, late at night mostly, while the evil around us slept, him keeping her secret this way, he told me all about her.

She moved onto a farm down the road from his back when he was seventeen and she sixteen; this was about two years before he wound up in Joliet. Right from the get-go he was smitten—that was his word—and he took to wooing her. He wooed her for more than a year, till he finally risked it all and asked her to marry him. She said that was fine by her because she loved him more than anything, but—and this "but" turned sour on Joe's lips—she couldn't marry no farmer. She had to marry a man of substance, by which she meant a man with plenty of clams on ice. She wanted to live in big cities in grand hotels and go to picture shows any time of the night or day; she wanted to see the world and sleep on silk and put on the ritz for the rest of her days. And she wanted to be a moving-picture actress.

Now Joe only wanted to please his Rose Allen, even as he didn't know much about striking it rich. But that didn't stop him from trying. He give hisself a year to get rich and promised her he would, so that she promised him she would wait, her face shining with love for him.

You can figure the rest; I don't got to say more, cept this: a tough guy what is courtly is doomed.

Anyway, that's some of his history. I got more to tell, mostly about that moving picture we seen a day after Joe got out of prison, but I'll hold on to that for now, till you're ready for it. Least you know now why Joe ain't no ordinary thug. Far from it. I told you, it was complicated, him a being a tough guy what defied science by having a heart what could love.

CHAPTER 4

"**D**amn," I said when I roused the morning after the premiere. "I got a cramp in my neck. And in my back."

Standing outside the Ford in his underwear, the ocean air making pimples on his skin, Joe laughed. "You ain't that old," he said, slinging his pants at me. He laughed again and raised up his arms, stretching, then whooping and hollering, he ran across the sand and splashed into a wave. He ducked under, then come up spouting water what glittered in the new sun, before he shouted a big old shout to say how good it felt, and how cold. Above him a couple of sea birds squawked. "C'mon, Pooch," he yelled, and dived under again.

But I wasn't no kind of damn fool. I got a body what wakes up in stages and don't take to shocks and jolts in the morning, what with sleeping the night in my automobile—we come west in a '23 touring Ford which I owned free and clear. It wasn't much built for comfort. Wincing, groaning, I eased from the seat and strolled down to watch him sporting in the Pacific. I envied him right then. Hell, I wasn't but five years older, but Christ, I felt ancient, watching him splash around— a big kid, he was, and near about as joyful and unbeaten.

An hour or so later, we drove along some orchards and bean fields, then a stretch of Spanish homes with red tile roofs giving way to more bean fields. We was headed for Empire Studios, which is where that moving picture got made, the one I told you about; the one we saw in St Louis. If we was going to find Symphony, that seemed like a good place to start.

In the hills above was a sign saying Hollywood Land; I couldn't figure why anybody would put them letters up there. I asked Joe why, but he didn't know, neither. They looked to be fifty feet tall, those letters did, maybe more. Maybe they was put there for aero-planes, like a beacon or some such; or maybe it was for folks what can't see good enough to find their way, that's all I could figure. After another couple miles, the road veered like it didn't want to climb those hills and in another couple minutes, there it was—Empire Studios.

Not that I could see much. This white wall stopped a body from seeing. It stood ten feet and ran for near a quarter mile, certain, with trees spaced along. Wasn't till later I learned they was eucalyptus and pepper trees; though I could tell the pine right off. Buildings stood up behind them walls, with Spanish iron bars, the twisted kind, in the windows. From the looks of it, it could be a prison, for all anybody could tell from the road. Ain't that a hoot?

The gate seemed as discouraging as Joliet's, you ask me. Sure, it was spruced up with a fresh-poured macadam road and a big old sign saying EMPIRE STUDIOS in fancy letters painted on the arch what led into the studios. And sure, there was tiny red flowers and blossoms—later I heard they was called bougainvillea—growing up the walls and onto the arch, with some ivy tangled up there, too. But pretty as it looked, there was these big old gates smack in the middle of the arch. Black iron gates of twisted bars, the same as the windows above. I said it, wasn't nothing encouraging about them gates, nor about the guard shack planted outside near the street.

The guard came out and leaned into my window, eyeballing Joe and me "You here to see somebody?"

Joe piped up, "We're here to see Rose Allen Frazier."

"He means Symphony," I explained.

The guard eyeballed us some more. I could smell the Blackjack he was chewing. "You got names?"

"I'm a friend of hers," Joe said, "and this here is my chauffeur."

That took me back a step, but then I figured he elevated me to his chauffeur so he could appear rich. Course it was foolish of him, what with the Ford wearing the residue of every mile of them past few weeks from Missouri, but that was Joe for you. He was a quick one, even if details sometimes escaped him.

The guard chomped on his Blackjack some more. "You got a name?"

"Sure, it's Joe Holder. What's yours?"

"Buster Keaton," he said and laughed at some joke I didn't see as funny. He had a list clamped on a board but he didn't look to it, saying instead, "I don't see a Joe Holder here." Then he gave me a nasty grin: "Nor his chauffeur, neither."

Now Joe wasn't ready to give in quick, him saying, "I got your name,

Buster Keaton, and I'm gonna to report you."

The guard said, laughing while he did, "You go right ahead."

He waved his board to where he wanted me to go. "Pull into that turnaround there and scram."

Which is exactly what I did.

Joe said, "What is it with the law in this town? You can't get nowhere because of them."

It wasn't till a few days later, when we found who Buster Keaton really was, that Joe stopped being sore about it, and we had us a good laugh at how silly we could be.

Well, we drove down the length of that wall and turned right on this side street, where the wall shortened and a wooden fence took over, while across the road was a field of alfalfa. But on its corner, across from another studio gate, a walk-in gate only, was a restaurant made out of adobe.

"I could use me some ham and eggs, "Joe said, and I was with him on that, so I pulled onto the lip of the alfalfa field where other automobiles was lined up, and we went into the restaurant.

The joint was cram full of cowboys; I swear, there had to be three dozen of them, with their boots and spurs and their chaps flaring wide, each of them sporting various kinds of Stetsons and ten-gallon drums and even a couple sombreros. Some wore lassos on their hips and most was holstered and packing pistols. Some had handlebar moustaches or bushy soup strainers, and some was smoking or working at a wad of chaw. Damn, they was authentic, and smelled it, too. And they was loud and kind of anxious.

Right off, my ears perked up when I heard Mr. Yancey Dix, that name ringing out clear. Joe looked at me; he had heard the name, too. Then we heard it again from another group, and we heard Mr. Dix was going to start rolling the cameras in a week or so. Joe grinned, saying, "Looks like we found the right place."

Me and Joe elbowed our way to the counter and ordered scrambled eggs and ham, while one sociable cowpoke, an unlit ciggy drooping from his mouth sidled up and said, "Could you fellas spare me a plate of grub? I ain't et none since yesterday mornin'."

"Now, Louie, you leave them guys alone," said this older cowpoke beside me, one with a belly on him and feathered sideburns under his hat. He told us, "Louie is a mooch, so don't pay him no mind. He don't like to spend his own money. He calls it e-conomizing."

Louie grumbled some and flicked his ciggy on the floor, grinding it under his heel. He was disappointed, till Joe took his arm and pulled the mooching cowpoke into the seat beside his. He spoke across me and told the older cowpoke, "It's okay, me and Louie got some talking to do."

"Suit yourself," the older gent said and renewed his interest in a plate of hotcakes and syrup.

After Joe ordered up eggs and ham for us and Louie, he said, "So Mr. Dix is making him a western. Did I hear you right back there, by the door?"

Louie dipped his head to slurp at his java. "Yep."

"Do you know him, Yancey Dix?"

"I know of him. He's moving-picture star and a director. Big as Fairbanks or Chaplin, the three of them as big as they come."

"That right."

"I read in *VARIETY* he been working for a year to plan this western. It said he wants to make a masterpiece about the Wild West. He wants to show on screen how the West got settled, but it's got to be authentic. That's what he said in *VARIETY*. And he said he's got a great love story to go in his masterpiece, a love story like no one has ever seen before."

"How about that?" Joe said, encouraging the cowpoke to go on, but that's when the plates was slapped before us, and Louie chowed down for a while, which is what me and Joe done, too.

Once the edge was off my appetite, I asked, "Why you fellas here? What do you got to do with Mr. Dix's western masterpiece?"

Louie sucked some egg from a thumb and said, "I told you, he wants to be authentic. So he's put out a call for real cowboys, and that's what we are. Me, I done rode for the 101, which is a ranch over in Oklahoma. You ever heard of it?"

Me and Joe shook our heads.

"Well," Louie said, after chewing at some ham and swallowing, "It's a real ranch, biggest there ever was, and it specializes in Wild West shows and rodeos, that kind of thing. Figure that gives me a edge, sure enough, cause I rode with Colonel Brady's Wild West Extravaganza—the 101 sponsored him—a few years back. I was one of the bandits who robbed the stagecoach."

"Damn, that's something," Joe said.

"Yep. Anyhow, in just about a half hour we got to show up at that gate out there, across the street. A casting director is going to sort through us and see which of us Mr. Dix wants to use."

Joe give me a sly grin, before turning back to Louie. "Can anybody show up?"

"Probably, but you two ain't authentic."

"That's so."

"Still, it can't hurt none. Hell, you could tell 'em your authentic western duds got stole."

"That's a good idea," I told Louie.

The fat cowpoke with the feathered sideburns snorted and said, "Clothes don't make the cowboy. Why you two so interested in Mr. Dix's picture show?"

"We ain't," Joe said.

"We ain't actors," I added.

"But we gotta get in them studios to find my fiancée."

"Your fiancée?"

"I ain't seen her in a while, and she don't know I'm here, so I can't figure no other way to let her know I'm here, except to look for her in the studios."

Now Louie said, "Dang, ain't no man should be separated from his bride-to-be."

"You got that right," said the fat cowboy.

A half hour later, Joe and me, wearing borrowed hats and chaps, stood disguised in the middle of a herd of three dozen authentic cowboys. Not one of them cowpokes wasn't in on it and willing to help in the hiding. Come the call, we moved right along, easy as you please, through that walk-in gate.

That's how it went; that's how we got through the gate. At the time I was grateful to them cowboys, amused at how they could be so sentimental when it comes to love. Now I ain't so grateful. Fact is, now I think of them, and though I don't mean them no harm, I curse the whole sorry episode. I got to, knowing as I do how this story will end.

CHAPTER 5

A fter we got through the gate and returned our disguises, we thanked them cowboys and they wished us luck. Wasn't too long before I figured we needed it, seeing how them studios sprawled out, taking up more than a hundred acres, it could have been. Finding Symphony might take a miracle. But that didn't stop us. We strolled along, searching, each of us big-eyed. Wasn't nobody what opposed our being there or said anything, neither. Not that I thought they would. Hell, I learned a long time ago, if you act like you belong in a place, don't nobody think you don't.

One thing I noticed right off about Empire Studios, it looked like a factory. I mean, there was these rows of warehouses, which I found later had stages in them so the actors could be lit up like they needed to be without no sun; or there was rows of open-sided sheds full of wood and canvas and tools and hand carts and machines for woodworking and painting and welding. And in them sheds or around them, guys wearing bib overhauls worked those machines, or they hammered and sawed and created walls out of canvas, walls what wasn't real but propped up with 2X4's; walls what slid on wheels, some of them. Next we came on a guy painting a fountain what could belong somewhere in Europe. It was made from plywood and chicken wire and canvas, this fountain was, but damn, it looked remarkable, it was that real. Other guys was making chairs from balsa which meant anybody what used one would find his backside hitting pavement pretty damn quick. I asked Joe about it, but he just shrugged, saying he figured them chairs wasn't chairs but built for their looks only. I mulled on it a bit before seeing his point: moving pictures ain't dependable; they only pretend to be.

After a while more, us turning a corner, a warehouse door beside us opened and out spilled a horde of beautiful dames dressed up like flappers. Giggling and buzzing with girl talk, they surrounded us. Damn, they were a pleasant distraction, even if none of them was Symphony. Naturally, as they moved on, I headed after them, till Joe grabbed my shirt and pulled me back. He didn't say nothing, but I could tell; he didn't approve of my womanizing just then, what with Symphony still to be found.

In time, the morning heating up and promising more heat to come, we walked into a Mexican square with its buildings being genuine adobe. Timbers still wearing axe marks jutted out their fronts and red tiles lapped over themselves on the roofs. They was two stories high, those buildings, with adobe walls running between them and actual stones paving the courtyard under our feet. The whole of it looked like it was from two hundred years before, when California belonged to them Mexican caballeros. Only, one thing wasn't true of that time, this being lines of rope running over the square.

These lines—they was seven of them—was tied to poles what stuck up from the roofs. Them poles was different heights, and they was round, like skinny telephone poles, only they didn't have but one line strung between them, that line running forty feet or so across the courtyard from one pole to a pole on the opposite roof. Five feet or so must have separated each line. Some of them lines was higher than the next one, and some just further along the roof, like telephone wires what weren't stuck on the same crosspiece, seeing as how these poles didn't have no crosspieces to them. And they was higher than telephone wires, them ropes was, though they didn't seem as heavy, nor as secure.

A guy was up there, too, twenty feet high, walking along one of them ropes, using one above to keep his balance. He could have been an acrobat, him being so nimble and easy at it, only he wasn't wearing no tights but a white shirt with sleeves rolled past his elbows and some dungarees. And he was barefoot, which got me to wonder why his feet didn't hurt, him walking like he done on that rope.

He seen us watching him and hollered out, "You guys going to the meeting tonight?"

"What meeting?" Joe asked.

"For the union. That meeting."

"We ain't no union men," I hollered up.

"I know that," the guy on his rope said. "That's why there's a meeting, so new fellas like you can find out for yourself what a union's for."

With that, he grabbed a rope and pulled himself along hand over hand—a monkey couldn't do it better— to a balcony, where he climbed over the ledge. "Here!" he hollered, and reached down, coming up a moment later and threw some paper at us which sailed down like a bird what couldn't fly no more. Joe caught hold of it, and he smoothed the pages, it becoming a pamphlet what said on the front, in big letters: *WORKERS OF THE WORLD, UNITE.*

"Didn't Guffey send you?" the guy hollered.

"Who's Guffey?" I asked.

"He said he was going to send me a couple guys so we could test this set-up rig."

Now Joe perked up at that, his eyes dancing over them ropes. "What's it for, this set-up rig?"

"That new Zorro serial."

"No kidding."

"We're gonna put laundry on 'em when they're ready. Gonna put some baskets by the poles, you know, make it look like clothes lines. Down there where you are is a hacienda, and up here is where they dry their laundry."

"How do you know that's what folks did in Zorro's time? Hung their laundry over a courtyard like this?" I hollered at him.

"It don't matter none, what they did. These lines are here for Zorro, so he's got something to swing from and be dashing like he's supposed to be."

"But how's it work?" Joe hollered.

With that, the union guy jumped onto a rope and swung from that till he was swinging in loops, a human pinwheel. Sudden-like, he let go and flew out, climbing in the air, and he snagged him a higher rope, and damn, if he didn't spin till he was near standing on his hands on that rope, balancing hisself on it for a moment before gravity pulled him down and he let go and grabbed him another rope, then flipped hisself so he was hanging from it by his knees and looking at us from upside down. That's when I seen he was ugly as they come, which was funny, because the rest of him wasn't, but his face sure was. He grinned and there was gaps in his teeth and ridges on the sides of his mouth which only made him uglier.

Now my momma didn't born no fool what grabbed the short end of luck like this fool was doing, swaying there twenty feet over us with no harness nor net neither. Could happen; one of them lines could snap and he'd be one sorry pile of broken bones at my feet.

"Ain't you scared of falling?" I hollered up, thinking he needed some wise advice to help him see the error of his dangerous antics up there.

"That ain't gonna happen, guaranteed. It ain't part of my plan."

I didn't know much about plans, but I figured they don't mean much if your brains is leaking on a Spanish courtyard.

"C'mon up," he said.

And, dammit, that's what Joe did. It seemed he was as much of a fool about danger as was the union guy hanging over us. He run over to some stairs and run up them and jumped on a rope; hand after hand he pulled himself along till he was hanging over the middle of the square, like the union guy was, only on a different, lower line. I near about choked on what he did next, cause he threw out his legs and got to swinging, faster and faster, till I could hear the sound of him swinging, till he flung himself up and caught the rope the union guy was hanging from, him hanging beside the upside-down union guy.

Seeing that near scared the bejesus out of me.

Then the two commenced to do acrobatics like they was testing themselves and not the ropes. First the union guy did a flip and a twist, snagging a rope with only one hand; and Joe did the same move. After that, he stood up on one rope, and I swear this happened; he did a back flip, falling past the rope and grabbing the one under it, using that one to swing out wide and float till he stood on a third rope, wobbling there, but nimble certain he wasn't close to falling. And wouldn't you know it, the union guy copied the same moves. Them ropes creaked and twanged, but didn't none of that bother Joe nor the union guy, each of them so busy trying to do a trick the other couldn't.

Now me, I don't need to prove myself none, so I shook my head. Sometimes there ain't no accounting for human behavior, why a guy has got to show off when it don't matter none. It ain't logical. But that's how it was. I'm just glad I ain't prone to such dangerous tomfoolery.

About this time I realized there was a man standing near me, watching the two of them twirling up there with no net, a man what looked near as scared as I felt. "Albert," he hollered up at the union guy, "don't break your damn neck, horsing around like you are."

"No sir, Mr. Guffey, I wouldn't think of it," sitting now on a rope, with Joe sitting beside him.

"Who's that up there with you?"

"Joe Holder," Joe shouted down.

"Ain't these the guys you hired to help me out?" Albert wanted to know.

"I haven't done that yet. It takes time to find good riggers and stunt men. You know that."

"Well," Albert said, "I think we found 'em right here and right now."

Guffey frowned at me. "This little one doesn't look up to it."

"I can handle it," I told him, real quiet.

"I don't know; it can get dangerous, our kind of work. You don't have the size for it."

This Guffey character had scraped on a failing of mine, that being I get riled when somebody talks bad about my lack of verticality, and right then I forgot I wasn't no damn fool what flirts with danger. I run up the stairs Joe did and jumped onto a rope and I did what Joe and Albert done; I spun and flew and flung myself into the sky, showing I was every bit as acrobatic as they was.

Joe laughed and so did Albert.

"All right! All right!" This from Guffey.

I stopped twirling. Like I told you—I ain't prone to tomfoolery cept when necessary or when riled—which I wasn't no more. Now I was just a sorry sap on a line twenty feet high with no net under me.

"What's your name, short stuff?" he hollered next.

I told him, and I told him I wasn't so short but I could knock the block off them what say I am.

Guffey blinked at that before he said, "Seems like I have found two new riggers and stunt men."

"You mean," Joe said, "we got jobs?"

"Exactly so. Albert, you take them over to the hiring office and get them signed up. But don't you bother them with that union bullshit, you hear? There won't ever be a union at Empire, and if you keep talking about it, you'll be out on your ass. I don't want to lose a good man. You hear that?"

Albert's face, the ugly of it crumpled up, but he answered, "The union ain't so bad."

"I'm serious, Albert."

Albert didn't say more, but I could see he wasn't happy. Guffey picked up the pamphlet Joe had dropped when he run up the stairs. "And don't let me see any more of these," he hollered, sounding even more stern.

Then he hollered, "I'll see you two tomorrow at eight along with Albert. We have plenty to do before they can start shooting Zorro next Monday."

After we was signed up—me skeptical that this was good idea, us working like this—an office girl gave us employment cards to get by the guards. Once we was outside the office and coming down the steps, Joe kissed his card. Albert asked him why he done that. Joe took a breath and told Albert about the premiere the night before, and about why we came to Empire Studios. Albert laughed hearing this, amazed that Symphony and Joe's Rose Allen was one and the same. Then he said, "If you guys are serious, I know exactly where she is. C'mon, I'll show you."

Joe looked to me, grinning: "Our luck has turned, Pooch; it surely has."

Me, I wasn't so pleased because I have learned in my doings luck is a fickle bitch. What it gives today, it takes the next. But I didn't say so, knowing Joe didn't appreciate my somber side all that much.

CHAPTER 6

Right here let me say this: back then, I never had no regular job. I'd been various sorts of a thief, like I done told you; and that's all I had ever been. This was why I tugged on Joe's shirt while Albert was leading us to see Symphony and let him know in a whisper my worry on this matter. He laughed and said, "Pooch, sometimes you kill me."

I wasn't none satisfied, but I didn't have but forty clams and some change in my pocket. Either we worked or I'd have to resume my thieving ways, but since I didn't know California so much as that, I swallowed my doubts.

Course Joe didn't know our finances was in such a sorry condition. Ever since I picked him up from Joliet—him being released three weeks after me—I done lied to him by saying my pockets was full of legit jack, this being an inheritance I collected while I been waiting on him. Joe took me at my word, him being the decent sort he is. It didn't bother me none, lying to Joe. You see, I just didn't want to disappoint him none. He'd become my friend, the only one I ever had. One night a week before I got out, he made me promise not to return to my thieving ways. Since it mattered to him, I promised. But I never meant to keep it.

So once I got out, I burgled several hotels and did some dipping at the race track, making enough to buy a Ford touring automobile and plenty more besides. That's right; I bought my Ford. One thing I never steal is automobiles, unless I mean to sell them quick, cause sooner or later john law will identify that automobile for being stole; and I ain't such a good driver I can outrun that kind of trouble steaming down the road after me.

Ten minutes later we stood on a western street. You've seen the street if you ever watched the oaters they made back then. It's still used, that street. I recognized it last week in a Hoot Gibson feature. On film it do look authentic, but that's cause the fronts of the buildings are genuine lumber and glass. You look behind, which them cameras never do, and you see ranks of 4X8s propping up each of them fronts. But what we seen was saloons and a general store and a barber shop what had a wooden Indian out front and a sheriff's office and other such places, looking open and ready for business. Only, there wasn't no people to do business—not a one—cept down at the other end of the street where a livery stable towered up. Henry's Livery Stable read a sign over the door—and under that sign, wearing a short-brim fedora, was Mr. Yancey Dix.

He was holding a pistol and saying something. Around him was ten or twelve gents, and they was holding tablets and pens. They writ down some of Dix's words, cept for this one tall woman what had no tablet but crossed her arms at what was said and nodded. She had on a leather dress with a vest to match, and she wore one of them cowboy hats with a brim rolled up in front and pinned to the crown, with gray hair hanging down from under it, which is how I knew she was old. The rest of her didn't seem old at all but sturdy and like she could outrun a horse. But what caught my eye and seemed peculiar was this holster slung on her hips, a holster weighing heavy with a pistol on either side. I asked Albert who she was.

"Minerva Masterson," he said. "Back in the day she was a trick rider and a shootist with Buffalo Bill Cody's Wild West Show. She was billed as Sure-Shot Minnie. You ever heard of her?"

I had—her and Annie Oakley—I heard of them both.

"Ain't she the one," Joe said, "who was one of Bat Masterson's lady friends? She asked him to marry up, but when he said no she took his last name anyway?"

"That's what they say. Don't know if it's true."

I didn't neither, but I was fair impressed by Joe's grasp of western folk lore.

"Mr. Dix hired her," Albert went on, "to consult on the western he's making. Plus, she's going to do some stunt work for Symphony. He's introducing her to the press, it looks to me."

"C'mon," Joe said, and we angled down the street. Them fellas what Albert called the press laughed at something Dix told them, and pretty soon we was close enough I could hear what he said next, him with a voice loud enough to rouse the angels: "Minerva, my dear, I do believe the time has come for you and me to square off."

He put his fists on his hips and I could swear, even if there was no camera, he was posing for one.

Minerva said, "I'm afraid my dueling days are over, Yancey."

The press chuckled and so did Dix, before he said, "Gentlemen, I've arranged a little shooting contest. If you'll allow me…"

He held his pistol to his shoulder and drew a line in the dirt with his foot, then his free hand invited Minerva to stand to the line beside him. Minerva held back to look at Joe and me and Albert before she toed up to the line.

"Gentlemen, if you will spread yourselves," and them fellas arranged themselves to the side so they could see these bales of hay what was piled up against a hitching rail. On them bales was twenty or so green and brown bottles.

Dix took out a kerchief and held it up, though why he done this made no sense, even as he waggled it some. Maybe he was testing for wind currents, for all I could tell.

Just then I heard horses galloping, and we turned to see two of them and their riders galloping down the street, dust trailing after them. On the one closest to us sat a chubby guy in a bowler with a monkey on his shoulder, a monkey what glared at us as the horse barreled by. The sight of a monkey took up my time so I never did see the other rider before he was past but I seen the white of his shirt. Once them horses got near Dix and Minerva, they slowed up sudden-like and commenced to dancing while the riders leaned back and pulled the reins tight to their chests. Right quick, them fellas of the press backed off to give those horses room, damn near falling over themselves, they was that fretful about hoofs flying near their heads. It got me to laughing, how they was scrambling around.

After them horses settled down the press laughed, too, though it sounded nervous to me. Dix said in his loud voice, "Ah, Symphony, my sweet, you have arrived on time."

With that, one of the rider's horses acted up and spun about so we could see the rider was no man but Symphony in a man's shirt and wearing those funny pants what puff out above the knee, with her hair piled up under a man's hat. She reined in that horse right quick, till it was standing obedient to this woman what was the master of him. While this happened, Joe trotted closer.

I trotted after him and pulled him to a stop, saying, whispering it mostly, "Think, Joe, not like this, dammit. Wait and see what happens first."

Joe eased off and nodded, but from our changing spots, we could see Rose Allen pretty good now, least the profile of her. Course she didn't see Joe nor me, or so I figured, what with her risen above us all and glorious in the sun, which glowed on her, and it shined in the threads of hair what had escaped her hat; and—I swear this is true—the dust what was stirred up, not a fleck of it touched her. It didn't dare touch her. She was blessed, you see, and not to be touched by dirt of any sort.

The guy on the other horse was not blessed, though, but sputtering and coughing. He took off his bowler and used it to slap at his coat, while on his shoulder the monkey shrieked and opened its mouth, gagging; and I recognized a trace of Albert in how he done it. Dix said to the press, "And of course you gentlemen know Rooney June, a key player in WESTWARD, THE WAGONS."

I couldn't tell which was Rooney June, even as the chubby man fussed with the monkey, which wasn't slowing its gyrations none. Dix snapped, "Koko, calm down. Now!" Koko had to be the monkey. It wore a little vest and cowboy hat. He chattered some, like monkeys do, but he calmed right down at the crack of Dix's "Now!"

Dix put an arm to Minerva's shoulder and nodded. "And now, gentlemen," he told the press before he took aim and fired off a shot. Glass broke and he took careful aim again, firing off another. It wasn't no wonder he hit all six bottles, what with how slow he took to aim, but still, I got to credit him: it was some good shooting. After the last one, he stood there, the gun smoking and straight before him, not moving an inch, so I figured it were a pose for that camera that wasn't there, a pose of him being heroic.

Could be the press thought so, for they applauded and so did Albert. Rooney June started to clap but he couldn't cause Koko grabbed ahold of his head and started clawing at it, shrieking while he done so. Rooney June yowled before plucking that monkey free.

Dix let go his pose and snapped again at Koko, and the critter settled down.

"My dear," Dix said, but before he could say more, Minerva Masterson pulled her pistols from her holsters and fired away. Them bottles didn't have a chance. Glass sang like it does when smashed to bits, some of those bits flying into the sun before dropping back to earth. The last one had a cap on it, and when it got hit, she shot the cap so it spun up, and she shot it again so it jumped even higher. How she done that was a wonder to behold. It didn't take more than four or five seconds, the whole damn onslaught.

She holstered them pistols and just stood there without posing, smoke drifting over her head.

Didn't nobody clap. Maybe they was too afraid to clap; leastways I was.

But Koko wasn't so awed as us human folk, for after a moment to take it in, he yowled and jumped from Rooney June to Symphony, and dug his fingers into her breasts. Her horse reared, but she yanked back on the reins and grabbed Koko by the neck—don't know a woman what wants to be pawed, even by a monkey—and flung him away.

"Koko!" Dix snapped, but this time after rolling along in the dust, the monkey went sudden deaf. He popped up and ran straight to Joe and Albert and me.

"Koko!" Dix hollered again and charged after the monkey, the press fellas scattering from his way, some of them already writing down what was happening, others of them trotting wide to get a good view of what could happen.

Koko ran right up to Joe and jumped in his arms. Why he done that, I didn't know then, not being much familiar with monkey habits, but later I figured it out. You see, the monkey done mistook Joe for Yancey Dix, they looked that similar.

Once safe in Joe's arms, the monkey threw an arm around his neck and just sat there looking up at Joe.

Joe patted its back and stepped out, carrying the monkey toward Symphony. She nudged her horse along till it was standing over Joe; he stopped to stare up at her. "Hello, Rose Allen," he said, real pleasant.

She glared down into him for a long moment. There wasn't no softness in her face, and her eyes was hard on him, hard and bleak. She shook her head once, denying him; and kicking her horse, she slapped the reins and the horse lunged off, heading back down the street from where it had come.

By now Dix had reached Joe and took the monkey from him. Stepping back, he sized up Joe, while Joe sized him back. Didn't neither of them seem ready to give an inch. I wondered what Dix was thinking. Did he recognize Joe from the premiere? Did he wonder why Symphony rode off angry like she done after seeing Joe? Or maybe he was thinking about shooting Joe with that pistol he was still carrying. Joe thought that's what Dix meant to do; he told me so later.

Anyway, Dix broke off the staring by offering his empty hand. Joe shook it solid, the two of them shaking man-steady hands, before Dix turned his back on Joe and returned, carrying Koko, to the press.

"Pooch," Joe said, "I think I got a rival for Rose Allen's affection; I surely do."

I didn't argue that none. I don't never argue the truth.

CHAPTER 7

A lbert told us how to get to Sunset Haven, but when we pulled off the Coast Highway and seen it, I couldn't account for its moniker. I mean, it was only four worn-out bungalows facing four other worn-out bungalows across the gravel we was driving on, our wheels popping. I couldn't account for how it was a haven.

Albert had him one of the two bungalows closest to the bluff. Earlier, back at the studios, Albert said he had an ocean view, and all for twenty-five bucks a month. That sounded good to Joe. Since Missouri, he been talking of the ocean like it were a wonder not be missed. Had to see him a whale, he kept saying; or who knows, maybe if we got a boat and go out far enough, we could see us a mermaid. Wouldn't that be something? Not wanting to disappoint him none, I didn't let on the only mermaids in this life was in books. Hell, it was cause he had this crazy idea we could maybe hear them singing in the dark that we slept in the Ford on the beach the night before. Even if we didn't, he fair glowed at the idea of being lulled to sleep by the sound of waves rolling all this way from Japan. But the bungalow we come to rent didn't have no ocean to see. It just had a strip of dead weeds and grass and the highway, which weren't that far off, ten yards or so. Trucks rumbled along pretty regular and I wondered at dead of night if they would still be rumbling.

Anyway, me and Joe give the bungalow the once over. It wasn't much, being a furnished two-room dump with a half kitchen, but we could afford it. Besides, Joe liked the idea of waking in the morning to the smell of the ocean and the sound of them waves down that bluff. Me, I don't go so much for sand and grit, but I did admit the air felt good, after that long hot day at Empire studios, though them trucks sure rubbed on a guy, lest he got used to them somehow. Maybe we could buy us a radio to drown them out.

The dame what rented it to us was a skinny ghost, the whole of her a tangle of shivers. Her fingers pulled at the handkerchief in her hands. Mrs. Benecke, she called herself. Mrs. Edward Benecke. She said that name two more times, like she were desperate to keep it alive. She said it in a damp little desperate whisper of a voice. And she said she was a widow. That word was what made her a ghost.

Didn't neither Joe nor me know what to say about that, so we give her some cabbage and took the key and left her standing there.

A hour or so later, after I got back from a grocery down the road, I didn't find Joe in our bungalow, finding him instead near Albert's bungalow, sitting on the landing of these stairs what run from the bluff down to the beach. His legs was dangling from the edge of that landing and he were staring into a sun what had mostly drownded in the ocean. "Pooch," he said, not even looking to see it were me, "I'm sad."

This wasn't no news to me. I plopped down beside him.

"It ain't right, what she done today," I told him.

"Maybe so, but I can't believe she meant to hurt me. Maybe she was confused. She didn't expect me, see? So she didn't know the way of it."

"Seems to me she ain't the girl you told me about."

"She is."

"Seems to me that girl done disappeared. I don't think you can find her, Joe."

"Nawh, that ain't so. She's there, but she's lost inside that Symphony woman, and I gotta rescue her. That's what I figure."

"How you going to do that?"

"I gotta woo her, that's how."

I wasn't certain she'd appreciate being rescued by Joe wooing her, but I didn't say so, telling him instead about the beans and franks and salad fixings I done bought at the grocery. Joe had him a healthy appetite, and I figured talk of food just might rouse him. But it didn't. He kept hunkered there, close to sighing like some tired soul what had given up. So I told him there was beer, which wasn't so hard to come by. There was a house in back of the grocery where a Mexican gent, after sniffing me out to see I was no copper, sold me four bottles at a quarter a piece. "That's good," Joe said, but I could tell the beer didn't matter none.

He said, "I don't much care for Yancey Dix."

"He thinks he's the cat's whiskers, all right."

"He ain't so swank."

I wasn't so certain of that, but I didn't speak up.

"And he ain't no cake-eater, neither," Joe said, but he was wrong. Plenty of ladies could fall for Dix; there ain't no denying that. Could be Joe knew this and was just trying to convince hisself different.

He asked me, "So how do we get her away from him?"

"Poison is good. Or a gun. We could get Sure-Shot Minnie to do the job."

Joe brightened some at that, saying, "Damn, she was something, wasn't she?"

"Must have been a looker in her day."

"Uh-huh."

After this, we sat there more, witnesses to the sun burying itself, when Joe got up to fix supper. Me, I stayed right where I was, my legs dangling over that beach and watching the waves sweep up the sand and pull back, making one of the loneliest sounds I ever heard.

I thought some more about Dix. He had me worried. He was a wild card didn't neither of us expect back in Missouri. I ain't no genius but I could see it plain: he had a hold on Rose Allen. I wasn't so certain Joe could break that hold. But I could be wrong, thinking now of something Joe said while we was in Joliet, him saying, "I'm written in her heart like she's written in mine." Now I ain't lying; them is his words, actual and complete, but they do sound phony, don't they? Well, it's like I said, Joe's a complicated guy. Maybe he could have been a poet, had he got him some proper learning. But, and this is my point here, when he said them words he was convinced of their rightness. Could be, he could break Dix's hold on Rose Allen. But then I thought—

Could he break Symphony's hold?

CHAPTER 8

The next few days we settled into work at the studios, with Albert showing us the ropes. We got assigned to the Zorro serial, which suited me fine. It was educational.

First thing I learned was about cameras, which was these boxes on stilts, they looked to be, with a crank on the side. One day more than an hour got spent setting up three of them, each of them aimed at the same spot from head on and the sides. When they was ready, the actors come out and acted, and all three cameras got cranked, chewing up film. I didn't see the reason of it, since a moving picture can't show but what one camera sees. Albert said this was so they could get different angles and later mix them together. I still didn't get the sense of it, so he said an editor does it all; he splices them films together so they look like one. But, I told him back, can't you just shoot it straight like you want, in the order you want? You don't need more than one camera to do that. Albert got sore then, and told me Empire was a fancy studio what can afford extra cameras. Me, I figured it for a waste of cabbage, but I wasn't running things, so it wasn't no matter to me, cept for being educational.

Back then moving-picture cameras ain't like the ones they use today. Back then they had motors what buzzed and clicked and clacked. Now they don't. I suppose they got re-invented when sound came along. Course on a shoot that wasn't the only noise. Damn, you'd be staggered by the noise surrounding the action, which is the name for what the actors do while them cameras clatter. Would you believe it; the director talked to the actors while they was acting, telling them what they was supposed to do. I didn't see how them actors could act and listen at the same time, but they did. And the lights? Hell, they sizzled and kept popping; it near to set my teeth on edge. And the actors talked as grand and lofty as if they was on stage, though I couldn't figure why they bothered, being as how the results was silent when they got to the screen. Once during a love scene, a couple guys played Spanish guitars, the music of them sounding Mexican. I asked Albert why they did this, and he said it was to set the mood for the actors. I didn't know about that, but leastways the director kept his mug shut so them actors could take care business. Ain't it peculiar, though, how much noise happened in the making of a silent photo play?

Anyway, the work kept Joe and me hopping so we didn't have much time for chasing down Rose Allen. Maybe that were best, cause Joe had him no idea how to woo her just yet. Besides, he was more curious about the making of a flicker than I was. He about wore out Albert with questions; and when Albert didn't have no answer, he went right up to somebody else and asked the question. He was educating hisself, he told me; educating hisself in a new art form, he said. Someday he figured he just might make his own photo plays. I didn't much think that likely but didn't say so. I ain't never got in the way of a man educating hisself.

Speaking of educating, Albert done took a crack at it, trying to educate Joe and me about a union. I didn't pay him much mind, cept one time when we was on them ropes adding wax so Zorro could use his whip to slide from one roof to another. "Boys," Albert said, "I'm not parlor pink, but Jesus, it ain't right nor fair, how profits get split up here at Empire. For every dollar guys like us make, a guy like Dix gets a hundred, two hundred, maybe more. But that's what a union's for; it makes sure guys like us get more of the pie, which is only fair, seeing as how what we do matters."

Joe asked him, "Who runs this union?"

"Why, the workers," Albert said.

"But they can't; they gotta work."

"That's so," Albert said. "Lawyers help us run it."

"Why lawyers?" I piped up.

"Because there's legal issues involved."

"Do they earn the same the workers do?"

"Of course not. They're lawyers. We gotta pay them more."

That did it for me. I ain't no genius, but I am a natural-born thief, and I can recognize a sting, sure enough. Besides, there ain't nothing comes out fair in this sorry old world, specially when lawyers and judges run the whole shebang. Hell, you had to give them lawyers credit. It were gorgeous, what they had going for them. Course I didn't say this to Albert. I didn't want to show him up for the sap he was, letting hisself be used like he was. Truth was, I kind of liked him, even if he was a red, not that he could admit it. He was a persistent cuss, even as Joe and me told him we wasn't joiners of no kind and not interested in his union. Seemed nobody else was neither, cause nobody took him serious, cept Guffey who bawled him out near every time he overheard Albert talking to us about that union. Still, it was funny, how he talked, even if he wasn't, as he claimed, parlor pink.

Along about the fifth day we had been working, I think it was, during lunch, he handed out some of them pamphlets: *WORKERS OF THE WORLD, UNITE*, remember? He were handing them to guys in bib overalls what was working in one of them shops making walls and such. Me and Joe told him he better not do it, knowing Guffey didn't have no tolerance for Albert's union talk. But he done it anyway, us tagging after, curious to see what could happen.

Which was this: Yancey Dix hisself showed up, with his short-brim fedora cocked back on his skull and Koko riding on his shoulder.

He glad-handed most of them workers and clapped them on the back, announcing he was there to check how his breakaway furniture was coming. Breakaway furniture is them chairs and tables cowboys smash up in saloon fights. I know you've seen them brawls. We all have. Hell, in the past few years—me making up for my deprived youth in Joliet—I done seen a hundred of them, maybe more; and it still amuses me thinking how, if they was regular chairs and such, the actor what gets hit is doomed to see the dentist—or the undertaker. Just goes to show, though, how reliable the flickers can be.

Soon, Dix seen one of them pamphlets and took it from a guy's hand and give it a gander. Then he looked up and seen Albert with his fist full of them. "Aren't you Kothe? Alfred Kothe?"

"Albert; yes sir," Albert said back to him.

"I don't think this is wise, do you? Why stir up trouble where there isn't any? Am I right, fellas?"

The workers all piped up, saying he was right.

"Are you a parlor socialist?" Dix asked, Koko chattering at that, as if he didn't much care for reds.

"No sir." Albert's eyes was big and his adam's apple jumped up.

"Then we better burn this trash."

With that, he had the workers collect all them pamphlets, including Albert's, and put them in a barrel of sand, and he set it on flame hisself with a match. While it burned, Albert, his voice cracking like it were fifteen, said, "Mr. Dix, about my photo play—the one I gave you—"

"You gave me a photo play?"

"I did, sir."

"I haven't read it."

"About a month ago—"

"Well, I'll look for it, Alfred. In the mean time, no more of those pamphlets, understand?"

Dix and Koko turned to the breakaway furniture, talking of it to some of the workers, while Albert slunk away. I near about felt sorry for him.

But later, back at Sunset Haven, Albert was cheerful and ready to learn Joe more on how to catch a wave and ride it in on the flat of his belly. He tried learning me, too, a couple days back, but I didn't get the knack of it and near about drownded. So I sat on the beach each late afternoon since and watched them sporting among the waves, content in knowing I was more likely to see old age.

CHAPTER 9

Albert got wise after Dix burned his pamphlets, because he didn't talk much more about the union. Least for a few weeks. I figured he was laying low for a while, measuring time till he could speak up again. That being the case, the three of us took to eating lunch on the roof of one of those Spanish buildings what had the ropes strung from it. Those buildings was offices for the studios, but they also acted, being a Mexican courtyard in Zorro's time. It felt good up there. It was early May, and the sun come gentle down on us, and was warm, while breezes kept it cool and smelled of orange blossoms and them pepper trees. Hell, you could see for miles from up there, it seemed to me, and I liked that fine.

One day, Albert showed up later than usual, bringing with him a skirt. "Boys," he said, "I want to introduce you to my girl, Miss Astoria Starr."

Now he'd been talking of her plenty for the past week or so since me and Joe been hired, and seeing her there in actual flesh—well, let's just say her alias humored me. I mean, this button of a girl with two moons for eyes could be never be so elegant as the name she give herself. But she tried, holding herself erect and walking slow, the parts of her waking up and still drowsy. I figured she was trying to be some kind of vamp, though she hadn't practiced enough how to be foreign. Her hair were wrong, for one thing, being pulled back tight to her skull, a roll of it stuck in a net at the back of her head. But she was pretty anyhow, though her bones was too close to her skin, showing she didn't eat like she should if she really meant to be a vamp.

"Let me guess," I said to her, "you want to be an actor."

"Why not? I bet I could give Theda Bara a run for her money." She batted her eyes and put her hands on hips and arched her back so her nubbins which wasn't quite breasts puffed out a mite, as if she was offering herself. All the while Albert beamed at her, and then at me and Joe.

Joe said, "Have you acted in a flicker yet?"

Astoria pouted a bit before saying, "No, but I will. I just know I will."

Albert said, "She's an office girl here at Empire. She started a month ago. I got her the job."

Astoria said, "It's my ticket to getting discovered."

Me and Joe blinked at her. "Discovered by who?" I asked.

"By Mr. Dix or one of them other hot shots they got here."

"Oh," I said.

She giggled and said, "I'm even going to acting school to get ready."

"I'm paying for it," Albert piped up, beaming like before.

"Not that I need it so much. I'm a natural actress." Then her voice dropped, shading on a whisper. "Maybe sometime I can show you how natural I can be."

I looked to Albert but he didn't seem to pick up on what I'd heard. Hell, was he deaf? Couldn't he hear this phony vamp wasn't the type what could stop offering herself to most any man? Course Joe got them offers pretty regular—not that they mattered, him being devoted to Rose Allen. But maybe she was just acting, and Albert knew it. Maybe she was just practicing to become a vamp. Maybe that's all she was doing. That, and practicing how to get discovered.

But I got to confess, I didn't much believe that thought.

Later, back at Sunset Haven, while Albert and Joe was riding the waves on their bellies, I took a walk along the beach.

I thought some more about Astoria, which got me to thinking about Rose Allen and if she was the same when she first got to Hollywood. Was she as phony and gawky in trying to get discovered? Somehow, I didn't believe that possible. I had seen her now in that movie back in Missouri and twice since, and I was convinced there wasn't no phony parts to her. Still—

Something burned in her, something what could scare most men; and I wondered if she burned like that when Joe first come to love her. Or did she burn like that after, him putting the fire in her? I can't say, cause Joe only hinted about this in a letter I ain't read but once, and that years ago right after it got writ. Even so, I got to try; and I got to say it like he would. I wasn't there; I know that, but here's how it went anyway. And even if it ain't true, it's close enough to be mistook for the truth, and that's worth it—

It was by a lake, the water lapping its music, with water flies skimming along its top, and pieces of the sun what got broken shining in the water.

They come on it sudden, and sit themselves in the grass at its edge, till the water pulls at them, pulling like cool water does on a day what is still hot in the late afternoon. In time they take off their clothes, each of them back to back, daring each other to get total naked, making a game of it, though they use their hands to hide their private places, not looking anyway, and run for the water, splashing into its cool and burying themselves from the other till only their heads are seen.

And so they swim and play and know the joy of each other, till somehow their nakedness don't matter no more, and he takes her hand and leads her from the water.

They lay in the grass and feel the warmth of the sun in it, and first all they do is look at each other, looking to see the wonder of the other's nakedness. Then fingers begin to explore while the need in them grows, it growing gentle and sure, and she lays back to offer herself, and he rises above and after reading her face, comes to her—

And after, the sun blanketing them, warming their souls, he pledges hisself to her. And she—

She slowly begins to burn—

It could have been just like that. It could.

CHAPTER 10

T he next day me and Joe acted in an episode of the Zorro serial. This is how it happened—

Douglas Cardwell was Zorro, and he was a Limey with a snooty accent; but he wasn't prissy about hisself. And he didn't lord it over working stiffs like me and Joe and Albert. Now and again, come a break in the shooting, he'd drift up to us like we was friends from his times on a London stage, and he'd tell us a story or two, expecting us to laugh where he meant for us to laugh, which was what we done. He had plenty of stories to tell and they was bawdy, some of them, but all of them was funny. On the screen he was just as funny, only not with words, his Zorro being a rascal what did enjoy monkey business. Time and again I watched him and his director plan out a prank, inventing it on the spot; and I do believe that was why his serial was so popular back then. It was playful and full of mischief and such—which meant Douglas was ever on the prowl to find a new angle for what could be funny without words.

Which explains why Joe and me become actors in the Zorro serial.

Douglas—he told us to use his first name; it didn't bother him, which was another reason for me liking him like I done—pulled us aside that morning and said he wanted to play a chase scene for the comedy in it, saying we was just the two to make the scene funny. And he told us it come with five extra clams for each of us.

Then he explained why it could be funny. I didn't see the sense of it, but Joe did, his grin matching Douglas's. I wasn't about to show I lacked humor so I told them it was a genuine gut buster, and I told them it was jake by me and worth them five extra bills, what I had to do; but I had my doubts, seeing as how I could get hurt if things went haywire.

Next thing I knew, Joe and me was being dressed up like Spanish soldiers in Zorro's time. It took a while, cause there wasn't no uniform to fit me and a costume guy had to pin up the legs and sleeves of the one they finally put me in.

After that, we trooped over to the Mexican courtyard with the Spanish buildings where the director run us through the gag a couple times so we got the sense of it. At first I was anxious, not being so eager for human flight with no parachute, and I pretty much stayed that way, even after Douglas and Joe proved they could hold up their part of the gag.

Finally we was ready, and the director called out "Roll 'em!" and the cameramen—there was two of them—started to crank away.

This is what they got—

I am sleeping against a wall, leaning my cheek on a musket what is near twice as tall as me. Douglas—only now he is Zorro—jumps over the wall and lands smack in front of me and grabs my musket. I wake up sudden-like and startled, and Zorro uses my own musket to conk me on the head. Zorro laughs, leaning back to do it, before he hands me back my musket. Then he runs up the stairs to the balcony, with me dragging my musket along, chasing after him.

At this Joe hears the commotion and comes out of a building down in the courtyard and sees it is Zorro and me; but before he can do much, Zorro picks me up. I drop my musket and start kicking. But Zorro ain't concerned, he just throws me over the balcony like I'm a human log what can fly. Only I can't, so down I fall near fifteen feet until Joe catches me.

By then Zorro has jumped onto the balcony rail and laughs again at what he has done, using his whip then to catch a line and swing from that to the roof, where he disappears.

The camera comes back to me and Joe and sees him cradling me like I was a baby, and it zooms in on how we look surprised into each other's faces—

After that, the director made us do it again, but not before Douglas pulled me aside and told me to relax and not be so stiff for them cameras. He made me breathe deep and give me a couple shots of good whiskey from his flask. I ain't much for hard spirits, but I downed it, and I'm here to say it soothed me some. So we played the scene once more, and after that, the director grinned and so did Douglas and Joe. They all grinned and said it was jake, a top-notch gag.

And it was. I don't know if you've ever seen it, but I have. It don't last more than thirty seconds, but it was funny, all right. Douglas Cardwell sure was an expert on comedy and could make it happen, even if Joe and me back then was no shades of an actor.

Anyway, Joe come up to me after it all, grinning. He punched me on the shoulder, saying, "Pooch, we done acted in a movie? Ain't that something?"

I wasn't so sure, rubbing my neck where he caught me the last time. It burned.

"Maybe if we do some more of this, Pooch, Rose Allen just might notice."

I wasn't so certain of that, Joe not being much of an actor, and neither of us likely to get asked to act again, but then I seen Dix standing off a ways, talking to Douglas. He looked over to us, and Douglas did too.

I realized he must have seen us do our acting.

When he seen we was looking at him, he stared back so I could tell he was measuring me and Joe, till he put a finger to the brim of his fedora to salute us and walked away.

I didn't know about Rose Allen, but Dix had surely noticed us. He surely had.

CHAPTER 11

Later, after Albert and Joe had ridden on the waves, me and Joe walked in the sand.

Joe said, "They were talking about us. Douglas and Dix."

"Whatever got said, it was serious."

"Maybe Dix is looking to get us fired."

"I don't see why. We ain't been in his way none."

"We ain't even seen Rose Allen since the day we was hired."

We walked along more, the waves spilling along my ankles every minute or so, till Joe waded in to his waist and stood there looking into the clouds what were building up miles off. I didn't ask him why he done this. Maybe he was looking for some trace of a mermaid or a whale. I moved up beside him, water churning at my breast.

He said, "It sure is big. Really big water."

Sand melted under my feet so I hopped around to stay by his side.

"Pooch, do you think Dix knows about Rose Allen and me?"

"Only if she told him."

"I don't—" but he gave up what he meant to say. Then: "Pooch, am I a sap for loving her like I do?"

"Pretty much."

We searched some more for whales and mermaids, the sun finally hitting the water, so threads of red gold was in the waves now. I wasn't comfortable, though. Joe was too quiet. It ain't healthy to be that quiet when a body's blue and leaking misery. So I said, thinking to cheer him up, "Why don't we go get us some nookie?"

Joe smiled a sad smile what said I was pitiful creature and not to be tolerated, him being that superior in his sorrow. He waded from the water, and I did that too, but after I let him go, I was that much hurt and pissed off; I didn't want to be with him for a while. He headed back up the beach and climbed the stairs to the top of the bluff where he disappeared. Mostly I just wandered along the beach and felt night reaching out, but it didn't soothe me none.

I ain't never understood the hold love has on this sorry old planet, nor why it matters so much, seeing as how its consequences is so dire. Big Larry Fornelli said tough guys can't fall in love; they ain't got the heart for it. Well, I had an answer for him, and here it is—it ain't healthy for a tough guy to love a woman. Don't matter how hard-boiled he is, it makes him sick. It breaks him. Just look at Joe for the proof of it. Hell, a tough guy like Joe gets steamed up over a woman and he puts it to her a few times and he falls in love. He forgets it ain't but nookie, and there's nothing fancy in a guy getting his ashes hauled. There ain't no love to it, only biology and chemistry and such like.

But this kind of thinking reminded me I ain't had a woman since that night in Chicago, the first night after Joe got out of Joliet. I had picked him up that morning at the prison gates and he told me to take him to the lake, which is what I done. He spent the day on the shore, him requiring open space and the smell of water, the clean brine of it, the water what could take him anywhere in the world. He talked about living the rest of his life on or near water like Lake Michigan. Big water, he called it, what cannot be dammed up or stopped. When the dark come, I took him for a surprise to a whorehouse.

When we got there and he seen what it was, he told me, "Go on by yourself, Pooch. I can't go in there."

"Why the hell not? It's been three years since you had a woman."

"I know, but I can't go in there."

That pissed me off. "Is this about you and Rose Allen?"

"You know it is, Pooch," he said, his eyes pouring into me how he loved her and meant to wait for her, only her.

I went into that house and took my pleasure without him, and when I come out he was standing in back of the Ford staring into the southeast. I didn't ask him why he was staring that way. I knew exactly why. He was staring at where Rose Allen should be.

I put such thinking aside and went to have me another woman.

Mrs. Edward Beneke's bungalow was directly across the gravel from ours. Before I could knock, she opened her door and left it open for me to come in, which I done.

I stood in the room's near dark. A clock ticked in the corner. It ticked very loud, louder than the trucks what rumbled along every now and then. There was pictures of a man on the wall. She didn't have to tell me who he was.

Mrs. Edward Beneke shivered. She pulled on the handkerchief in her hands like it was a rope. I supposed she knew why I was there, but didn't know what to say about it.

"I acted in a moving picture today."

"I don't go to them very often."

"Why not?"

"Oh, I don't know. They don't matter any."

"Probly so."

"If I see one, I forget what I've seen. It's like they become ghosts in my memory."

We didn't talk much more. After that, we went to her bedroom. There was another picture of the man over her bed. It didn't bother me none, but I wondered when she opened herself to me, while I poked into the tiny warmth of her, if she mistook me for him behind her closed eyes. She probly did, and that was fine by me. When it comes to loving a woman, don't hold no grudges. That's my motto. Everybody had ought to copy it down a thousand times till they get it right in their heads.

CHAPTER 12

The next morning, sleep still hanging from my bones, I crossed the gravel and went into me and Joe's bungalow. Java was brewing on the stove, and the shower was running. I poured me a cup and the shower stopped. A minute later Joe come into the kitchen, drying hisself on a towel, wearing him a big grin and nothing else. I poured him a cup to show I had no grudge and he took it, saying, "Pooch, I got me an idea. It's a good one, too. I'm going to write a letter to Rose Allen. That's what I'm gonna do."

I slurped at my java, but he didn't drink his, putting his cup down after a sip and running off to the bedroom, shouting, "I writ it last night." He come back into the front room holding out his letter for me to take.

I took it and while he hurried up to dress in the bedroom I seen it was writ in pencil and had a lot of rub outs. It looked dirty from the rub outs, but I read it. It started out "Dere Rose Allen," I remember, that word "Dere" being rubbed out and re-writ more than most any other word, like he wanted to use some other word but wasn't sure he should and so he settled on dere only after he tried a dozen others. I can't remember more of the exact words, it being near to ten years since I read them. Sides, he didn't write so good as me and left out commas and stuff, and his spelling was piss poor, which was why that letter wasn't easy to read. But I read it anyway and this is what it said mostly. It said he had to see her and it told her where and when. It told her he would wait every day for week for her to come to him at that time. But it said more. It talked of that hot day at the lake when they loved each other for the first time, and it talked of other times after that when they loved each just as much. It told her to remember the promises. She can't forget them promises. It was a sad and desperate letter; that's how I remember it sounding.

After I read it, I came into the bedroom. "It's a good letter, Joe. It's honest, it is."

Joe was brushing at his hair and he stopped to grin. "It's the ticket, all right."

"But you got write it better than this."

"It says what I mean it to."

"I don't mean changing the words none. I mean you got to write it on fancy paper in ink."

Joe perked up, his grin back. "And I got to put it in an envelope with her name writ on the front, real fancy."

"Astoria could do it. Write it up fancy."

"Yeah. When we get to work, I'll go see her. I'll get some paper from her. I'll write it up clean with ink and I won't make no scratch outs. Then I'll get Astoria to put her name on the envelope."

"That's good, Joe, but make sure it's Symphony she writes down. Then have her give it to one of them kids what run the messages. He can deliver it to Rose Allen."

When we got to the studios, he did like we said. I wasn't there but it took him near an hour to do it all, him saying when he got back to where me and Albert was working, that he writ it nine times before he got it perfect. The rest of that morning he was anxious and Albert told him not to worry so much. But he kept right on being anxious.

At lunch we was sitting on the roof. The three of us had took off our shirts to let the sun's heat sink into our skin. That's one thing about being free and out of Joliet. It give me and Joe plenty of time to get sun brown. Joe looked healthy that brown; and ugly as he was, Albert looked like a heathen what feeds on raw meat.

Then, would believe it, Yancey Dix hisself popped up on that roof. He slapped his hands and rubbed them to get the grit off them, he having to climb the same ladder we climbed to get up there. He adjusted his fedora against the glare and strolled up to us three. "Hello, fellas, how are you doing?"

We said hellos back while squinting up at him, the sun making his head near white and hard to see. I figured he stood like that on purpose, just so we couldn't see him that clear, and he could lord it over us.

But Joe wasn't having it none, and he stood up, so I did too, Albert standing last of all.

Dix said, "Pooch, isn't it?" offering his hand.

I nodded and shook his hand.

"And you're Joe Holder."

"That's right," Joe said back, shaking Dix's hand when it come to him.

Dix said, "Doug told me I'd find you up here."

Didn't Joe nor me say nothing, even as I could tell Dix expected us to. "Boys," he said, "Doug and I have been talking. He spoke highly of you two."

Albert piped up, "And me? What about me?" offering his hand to Dix.

Dix ignored his hand but he put on a smile that wasn't no kind of real. "You too, Alfred."

"Albert, Mr. Dix. Albert B. Kothe, remember? I'm the guy who gave you that photo play about six, seven weeks ago, remember?"

"Really? I haven't read it yet."

"But you will, right, Mr. Dix? You said you would."

"When I get the time, I will indeed."

"I know it's good, Mr. Dix. It's got a part you're perfect for."

"Well, not just now, Albert, not with my own photo play so close to production. In fact, that's why I'm here.

"Boys, I have had you three assigned to *WESTWARD, THE WAGONS.* The shooting starts in ten days."

"But what about Zorro?" I wanted to know.

"I've talked to Doug. He's fine with it. He wraps up the serial by next Friday, and if he needs a few days more, we can work it out."

Joe looked suspicious for a moment, before he brightened some by smiling a slow smile and said, "It's jake with me."

Albert said, "Damn right, it is."

It wasn't jake with me, though. It smelled sour somehow. I mean, I ain't no genius but I pretty much could bet my life Mr. Dix don't never make a habit of climbing on a roof to chase down three set-up riggers and stunt men. Turned out, I wasn't wrong.

Dix asked me to follow him down from that roof. I hung back, though. I couldn't figure he needed to see me without Joe or Albert. But he asked me again, using a hand to show me the ladder. I give Joe a look, but he just smiled and said, "You better go on."

Which is what I done, Dix coming down right after me. After I got off the ladder, I could see Joe and Albert's faces side by side above Dix. Joe give me a wink to tell me it was funny, what was about to happen.

When Dix got off the ladder, he headed into the shade of the balcony, expecting me to follow, which I done. I looked up but from under that balcony but I couldn't see Joe and Albert no more.

"Pooch," he said like he was warning me. His face was grim; it was hard. He reached in his coat and pulled out an envelope and held it so I could Symphony writ on it in fancy letters. I knew what was inside, though he didn't let me have the envelope.

"I think, Pooch, you need to talk to your friend, Joe. I think you better tell him Symphony does not keep secrets from me."

"Did you read it?" I asked.

"I think it's best if you speak for me on this matter. I want you to do this so there is no unpleasant incident to follow, no spiteful tantrum from Joe with a threat of fisticuffs. Make it plain to Joe; no matter what he does, he can't beat me. Make it plain Symphony is mine now. Do you understand?"

"Mostly, 'cept I don't get it: why assign him to your moving picture if you don't want him around Symphony?"

He smiled and I could see why women swooned over him and his electric eyes. He said, "It amuses me. I mean no offense, Pooch, but Joe amuses me."

Putting the envelope back in his coat, he walked off, leaving me there to wonder how Joe amused him. I mulled on it plenty, but I couldn't find an answer. Then I mulled on why Symphony showed Dix Joe's letter, and all that did was scare me. I didn't much see how the woman could turn on Joe. Sure, he was a tough guy, but he done writ her name in his heart. And her? She done rubbed out his name from hers, and that's what scared me, cause when Joe found his name was erased he was likely to go wild and fly off the handle. Somebody could get hurt—probly Dix, knowing Joe, which wasn't smart of a convicted felon. It could send him back to the stir, and for a brutal long time. But mostly it scared me for another reason, that being I didn't know how to protect him none. Could be, he'd hear from somebody else about what Rose Allen done with that letter, and there wasn't nothing I could do to stop it. But that didn't mean I had to tell him. I couldn't do that; it was too cruel. I didn't want to hurt him. I told you, he was my only friend, and if I told him—

Hell, I just would not tell him; leastways not just yet.

Come five o'clock, when we cleaned up in the washroom, he told me to go home without him. I watched him comb his hair real careful, getting the grooves straight and glossy, and I didn't say a word about Dix reading his letter. And then he did something he never done before, he slapped bay rum on his face and rubbed it in. I didn't say nothing, dammit, but done like Joe told me. I went home without him. It made me sick doing that, but that's what I done.

Around eight or so, it being finally dark outside, I sat in our front room under the floor lamp, reading a *TRUE STORIES* moving-picture magazine and listening to Bessie Smith on a radio I done bought a few days before. The sound of her music mostly drownded out the trucks what were rumbling along the Coast highway.

Joe come in full of ache, the whole of him chewed up and miserable, his hands dug deep in his pockets and lost there. He said, "She didn't show up."

"Maybe she will tomorrow," I said.

"Yeah," he said, "maybe tomorrow."

I got sick all over again, thinking of tomorrow. But I still didn't say a word about Dix and the letter. It didn't seem right to talk about it.

CHAPTER 13

F act was, I never did tell him about Dix and his letter. I never could find the sense of the words for telling him, nor the will to do it, which is why every night that week he come home sad and chewed up and full of ache that Rose Allen had refused to see him.

That Sunday, us not working at Empire, wasn't no better, what with Joe riding the waves on his belly much of the day and into near night before he staggered from the cold of it, tired and moping sore and disconsolate along the beach and up the stairs to our bungalow. But come Monday he was fresh scrubbed and resurrected; he had him a new idea, one that was a pip, or so he said.

He had me take him to work early so he could stand just inside the gates to Empire Studios. He stood by an office wall near where roses grew, and while he waited he kept pulling at his clothes or brushing them, or straightening the seams. Or he combed his hair, though it didn't need it none, the grooves of it still straight and smelling of Vitalis. But mostly he stood with a hand in a pocket and the other hanging free, standing like he was a man easy with himself and knowing the world agrees.

It near about made me laugh, him posing like that, and without a camera in sight.

After about half an hour, Rose Allen drove through them gates in a polished Cadillac Coupe, a green one with white walls and the top down; and its headlamps shined with the sun bouncing off the silver of them. Winged victory was the radiator cap and she rode over the grill, the tilt of her head matching Rose Allen's tilt, the both of them riding grand and serene before the world.

Joe stepped out to show hisself. He didn't do nothing but stand there, and she seen him, right enough. There wasn't no way she could miss him. But she drove on by without slowing none nor even turning her head to see him. She drove down the road like Joe wasn't fresh scrubbed and smelling of Vitalis just for her.

Joe didn't say nothing about it the rest of the day, him keeping curious quiet and not saying much of anything. The next morning we tried it again, but it wasn't no different, she just glided grandly by in her Cadillac coupe, like she was a duchess and not to be trifled with.

Again, Joe was quiet about it, but I could tell it hurt, what she was doing to him. But it didn't stop him from trying none. That Wednesday he was there again, only this time she come with Dix riding beside and Koko on his shoulder. Dix raised a finger to salute us when the Cadillac glided by, and Koko chattered at us before showing his teeth; but Rose Allen didn't even turn her head nor change the stillness in her face.

Now you or me, we don't need no Western Union to get the message, it being plain that Rose Allen done cut him from her heart. But Joe wasn't opening no telegrams from nobody, specially his Rose Allen. I tried telling Joe to read it for what it was, telling him this the rest of the day, but Joe wouldn't hear of it, him turning surly deaf every time. So I give up trying, and come Thursday, there he was again, standing by them roses, waiting, and waiting, him more desperate now than he was the Monday before.

But it wasn't no different; the Cadillac coupe glided past and Rose Allen refused to see Joe. He turned to me, and his face was worn flat and bleak by its suffering, and it was pitiful confused about why she didn't stop for him.

It ain't right for man to suffer like that. It ain't humane. And I don't care none what you think, I'm glad I done it. I'm glad I done told him what we could do.

That afternoon we left work early and I parked my Ford touring automobile, with me and Joe in it, under an oak tree down the street from the gates of Empire Studios. Joe kept slapping on the door, he was that anxious, but I didn't mind. I only wanted this thing done and buried, with Joe finally satisfied that Rose Allen was no longer his. Sure, he might grieve some, but a trip to Frisco ought to set that right in time. I figured it couldn't fail, my plan, if we was patient, which I certainly was, even if Joe couldn't sit still and near about broke his eyes staring at every vehicle what come through them gates and headed down the road.

After an hour or so of waiting, the gates opened and Rose Allen drove her Cadillac Coupe through and past the guard shack, just like I done figured she would. Turning onto the street, she headed west, right past us. I waited till three cars passed going her way before I swung in a u-turn and drove along behind her, them three cars between us. Joe slapped the door some more, like my Ford was a horse he wanted to hurry on. I told him to knock it off. This was delicate, trailing her like we was, and not to be hurried. So he calmed down and complained when I let another automobile slip in front of us. I told him it didn't matter; I wasn't going to lose sight of her.

I couldn't lose her, truth be told, she was driving that slow and easy. In time she turned on another road, with us following without no automobiles between. I hung back a ways, not wanting to scare her none. That wouldn't be wise, not if we was going to follow her to where she lived so Joe can go up to her door and knock. She'd have to talk to him then, cause Dix was at the studios; we was certain of that. And there wouldn't be no guards nor nobody to stop Joe from talking to her—and hearing the truth of it. He could hear she was a moving-picture actress now, and rich to boot, and she didn't need a tough guy what was an ex-con like Joe no more. She had a classy guy now, a real sheik, in Dix. She could say this from her own lips. And maybe if Joe was lucky she'd be cruel in this telling. Maybe she'd slap him. Least that's what I hoped; that she'd slap him hard, so he couldn't doubt none she had lost the yen for him.

Rose Allen's Cadillac coupe disappeared around a curve and we come around it and seen she was parked at the side of the road. I pulled up behind her Cadillac coupe. She got from her automobile, and when Joe seen this he opened his door and got out to go to her.

Now, this wasn't like I planned but I ain't no fool. I seen it could work just fine this way, on the side of a road what ain't no place to either of them. Beside us, a hill swooped down into that chaparral what grows in California, and I could smell the dryness of it in the last of the day's heat. I shut down the engine and opened my wing window so I could listen, them being right in front of my Ford and me watching through grime on glass.

Joe leaned in to kiss her, but she got wood stiff as soon as he put his hands on her arms, so he never finished the kiss and let her go. He said he was sorry, saying it low so I couldn't much hear it.

"Joe—" she said, breaking it off. I guess she didn't have no words yet.

"Rose Allen, I—"

"It's Symphony," she said. It was sharp, her saying this.

"But—"

"There's no—no Rose Allen anymore, Joe. I left her back in Missouri, along with the rest of her past." Her face was grim as a judge's and it didn't have no pity—none at all.

"But we promised each other—"

"They don't matter, those promises. We were kids."

"I meant mine. I did."

She stared into him and then looked at the Ford, at the dust glare of its front glass. Maybe she could see herself there, reflected. Least I think she could. Or maybe it was me she saw, but that didn't figure, cause her face broke up then and it was sad and full of hurt. It lasted only a moment or two, but I swear I seen it that way before it was grim again, with her turning to pour that grim into Joe. She said, "Let it go. It's time, Joe. You—you have to let it go."

"I—I can't." His voice wobbled.

"Joe, don't," she said, which was an echo of what I was thinking. It wasn't proper for Joe to cry.

"All I can think is how much you matter to me." His voice still wobbled but he was trying to firm it up.

"I—I have no room for you, Joe. And I don't want you following me like—like this, or staring at me or sending me letters. I want you to leave me alone."

"No. I can't do that." He was angry now, it low and burning thin, him trying to hold it back by staring into the ground.

"I mean it, Joe."

"No. No. I ain't walking away, dammit."

"Joe, look at me. Look at me now."

Joe done this.

"It isn't healthy, this obsession with me."

"You think I'm sick? In the head?" His voice wobbled again, and he wasn't that far from tears, it seemed.

A breeze come up and run over them, kicking up dust so the sun glowed in it, glowing around them.

Joe swallowed away them tears and said, "I ain't sick."

"Yes, you—you are, and it has to stop. Do you understand?"

Joe stared at the ground more.

"I'm not kidding, Joe. I'm not."

With that she walked quick to her Cadillac coupe and took off down the road, dust kicking up and spilling over Joe.

Joe stared after her a moment and then he got in the Ford and told me, the anger coming off him now in waves, "What are you waiting for? Let's get after her."

"I ain't gonna do that, Joe. It's crazy to do that."

"Godammit, go!"

"I ain't doing it." And I glared into him, standing up to his anger, till he grunted and opened the door and took off running down the road after Rose Allen's Cadillac coupe, which wasn't but a green dot by now and close to disappearing.

Now I just sat there a while and listened to the air tick in its quiet. It was right to let Joe run off his anger. He didn't need nobody to help him do that. He run until he was near a half mile off and then he stopped and put his arms on his waist and then he ran some more after Rose Allen. I let him go on till he was small and then gone, and I still waited until I set the lever and cranked up the starter and eased onto the road, coasting along till five minutes later I seen Joe standing in the middle of the road, his shirt stuck with sweat to his body, and him panting. I stopped.

He got in the automobile and said, his anger gone now, and the whole of him determined, "Let's go see Dix."

CHAPTER 14

Right now I got something to say. Something you got to hear, specially after what I just told you. Joe wasn't no crybaby, dammit; and he wasn't sick in the head, neither, but he was something else. He was a victim, pure and simple—a victim of a place where good hearts don't matter none; a victim of a time where devotion to a woman ain't but silly wrong.

Aw, I could cry from the memory of what happened next—

We found Yancey Dix at the Egyptian on Hollywood Boulevard. He was in a moving picture called *CITY OF JAZZ*. Joe didn't tell me why we wound up there, but he didn't need to. I knew why. He had adopted him an enemy, and Yancey Dix was a slick enemy and a formidable bastard what could not be strong armed, which stymied Joe, him not never meeting Dix's like before, least not during his criminal past. So, now: he had to be crafty and like a spy. Only, in his sorry state, it was half-cocked and out of character for a tough guy to snoop around so as to find him an edge to topple Dix.

But I was too polite to tell him this, which was why I bought us tickets, and we went through the columns and in the doors and was floored. A sunburst was painted into the ceiling, I kid you not. A sunburst so huge and grand it near could blind a guy, or so you'd think. And there had to be more than 600 seats, with maybe a 300 of them used up with people what was sitting under the sunburst and worshipping, for all I could tell.

We took us seats in the back and pretty soon *CITY OF JAZZ*, with Yancey Dix's name over the title, jumped onto the screen, while an organ busted out, the sound of it loud and alive on my skin. It played *JOHNNY COMES MARCHING HOME AGAIN*, which matched up with what we seen, this being a ship what steamed into New York Harbor. Then that picture cut away to doughboys standing at the ship's railing, shouting and waving and showing they was happy to get home from the

War. Then the camera zoomed (though I didn't know camera terms in those days) on a face and panned across other faces, each of them beaming and hungry to get off that ship. But that pan shot stopped and stayed on Yancey Dix.

Dressed up like an officer, he was, with his feet planted wide and his hands on his hips, the camera staying on him long enough so you could see he didn't take shit from the world and so you could see he was a gallant and proud figure of a man. He dazzled, that's what he done. Even when he wasn't the only one on screen no more but talking now to other doughboys, my eyes was stuck to him.

Now don't get me wrong. He wasn't no actor, not really. Still isn't. An actor is some fella like that Cagney kid. Have you seen him? Mostly he does them gangster flickers for Warner Brothers. Now he gets it right; he's just a regular egg what gets caught up in evil, Cagney does. He don't never pose like Dix but steps up and says what he has to say and listens to what gets said back to him before he pops off again. No muss; no fuss. As natural as they come. But Dix was the opposite, him being unnatural and more than ordinary. Course that was the acting style back then, but you can still see him that way in the talkies he's made since, though he's toned it down some. You can see he ain't never a character but always hisself, Yancey Dix; and ain't he a wonder to see? Ain't he purely dazzling? After a few minutes, it near about made me down-hearted, for I knew while *CITY OF JAZZ* unfolded, Joe wasn't likely to find an edge. Not with a guy like Dix, a guy what could dazzle.

The moving picture itself was a tale of a man, Dix, what joins the fast crowd in New York City and hops from speakeasy to speakeasy, running wild and carousing, the organ playing jazzy hot and modern. The reason he runs wild is a woman, a rich dame what ain't right in the head and careless. She drives her automobile fast and drinks while doing it; and damn, she did look good up there, looking ripe enough to get most any man's pecker dancing, including Dix's, which was understandable, him being that hungry for a woman after winning a war. Course we didn't see him banging her none; it was only suggested, seeing as how them what makes moving pictures claim they is protecting us from sin and corruption. Ain't that a hoot? But none of us is blind. Ain't none of us fooled. We know sex when we see it. And when we hear it, from how that organ sounded.

Anyway, there's another dame and you know who that is—

Symphony. She's rich but she ain't no gadabout nor careless. Instead she feeds the poor and such like good works. She and Dix meet up and she takes a crack at turning him from his wicked ways, claiming a war ain't no excuse for bad behavior. You can pretty much figure how it ended up. Ain't nobody want to see a good man turn evil. We don't go to moving pictures to be reminded of truth.

As for Joe, while all this was acted out on the screen, he sat quiet and solid. Now and again, I turned to see how his eyes was moving and searching for an edge, though I couldn't tell none if he found one. I don't think he did, cause after it was over, when we come into the lobby, Joe walked up to a poster hung on the wall, a poster of Dix and the careless dame over one shoulder and Symphony over the other. Joe stood under it for a minute, maybe more, craning his neck up, baring his throat, which was funny, cause somehow, standing like that, he looked shrunk up under Dix.

Then Joe give me a doleful look and said, "Pooch, let's get drunk."

Now there's something you have to understand. Joe wasn't no serious drinker. He'd have him a beer or two, now and again, and that was enough. But not this time. We stopped at the Mexican gent's house behind the grocery and bought us a quart bottle of something called Smoky Red Bourbon.

Back at our bungalow, he cracked open the bottle and after an hour it was more than half gone. I done took a few sips so as to commiserate with Joe, but I ain't built to be no serious belter of a gin mill's home-made worst.

Neither was Joe, from the looks of it, for he stood up from the sofa, losing his balance, and teetered across the room till he collided with the wall, bouncing off it and teetering back until he caught hisself on the sofa's arm. Righting hisself, he sucked on some air, and I figured he was fighting a need to upchuck. Now we didn't need no puke to spruce up our carpet, and since he couldn't make it on his own, I guided him to the front door where he could suck up some ocean air and get his gut to settle down. He stood there, teetering for a good minute. Then, without a by-your-leave, he lurched into the night.

I followed after and grabbed his arm. "Where you going, Joe?"

"To the beasch," he said.

"It's late, Joe. You don't want go to there."

"Do so."

He threw aside my arm and lurched on, the gravel crackling under his feet. I trotted after; I tried to reason with him, I was that worried: "C'mon, Joe. We got a big day tomorrow. We gotta get some shuteye."

Joe lurched along like he was permanent deaf.

When we got near the stairs, Albert come out of his bungalow and seen what was what. He trotted over and I told him, "Take his other arm. We've got to get him into bed."

We grabbed Joe and both of us tugged but he didn't stop none. I said, "C'mon, Joe, you can't go down there."

Yanking and twisting, Joe pulled himself free of us and tottered down the stairs. I near about swallowed my teeth when he tumbled down the last six or seven of them steps, with us chasing after.

He stood up and stared at us for a moment, saying, "Gots to find a mermaid, tha's so."

Albert stepped in front of him, blocking his way, and Joe didn't hesitate to throw a fist and it connected, sending Albert flying back into the sand. Then Joe turned and pushed me with both hands, pushing hard, like his arms was steel poles, and I wheeled back and wound up on my butt in the sand across from Albert. The two of us blinked at each other. We knew there wasn't no help for it, that we was pygmies in a land of giants.

Joe lurched to the water and crashed into the waves, till he could swim, him then raising his arms and going further, pieces of white flying over where his arms landed stroke after stroke.

"Oh Christ," I said and both Albert and me ran into the surf, but Joe was too far gone for me to catch up, though I tried. I flailed and kicked and went out more than a hundred yards, fighting the tidal wash and current, but I wasn't no match for an ocean and so I turned back. Albert swum right past me, him being a regular water monkey.

I paddled slow back to shore, nursing my worry. Knowing how stubborn Joe could be and unaware of consequences, I didn't doubt he'd try to swim to Japan, if need be, to see him a mermaid, and thus be drownded in the trying. Or maybe that was his intent all along, to drown. Hell, he was drunk enough to try something crazy as that, to sink into the Pacific and be done with both Dix and Rose Allen, which was a wicked idea and not true nor worthy of Joe. So I cursed myself for such ghastly imagining and told myself he would likely drown only cause he was drunk and tired and lost in all that cold bottomless water. A victim done in by pain and physics and physical limitation, him too far out to return to shore; and not no pitiful sap what done give up on himself.

In time, Albert come out of the waves and plopped down beside me. So now, the two of us forlorn, we hugged our knees. There was nothing we could do but stare at the tattered water and how the moon's light was scattered in a corridor headed for Japan. But Joe wasn't swimming in that corridor.

Neither of us said it. Neither of us wanted to admit Joe was probly dead and drownded by now. But we mourned anyhow. That's what we done, each of us trembling and mourning and afraid to say a word to recognize the horror of what had happened to the finest man we ever knew.

I don't know how long we sat there, it being probly close to an hour when a blackness come into the moon's light at the edge of its corridor, a blackness of a spider walking on water, a blackness which slowly come closer to us, so we stood up and waded into the ocean, me not daring to believe what I seen, but soon enough daring to believe it exact; for Joe rode in on a wave on his belly till he stood with water milling at his waist and washing away. He stared into Albert and me, panting, before he come up to us—trembling, sure, but only from cold and not from no fear for his own mortality.

Suddenly he grinned. I swear that's what he done, water from his hair glinting on his lips and teeth. He grinned a grin what said he was sober and young again, and resurrected.

Albert piped up, "Did you see that mermaid?"

Joe laughed. "I had my hands full out there. If I had, I might've drownded from the shock of it."

Albert laughed.

I didn't. Instead I scolded him, saying, "You scared the hell out of me."

"I'm sorry about that."

"Us sitting out here freezing our asses off. I thought you was drownded."

"That can't happen, Pooch. Ain't no ocean can swallow me."

I knew better, but I let that one go, preferring his renewed swagger to the haggard and pitiful creature what had got spifficated on Smoky Red Bourbon.

"'Sides," Joe said, "it did me good, going out there. It set my head straight."

Well, if that meant he was giving up his Rose Allen and ready to head to Frisco, I would forgive him, which I near done, but he ruined it by saying something peculiar and definite, something what has become dreadful over the years, him saying, "Pooch, it can't go like this. It can't go like this at all."

CHAPTER 15

In the next couple of days it seemed Joe had got hisself converted. He didn't moan and carry on no more about Rose Allen. He didn't even mention her name, nor Dix's neither. He took to smiling or singing to hisself, or whistling too; and he chattered about how some day he might just become an actor, wait and see if he didn't. He was like a man what had returned to his certain and pleasant self.

All this pleased me, and it pleased me most cause he didn't turn deaf when I talked of seeing Frisco, but said it was a good idea to go there so we could see them redwood trees. He said it was right and not no heresy, us going to know them trees, even as we didn't have no religion or god. He said it could still renew our souls, like I been preaching since Missouri, him adopting my very thoughts on the matter, till he done promised after *WESTWARD, THE WAGONS* got made, we'd take us a vacation there.

But there was more to it. He shaved hisself regular every day, saying a fella has got to look right to be right with the world. On our next day off he bought some new clothes, and damn, they looked good on him, falling all elegant and smooth from his shoulders. He even bought hisself a short-brim fedora like Dix's, which bothered me some, but not so much as that, for Joe wore his cocked at a different angle than Dix did, and so made the hat his own.

Like I said, he done got converted, proof of this being what happened one day while Albert and me and him was eating sandwiches on the roof of the Spanish building, this being but two or three days before we was going to work on Dix's moving picture.

"Albert," Joe said, "you know this town pretty good, don't you?"

"I'd say so."

"That being the case, where can a guy go around here to meet a girl?"

My god and hallelujah. He really has put Rose Allen from his heart, or at least was trying.

"Well," Albert answered him, after swallowing a bite of ham and cheese. "After our meetings some of us union guys go to this dance hall down on Broadway. That's downtown, you know, in L.A.. In fact, I met Astoria there."

Joe shook his head. "I can't go to a dance hall."

"Why not?"

Joe shook his head more, saying, "I just can't."

Albert frowned and said, "Joe, I told you, just cause we want a union, it don't mean we're reds."

"It's not that. It's just—" Joe's sandwich dangled from his hand, and he picked some at the crust.

"Hell, even if we were reds, so what? Being parlor pink ain't a disease."

Then Joe blurted out: "I can't dance, dammit, that's why. I ain't never learned."

Albert and me sat there a moment blinking like we was two vultures in a tree, then the both of us busted out laughing. It was a genuine gut buster, which only got funnier cause Joe looked so hangdog watching us.

Finally Albert settled down and said, "That ain't a problem, Joe. Me and Astoria, we can teach you how to dance."

Which is exactly what they done that very night.

Astoria brought a Victrola, and it was a handsome machine, being made from walnut and with red velvet inside the lid. But the arm with the needle was a strange contraption what looked like a squared off U with a wheel on the end. I had never seen its like before. We set it up on a table just outside the door of Albert's bungalow, there not being no room inside to do a proper Charleston or Turkey Trot.

The inside light come out the open door and the window, it laying yellow and soft so the gravel looked near golden white. Joe and Astoria stepped into the light, and Albert showed Joe where to put his hands, one on her waist, the other holding her hand. At first there weren't no music, but Astoria and Albert counted off time and showed Joe where to set his feet and how to bend his knees and turn his feet out and in and how to swing his arms. Once he got it down—him learning it fast and without much repeating—it was my turn.

I worked the Victrola, though it took a minute or so to figure the science of it. I'd take a black disc from a box Astoria also brought, a disc what she called a record. I'd put it on this plate inside the Victrola and set the arm and turn the crank, and that music lifted up full of horns and rhythm, a sound to beguile most anybody's feet, mine included, into jumping and thumping for the joy of it. But I never let my prancing interfere with my duty to the machine, making sure it was cranked and playing out till the sound of it matched the waves what rose from the ocean. Songs got played what had peculiar names: *CHARLESTON DANDY* and *AFRICAN SERENADE*; *AIN'T SHE SWEET?* and *LIVERY STABLE BLUES* and so many others, and I could hear the South in them all. I could hear why folks called it coon music; I could hear the heat of it and how it didn't care none for the rules of the music what come before it. And after a disc done ended, while I put on a new one, the beat of it stayed in my head so I thought it was part of the night itself.

But this wasn't no lesson meant for me; nor the music, neither. It was music meant for Joe, and he took to dancing in no time at all. And he was stylish smooth at doing it. He only needed Albert to tell him once, early on, to jazz it up some, showing him what to do on the side, so Joe copied the moves and put in the jazz; and damn, you could swear he was born knowing them dances in his bone and muscle, and they awoke now to ease out full-formed and natural. Soon enough Astoria didn't do more but flow along from his lead, her face alive with the wonder of it all, a face what told Joe she was willing if he was.

But Joe, if he recognized what I seen, paid it no mind, and Albert was blinded by lust and couldn't see what was plain in his face. Me, I most wanted to laugh at the girl, since I didn't take her for a dame to which flirtation come easy.

After a while I played a disc with a label what read *I WANNA BE LOVED BY YOU*, sung by some baby-voiced girl called Helen Kane. It was a sweet song and silly to boot, and it had a line in it what goes like this— "*I wanna be loved by you/ by you and nobody else but you.*"

Now, I ain't no warbler, but you get the idea. Joe took a liking to this song, having me play it five more times till he got it square and could sing the song as pretty as you please. But after the lesson was over, us back in our bungalow, he sung it more and when he come to them words I just sung to you, he sung them different, singing them a mite slower and melancholy, so I knew he was singing them words to Rose Allen.

The next night he gussied up, putting on his new clothes and splashing on bay rum after a shave and combing grooves slick with Vitalis in his hair, with the part looking specially crisp. He wanted me to go with him, to this dance hall on Broadway, but I told him that wasn't proper etiquette when a man goes to meet him a dame. After all, it only took one guy to do the sweet talking. Joe didn't argue much, but I could tell he was anxious and sorry to be on his own.

Anyway, he cranked up my Ford touring automobile and hit the road, headed for Los Angeles.

I drifted over to Albert's for a while, but he was anxious too and when Astoria showed up, I could see he wanted me to leave, so I done that. Ain't no man should get in another man's way when it comes to lust and it circumstances. I thought about visiting Mrs. Edward Beneke, but it was only a thought. I wound up back in the bungalow, where I turned up the radio, listening again to the bluesy sounds what ran into the night through my open door. Truth be told, I was as anxious as Joe had been an hour before. But there wasn't no help for it, so I settled into my wait, and in time the anxiety drifted off. I done shut my mind off mostly. I ain't no philosopher and my thinking ain't so deep it mattered anyway. Now it was just me and the night.

But along about eleven or so, my Ford popped over gravel and stopped and the door slammed and, a moment after, Joe come in. He was smiling and shy, it seemed, and near like a kid what is pleased with himself but embarrassed about his shenanigans.

"So?" I asked. "Did you get any?"

"Aw, Pooch, it wasn't like that."

"But what happened?"

"I danced."

"And?"

"And nothing. It was only dancing."

I didn't press him none; it was his business, this healing from Rose Allen. I figured it would take more time before he was comfortable and could chase down nookie. He had to work up to it gradual, that's all. But I decided to give him some advice, saying, "Next time stay out longer. Most dames ain't willing till after midnight."

Joe laughed and said, "This ain't about fucking, Pooch. It never was with Rose Allen, and it won't be with whoever's next."

"Then what's it about?"

"It's about what comes after the fucking."

"Only thing to come after is more fucking, if you got the time and she's still willing."

"That ain't so. There's soft words and laughing and stories. Her stories and mine and meant only for us. There's knowing the two of us can spit in the eye of anybody that gets in our way."

"Spit in the eye of—Hell, you mean guys like Dix. Rose Allen ain't never going to spit in his face."

"Maybe you're wrong, Pooch."

I wasn't, but you can't reason with a starry-eyed boy-o what reduced the world to the lyrics of a silly song—*"I wanna be loved by you/by you and nobody else but you"*—him thinking that if he sung them lyrics enough, like it was a prayer, he could make love true and certain.

What a hoot. What a wonder, how he could trick hisself so.

Hell, Big Larry Fornelli said it said it better, if you ask me, cause at least it was honest – crude but honest – him saying it's only love when a guy is comfortable enough to fart in front of his woman.

But I didn't say this to Joe. He didn't appreciate irony none.

CHAPTER 16

The next morning I jumped from my sleep with a pounding on the door, it being that sudden loud, followed by Albert shouting, "C'mon, fellas, me and Astoria got something to show you!"

Now you should know I sleep naked since I left Joliet. My skin is free, sleeping naked. So I rose from my bed, while Joe sat up in his, and I sported a piss boner. Before I could reach for my pants, the front door banged open and a moment more Albert and Astoria bustled up to the door of the bedroom.

Astoria giggled at seeing me, but I didn't much mind, seeing as how not all parts of me is short. She held up her hand and waggled it, and on a finger of it was a ring. Albert stood beside her, saying, "Fellas, she said yes not ten minutes ago."

Joe hopped from his bed—him in his underwear and not so naked as me—and went to pump Albert's hand and kiss Astoria on the face. She blushed and Albert planted a grin on his ugly mug.

I shook his hand next, but when he finally seen my nakedness, his grin drooped. He said, "Baby, maybe you better wait outside."

Astoria giggled some more and give me and Joe an eye what said, Ain't I something? Ain't I the bee's knees? After a last look at my pole, she near winked at me and left the room.

Albert said, "Boys, can you do me a favor? I got to take the morning off. We got to go tell her folks. Can you tell Guffey for me? Tell him I'll be there by noon."

Joe said, "Sure, Albert."

I said, "Guffey ain't gonna like it. You know we're starting on Dix's western today."

"I can't help it none. Besides, I'm no wage slave. I am a man who has got a right to live my life as I see fit."

It was no skin off my teeth, but I knew Guffey wasn't pleased with Albert after yesterday when he found Albert in a workshop handing out a new pamphlet what said the working class was the true masters of the world and other such nonsense. Guffey bawled him out good for that. But seeing him now, the sap of life rising in him, I didn't have the heart to warn him more. Sides, he had his hands full, him getting engaged to a dame like Astoria, a phony vamp what was willing to offer herself to most any man. I didn't figure wearing a ring mattered none or could change that any. I told him not to worry none. I'd explain it Guffey.

Later while me and Joe was in the Ford headed for Empire Studios, Joe said, "Wonder what he did to get her to say yes."

"He probly lied to her. Ain't that usually the way of eternal love?"

Joe only shook his head and pulled a long face. "Pooch, sometimes I worry about you. You ain't got no poetry in your soul."

And thank god for that, which I kept to myself.

That afternoon Dix come up to Guffey and told him to head out for some ranch in a place called Encino and see if some horses had been trained to take a fall from wire. Guffey grumbled it wasn't right, treating a horse that way, saying a rider could lay one down as good as a wire tripping them. But Dix wasn't in an agreeable mood, saying what he wanted had to be dangerous-looking, with dirt and clods spewing up after a horse hit a wire. He wanted them clods flying right into the camera.

As Dix headed off, Joe asked Guffey if he could go along to the ranch, him eager to learn something new about moving pictures. But I wasn't eager and I ain't no sadist. I don't much care to see horses running into wires what trip them up. It ain't that I'm squeamish, you understand, but a guy's got to have some principles, even if it's only for some dumb beasts.

Since nobody told me what to do, I ambled after Dix and seen him go into a studio with the number six by the door. I went in after him, curious mostly and filling my time as best I could.

Inside, that studio looked like a hollow shell of a barn, most of it dark, though down at one end, past some crates and dollies and carts and stacked-up furniture, light burned—hard throbbing light what come from a crowd of head-level theater lights on poles and more hanging high from rods what stretched just under the ceiling. As I drifted in the dark finding a place to be, they sizzled and popped. Dark men adjusted some of them lights, aiming them into a room what had only three canvas flats for walls and no furniture. Each of them walls had windows what looked onto hills and trees and a river, though none of it was real but painted on a backdrop.

Symphony stood in that room, standing in the place where the lights was aimed. From the bright of them, she had ducked her head, and even from where I stood, I could feel the heat of them.

At the edge of the light, Dix talked to a light man and then told Symphony to look up, which she done, and the light man tilted his light, and when Dix told him to tilt it more, the light hit Symphony full in the face.

I edged deeper into the dark, till I come on a crate where Minerva Masterson sat. I eased up to her, saying, "Damn, it's got to hurt, all them lights."

"Can burn the eyes bad. Been known to happen."

Symphony stood without moving, but I could swear she trembled from the effort of facing all that light, trembled under its weight, a halo around the whole of her.

Minerva said, "Dix is punishing her."

"Punishing her?"

"He coulda used a stand-in, but he's not."

That didn't surprise me none. He reminded me of a big guy back in Joliet, a Polack, what set hisself up as an unofficial boss of a cell block. Every now then he'd clobber another inmate just cause he could or cause it was a warning. Mostly I figured this Polack as scared to lose his place, so that's why he clobbered them. I could see it was the same with Dix. Still, it wasn't right, what the Polack done, and it wasn't right what Dix was doing.

Dix clapped his hands and said, "Right, then! That's it!"

The lights popped and began to die off, one after the other, till only two from above was left to burn. I shut my eyes, but the glare of all them lights was printed in my darkness, so I opened my eyes to see a workman with a roll of tape pull off a swatch and set it on the floor just under Symphony's feet.

"Why's he doing that?" I asked.

"It's a mark. Tells Symphony and the lighting technicians exactly where she has to stand when the cameras roll."

Dix had got hold of a big white feather somehow, and he waved it in front of his face like a fan, waving it lazy slow, with his wrist turned in. He was showing Symphony how to use it.

She took the fan and waved it without no bent wrist, and Dix shouted out, "No! No! No!" grabbing the fan from her. Dix again waved it with a bent wrist.

Symphony stared nails into his face, but she took the fan from him when he give it to her and fanned herself as before and not like Dix wanted.

Dix exploded, "What is the matter with you? Don't be a damn prima donna, my dear. It is not becoming nor lady-like."

Symphony turned in her wrist as he wanted, but instead of fanning herself, she slapped Dix once, twice, three times with the fan. It didn't hurt him none, it being a feather, you see, but it left a mark of startlement on Dix's kisser.

Most everybody else froze up right then. They was moving-picture folk and sensitive to drama, even if it was real.

Symphony dropped the feather fan and stalked off the stage and disappeared through a door, leaving Dix to blink before shouting out, "Get back to work, damn you all!" which was what most everybody did.

Cept for Minerva. She chuckled some and said, soft so none but I could hear, "Dix is losing his hold on her. About time, that's what it is. Give it another six months and she'll be on her own."

"That ain't likely," I said, offering a bit of a laugh.

"Without a man, and better for it," she said, the tone of it daring me to say different.

When I didn't, she stopped glaring at me to jump from the crate and walked straight to the door Symphony had used a minute before, leaving me there to study on what she just said, it troubling me that a woman could be better on her own.

I mean, why on earth would a woman what to be on her own? It didn't make no sense and therefore upset me cause I don't take kindly to a world what don't necessarily work how I think it should. Hell, if a dame was on her own she'd screw it up about as sure as a man does, and that's a truth can't nobody dispute. But I kept thinking—why would a dame want to do things alone and without no man? It didn't seem logical, nor nowhere near as much fun. But then I ain't a woman, thank the Lord, so I guess my feelings on the matter is tainted and of no value anyway. Still—

You got to know this: Minerva was wrong about Rose Allen. I say this cause of what happened that night.

CHAPTER 17

Joe and me was in our bungalow, the radio singing soft and blue. The two of us had been playing cribbage at a nickel a game, when he went to drain his lizard while I wandered out to the tiny porch we had, to measure the night.

I noticed the lights of an automobile stopped at the turn off to SUNSET HAVEN, lights what waited till a truck rumbled past before turning left and bouncing slow along the gravel through the weeds, and as the automobile come into where the bungalows was, I seen it was Rose Allen's Cadillac coupe, only with the top up.

The automobile swung a loop and eased up behind my Ford and the door opposite opened; and Rose Allen stood now, with the roof of her Cadillac between us.

"Hello," she said, offering me a small smile.

But it was useless, that smile. I wasn't about to offer no welcome in return, I can tell you that, specially now that Joe was healing and planning on a return trip the next night to the dance hall downtown. I give a quick gander inside but Joe was still in the toilet, which suited me fine. I hoped he'd stay there till I could get Rose Allen gone.

I hustled fast around the car, hissing at her, "You don't belong here. Go on now, get out of here."

She blinked and read my face a moment before putting on that same smile so I could see the dimple what came with it. "I—I have to see Joe."

"He don't want to see you none."

"Please, I have to see him."

"He ain't got no room for you no more."

I said this to be nasty and as an echo of what she'd said to Joe at the side of the road, with me staring at her through the dust gold of my Ford's glass. The smile drained off, while she remembered them words and the others to go with them, remembering how she had betrayed Joe and flung aside her promise to him; or so that's what I wanted the agitation what now touched her face to mean, before she got back into her Cadillac and drove off, letting Joe go, just as she told Joe to let go at the side of the road. Then I thought of Minerva and what she said about Rose Allen. That's when I knew she was wrong, for Rose Allen wasn't never designed to be on her own.

Before I could hurt her more with her own words, Joe said from the door, him sounding amazed and urgent, "Rose Allen."

"Joe," she said and stepped away from me, stepping out to meet Joe as he circled the automobile.

He stopped and they stared at each other, the two of them awkward close and not going no closer but wanting to touch and know each other again. It bothered me to see them like that, as still as that, and as hungry for each other, so I said, "Joe, this ain't a good idea."

Rose Allen wore a desperate look at this, the desperation rousing some pity in me, but I swallowed it back and stared my disgust into her.

Joe reached over to shut her door and I stopped him by putting my hand on the door. He shifted his head to look at me. This wasn't my business none, that's what his look said. But I stared my uneasiness back at him, till he said, "Pooch."

That's all he said—just "Pooch." But in that word was a warning and an apology, too. In that word was all his hope. Which was why I wilted and let him shut the door.

He took her hand now and held it in both of his, and in the yellow of the light I could swear he was near tears even as he was smiling. And she was that way, too. Right then, I knew—Joe could never rub her from his heart, no matter how many dances he learned. As for Rose Allen, I can't pretend I knew her reason for tearing up, but I figured shreds of Joe still clung to her heart, reminding her of their tender time in Missouri. I didn't know what to do about this, except to stand useless while a tiny fear sprouted up in me.

Joe led her now past me and around the Cadillac, leading her into our bungalow.

I didn't follow them. I ain't no kind of fool and know when I ain't wanted.

I wandered to the bluff and stared some at the black swells in the ocean and watched the white of their teeth run onto the shore, feeling most sorry myself when Albert and Astoria, arm in arm, come up to me, Albert saying, "That's Symphony's automobile in front of your place."

I give him a sour look and turned to stare, as they did, at the Cadillac.

Albert said, "Mr. Dix won't like this."

Astoria said, "Maybe he knows she's here."

I didn't think so, remembering what I had seen that afternoon in the studio. She had left Dix full of anger and not so ready to forgive. Could be, she come here to punish Dix for punishing her. But I didn't think this likely, it being more likely she had come from regret and shame for betraying Joe like she done, and cause she needed him now, knowing that Dix was her villain, too, and a man what didn't value her like Joe did. Could be, I'm wrong, but I won't take it back none.

Astoria said, her voice keen to say it, "*SCREEN ROMANCE* says Dix discovered her in the desert. She jumped off a train because of a masher, because he, you know, wanted to ravish her. So she jumped off and got lost in the Mojave. But she was lucky because Dix was there. He was making *SCIMITAR NIGHTS*, you know, the one where he's an Arab bandit but like Zorro, dashing and true in his heart. So, anyway, he rides on a camel over the desert and finds Symphony lost in the dunes, and he brings her to civilization, which is Hollywood, of course. I think that's a wonderful story, don't you?"

"It ain't true," Albert said softly. "I was there when she got discovered. She was an extra in *A NEW TOMORROW*. She was the nymph in the fountain, remember?"

"Oh yeah," Astoria said. "I saw that—oh, but I like my version better, don't you? It's so romantic, being found by Yancey Dix under the moon in a desert."

Albert laughed and said, "I like that better, too. I like it just fine."

Astoria got thoughtful and sounded full of yearning, her saying, "I wish Yancey Dix would discover me. It ain't like I haven't been trying to get him to."

Albert leaned in and kissed her, saying, "Wait until he reads my photo play. I'll tell him about you, that you're the only one who can play Emily. He'll see that, I guarantee it."

Astoria giggled. "I know, Albert, honey, but why does it got to take so long?"

Albert stared some more at Rose Allen's Cadillac. "Maybe we should tell Mr. Dix about this."

"No!" I shouted, the sound of it startling both him and Astoria. "Don't none of us tell nobody about this."

Reaching out I took their arms and I shook each of them. And I squeezed my "No!" into them. "Not one damn word, do you hear me?"

They nodded and I could see Astoria was leaking tears. She folded herself into Albert's shoulder while he led her back into his bungalow.

I didn't mean to make the girl cry, but I didn't have no time to brood over it, I was that scared of Dix and what he could do if he heard about this night. Course, sooner or later, he was going to hear about it, probly from Rose Allen herself, she punishing him hard to show she was the unofficial boss and not Yancey Dix. But it was unpleasant seeing the future like this, so I wandered back to the Cadillac and hid myself behind it, peeping over the hood to see into the door of mine and Joe's bungalow.

They sat on the sofa, with Joe leaning in and talking earnest soft to her, the sound of the words too dim to hear from where I stood. She listened to him and spoke back after a time; and as she did, Joe's face said he had found his joy, which made me sad, for I knew what that joy was going to cost him – and cost me. But there wasn't nothing I could do but peep over the hood and watch him sink into the horror of his love.

I wished Big Larry Fornelli could see this. He'd see it true. He'd see there ain't no scientific hoo-doo to it. He'd see a mystery what can't be explained by science, that mystery being a tough guy what done writ a woman in his heart, writing her permanent and deep, making a tattoo of it, a stain of a tattoo what marked him for a life of sorrow and misery. Course Big Larry Fornelli couldn't see that sorrow and misery. All he could see was what I saw—the glow of Joe's joy and resurrection, a joy and resurrection what would turn rancid in its time. And that was the mystery, how a tough guy like Joe could do this to hisself, mark hisself this way, with the stain of a woman what will betray him again like she done before.

Now Rose Allen lifted her head and read his face and her hand come up to trace his lips. Joe kissed the tips of her fingers. No other part of them touched, just her fingers gentle on his lips; and that's how they sat for long seconds, till Joe raised his hand to take hers—

And they kissed—

After, they stood and there was no words; they had found peace. It was false, that peace, but neither would admit this—not now; not as they breathed in unison and came to discover each other again. Her hand touched his chest and lay there and I could see his hand, the back of it, smoothing her cheek.

They moved from my sight, moving slow into the bedroom.

Now I ain't no pervert; I didn't go banging into our bungalow demanding I get to watch from my bed. Still, it was an inconvenience, cause it was cold out. Though I couldn't see them, I knew clouds was hanging dense and low like they do at night on this bluff.

There wasn't no help for it. I walked across the gravel and knocked on the door. In time, Mrs. Edward Beneke welcomed this poor child into her scrawny arms.

CHAPTER 18

The next morning I peeped between the curtain flaps to Mrs. Edward Beneke's window while sipping cups of java and eating stale Danish. I peeped for most of an hour before Rose Allen and Joe walked from our bungalow, them holding hands like love-loopy kids; them wearing smiles what Adam and Eve might have worn after they walked out of that garden and realized they was on their own. Smiles full of light; smiles what said they didn't need nobody but themselves.

Stopping by her Cadillac, they talked, till she leaned up and touched her lips to his. He opened her door, like the regular gentleman he wasn't never trained to be, and closed it after her, which near made me laugh if I hadn't stopped myself. Being courtly could look silly. They said more, and then the automobile eased off, swerving around my Ford and headed for the highway.

That's when I ran from Mrs. Edward Beneke's bungalow straight for Joe, who was staring at the automobile, him staring into the lip of a new sun just breaking from the hills across the highway. I meant to have it out with him. A resurrected man don't act this way, I wanted to tell him. A resurrected man don't crawl back into the swamp what near drownded him before he escaped.

Joe heard the gravel under me and turned and I stopped, bowled over by his face, it being tender and sweet in its joy, him almost a priest what had just heard actual words from his god. Now I ain't no brute. I ain't that kind of criminal, and that's what I would be, a criminal brute, if I said what was in my mind. It would be a sacrilege to say it, and a violation against Joe. Sure, he was love-loopy and it was wrong of him, but sometimes a guy has got to leave it alone, if only so he can prove he ain't no brute. Which was why I shook my head and said, "We're late for work."

Course, these years since, I sometimes think I should have said it anyway. Being a brute for the sake of another guy ain't really criminal, is it? Maybe if I had said my mind, Joe would not have—

Aw, that ain't so. What happened to him was unavoidable and necessary, I suppose. I know that now but I didn't then or the next night when Rose Allen returned, pulling her Cadillac coupe up behind mine.

Joe and me was playing more cribbage, and when we heard her automobile on the gravel, the white of its light filling our room as it made its loop, Joe didn't say nothing. He just looked at me with eyes what pleaded. It's my bungalow, too, I near said, but I could see it mattered that much to him. So, I stood up, and Rose Allen's door opened and closed. Joe said, his voice low from wanting, "Pooch, thanks, pal."

Rose Allen reached the door and stopped, looking past me at Joe. She wore a green dress what had beads sewn in it and some kind of cowl what had beads on that, too. Them beads glistened like they was drawing light from Rose Allen, which was very likely, for she glowed. That ain't no surprise, you knowing this from having seen her on the screen, but she wasn't on no screen in our bungalow. She was her own self and still she glowed with that fire what burned in her, so a guy couldn't help but hold his breath while he warmed himself in her light. But I shook off the glow quick enough; I wasn't in no mood for glowing.

I slunk past her—she giving way so I could—and stood on the porch, hearing them behind me, hearing them waiting. Well, they could wait a moment while I considered my options, deciding finally to crank up the Ford and head for a moving picture. But I hadn't drove but five miles or so, when I decided I didn't want to see a flicker, and I was still full of the ham and eggs I had for supper. No point stopping for another meal. I had nowhere to go, and it was foolish to drive into the night with no destination, unless I headed for Frisco.

Hell, why not leave Joe to his fate? I didn't owe him nothing, and it wasn't healthy nor proper to watch him get chewed up cause he don't know about love's cruelty. But this was only a moment's swerving, and selfish to boot. I didn't head for Frisco. I couldn't desert Joe. I had a duty to him, even if he didn't know that yet.

I returned to SUNSET HAVEN and pulled up behind Rose Allen's Cadillac and shut down my engine. I sat, not having no place to be, and felt the wet in the air creep into my windows. I could hear the radio from our bungalow, it playing that Cole Porter fella, something about "anything goes." I wasn't too certain of that, not by half. If it was true, Joliet would never have got built, would it? And my thieving would be a virtue to be blessed, ain't that so? It goes to show, music like the moving pictures don't care none about the facts, and that's a pity for all of us.

Maybe twenty minutes later Rose Allen ran from the door, running into the yellow light what spilled from our bungalow, with Joe coming after. He called her name and she stopped and stood, trembling, or so it looked, till Joe come to her on slow feet what crunched under him, and he stopped, him right in front of me, and said, "You owe me that, Rose Allen. You know you do."

She turned, and in her eyes, glistening in them, was tears. "I—I'm here, Joe."

"Yes, you are."

"Don't expect more."

"I won't."

Putting a hand on his chest, she said, "I don't—I don't love him, Joe. Not really."

"And me?"

"Don't ask that, Joe. Not like this."

"I—I'm sorry."

"Isn't it enough that I'm here?" she saying this small-like, the whole of her open and ripe for hurt, with her eyes glistening with them tears.

But Joe could never hurt her. He took her hand and walked her, gentle as you please, back into the bungalow, their shadows stretching long behind them across the gravel, till they was gone, too.

What I had just seen of Rose Allen, it was an echo. It reminded me of how I seen her for the first time, seeing her in that moving picture theatre in Hannibal, Missouri.

I promised I'd tell about this when the time was right. So, now it's time—

CHAPTER 19

After we left the whorehouse in Chicago, we drove into the night, heading southeast, heading for Rose Allen. Joe done slept most of the way, him wearing the beard of a man what ain't shaved in three days. And his clothes looked no better, what with a prison-issue suit wrinkled into bunches and a shirt under what had wilted, specially at the collar, not to mention them clothes stunk of sweat. That's why, come about nine, I pulled into a garage on the outskirts of Hannibal. It was closed for business, a sign in the window said, and that was fine. We wasn't there to buy gasoline. Rousing Joe, I told him he was too ripe by half. Even in prison he scrubbed hisself regular and smelled sweet, and just cause he was free it wasn't proper for him to forget that. I told him he wasn't no grand sight for his lady love, and that we couldn't go no further till he got clean and smelled it.

Down the street in a general store, I bought him fresh clothes, soap and a razor, and tooth powder and a brush. While I done this, Joe hooked a hose onto a faucet on the side of the garage, and he stacked up some crates and barrels to make it private. He stripped hisself naked. When I got there, he was whooping in the cold of the water, throwing off drops what gleamed in the sun.

While he shaved, I done stripped myself and washed, him saying like he just discovered the idea, "I'm scared, Pooch. I ain't never been like this before. But I'm scared."

I laughed. I didn't mean no harm by it, but a tough guy didn't have no business being scared. Improbable, that's the word for it.

But Joe didn't appreciate my laughter, him sulking cause I did.

"Aw, hell, Joe, it's been, what, five years since you seen her?"

Joe nodded.

"Probly she's as scared to see you."

Joe thought on that, while I let him know, "A lot can happen in five years."

"That's what scares me."

"Could be, things won't be the same with her. Could be, she don't feel the same, cause if she did, Joe, she'd have writ you letters during them years. She'd have writ you a hundred letters. And she never did. Not even one."

Joe thought some more on that, while he pulled on his new shirt and buttoned it. Then, his voice low and stubborn, he said, "I can't listen to you, Pooch. It's wrong to listen to you."

So, I didn't say more. We got us late breakfast instead and after that, we drove to Rose Allen's farm.

But she wasn't there. An old lady come from Rose Allen's house and told us Rose Allen had left the farm back in spring of '20, this being about the time Joe got arrested and put on trial. She left under a cloud of shame, the old woman said, and not saying more to explain. About three or four months after that her father sold the farm and that was the last the old woman had heard of any of them Fraziers.

We drove next to Joe's brother's place, and we waited the day on his porch, till Jimmy come home from work. He looked some like Joe, though his features was more blunt, specially in the nose and around the mouth. And his clothes didn't hang natural on him like they done Joe, probly cause he was shorter and thicker in the waist.

Anyway, they hugged and talked and such, Jimmy excited Joe was out of Joliet. Jimmy took us to a diner on the river and while we chowed down, Joe asked Jimmy what had happened to Rose Allen.

Jimmy frowned, hearing her name, and didn't say much, saying only this, saying it somber, "After we get done here, I'll show what's happened to her."

Joe kept nagging him to explain, but Jimmy wouldn't say no more about Rose Allen. Instead, he looked at Joe like he felt sorry for him. Real sorry. Then he took us two blocks up from the river to a theater called The Argonaut, which was an odd name, given it wasn't much more than a hole in the wall, what stank of ciggy fumes and dust and dank curtains. We sat in the back and soon enough the lights went down, and a moving picture started, a piano down in front playing along. It was called *LOST AT SEA*.

Maybe some of you has seen it, but that ain't going to stop me none from telling what it's about.

This photo play started with a shot of a boat in the rain, a boat built for rich folks, like the Titanic. Then it cut to the dock, where them rich folks bustled about and walked up the gangway, pushing aside a girl what got in their way. The girl wore a cape with a hood but you could tell she was poor and not welcome amongst these people. But then she stopped near the gangway and looked up at the boat. The hood fell away and her face—it drenched and vulnerable—was visible now, and that's when Joe gasped.

Now I ain't being dramatic here—he *did* gasp, and he stiffened up and I seen his face watch her face. In the flickers of them shadows, I seen how stunned it was, and I heard him then, hearing the wonder in his voice, though it were a tiny voice and mostly a whisper, "Rose Allen."

Every few seconds during the next five minutes of that photo play, he said her name again, saying it regular and low, like a chant to remind hisself that it was really Rose Allen he seen through the threads of ciggy smoke what churned between him and that screen. It unsettled me, that's what it done, hearing him repeat her name, till I punched his shoulder and told him to knock it off. He looked at me like a man what had been lost in a cave for twenty years, before he turned back and sunk into that world on the screen once more.

After twenty minutes or so, Symphony—who was a stowaway—falls asleep in one of them rescue boats what hang off the sides of ships like the Titanic. A couple of drunk rich guys, not knowing she's in it, lower the boat for a prank, lowering others, too. And so Rose Allen sails alone into the sea, among a flock of rescue boats.

The next morning, the boats are small and the sea is immense and flat and near still. A card pops up what reads—*A WAIF AFLOAT IN A LIMITLESS WASTELAND*—followed by a shot of Rose Allen waking. She sits up and realizes she is lost while a hand rises to her cheek. Strings of hair move in the wind. And her eyes slow glisten with tears, while the undeniable beauty of her face is stripped bare with the awfulness of being utterly alone. As alone as an orphan star in the whole of empty night. It near about made me cry, seeing her like that.

Hell, it ain't no surprise why Joe was devoted to her. Any man would be, she looking that beautiful and ripe for rescue.

Which she was. A fisherman finds her and takes her to New York and the rest of the photo play don't matter none, it being an ordinary Hollywood story, with her marrying the fisherman what saved her.

So, there you have it, just like I done promised. It was that moving picture what sent Joe and me to Hollywood. We had come to rescue her.

CHAPTER 20

About ten minutes after Joe and Rose Allen went back into the bungalow, I got out of my automobile and got into her Cadillac. I done it cause I was curious, but mostly cause I wanted to find her secrets. All women has got them. So do most men. And let's face the truth. I was born a thief and therefore inclined to find secrets. And on the back seat I found one.

It was a gift, a box wrapped up in tissue paper and a bow, it being the size of a square shoebox. Probly I shouldn't have done it, but I did—I stole that box.

I know; I know—I promised Joe I'd stop my thieving ways while we was in California, and until this very moment, I had done just that. But old habits can't be broken that easy, specially when it comes to the mystery of this woman what now calls herself Symphony. 'Sides, I wanted to knock her off her pins. She ain't no fool; she'd figure in time it was me what stole the gift. And that's how I wanted it, with her scared of me some and worried what I'd say to Joe.

Back in my own automobile, after seeing it had no name on it, I opened the gift to find it was a baseball and a glove. Well, now—what did that mean? I put the glove on and slapped the ball into it for a while, smelling the newness of the leather, but I couldn't answer my question, cept for this: the gift had to be for a guy. Could it be for Dix? Nawh, he wasn't a baseball man. Baseball is for ordinary eggs what ain't moving-picture stars. Dix was a tennis and polo man; he was a guy what played with the rich and not us ordinary eggs. And it couldn't be for Joe since he had no interest in baseball. So, then, it meant there was another guy, a guy didn't neither me nor Joe know a thing about. Well, now—ain't that curious?

I stashed the glove and ball under my seat, and then I got a good idea, a perfect idea. I got from my automobile and squeezed into the backseat of the Cadillac. It was comfortable there and I stretched myself out, which I couldn't do in my Ford. It even had a car blanket I used to keep the chill off while I dozed through the night.

Come morning I heard Rose Allen and Joe walk on the gravel, while I stayed flat on the seat under the blanket. Then it was silent and in that silence I knew he kissed her, till the door opened, and as she sat, I heard Joe say, "I been thinking – maybe we should tell him."

"No, Joe. He—he must never know about this."

"But—"

"I'm serious."

It was quiet again, but I could tell they wasn't kissing in that silence. Then she said, softly now, forgiving Joe. "I—I owe him that much, Joe, after what he's done for me."

She started up the automobile and Joe told her goodbye. I stayed flat till we got onto the highway when I popped up and said in her ear, "Pull over here. I want to talk."

She jumped at my words and the automobile spurted ahead till she got it in hand and did what I said, pulling over. Least this way I didn't have me no long walk back to the bungalow, me seeing it through the weeds behind us.

"Your name is Pooch, isn't it?"

I give her a glare.

"Joe's friend," she said.

"We was cellmates in Joliet," I said.

"I thought it must be—be something like that."

Three trucks rumbled by, one after the other, and the Cadillac shuddered.

But that didn't stop me none from glaring into her. I was looking for the ruthless temptress I figured she had to be—dammit, I didn't see nothing like that, seeing instead the face of a troubled soul what probly didn't mean to be no siren. I said, "Joe ain't sick in the head."

"I never thought he was."

"He's love-loopy, that's what he is. And you ain't making him better by coming around here."

She pulled her head back, as if she had to get away from me, but my words charged right into the space she left, "It ain't right. None of it. You got that Dix fella to contend with, and it ain't right, you setting him up against Joe."

"I'm not setting up anyone," she answered sharp, taking back her space.

"Maybe you don't mean to, but—"

"It isn't what you think."

"So what is it? Are you guilty and ashamed for what you done to Joe? Is that it?"

"Some, yes. But—"

"But nothing. Joe ain't in your class no more. We both know that. So why are you here? What do you want from him?"

"A kind word," she said, sounding as hard as me. "Just a kind word and a night's comfort."

"Jesus," I said mostly to myself.

"Pooch, I don't know if you can believe this, but Joe matters to me."

"And what about Dix?"

I could see I had stabbed her good, but she shook her head once and said, "Joe and I have a history—and we have more."

"What more?"

Her eyes shrunk up at this, and she got sad, the trouble in her soul now riding full on her face. I knew she wasn't going to answer my question, so I said, "You can't come here no more."

"I know, Pooch. I—I knew that last night."

"It just ain't—"

"I won't come again. Is that what you want to hear?"

It was, but I wasn't going to give no satisfaction by agreeing with her. I thought then of the ball and glove, but I couldn't bring that up or she'd know I done stole that gift. Still, it was on my tongue to ask who the fella was, the fella what liked baseball so much she bought him a ball and glove. But I didn't. I didn't want her to know I was onto a secret of hers. I didn't want her to know I had my own secret about her. Instead, I leaned over and opened the door on the passenger side and I squeezed past the seat so I was standing on dirt. I turned back and stared at her more before saying, "Joe's a good guy, but he ain't so smart as you and me. Could be, he don't know when a dame's using him."

She read my face and nodded. "He's lucky to have a friend like you."

There wasn't more to say, so I backed off and shut the door and she eased her Cadillac onto the road and drove off.

I stood there smelling gas fumes and feeling the air shift when another truck passed me by. I didn't want to admit it, but I was pleased with what she said. I was pleased cause it was true. Joe was damn lucky to have me for a pal.

CHAPTER 21

I wasn't so foolish as to tell Joe about my talk with Rose Allen, or about the ball and glove I found. I didn't see no need to complicate matters for a love-loopy tough guy, specially when he done turned housemaid.

I ain't kidding none. That evening, after we got back from work, he didn't ride the surf on his belly like usual. Instead, he dusted the furniture and aired out his bedding and swept the floors and washed the windows. I pitched in, since the bungalow lacked any recent polishing. After an hour or so the place looked as polished as that tired old palace what cried for paint could ever hope to look.

After that Joe hovered around, mopping the kitchenette floor for a second time and I told him to knock it off. Ain't no amount of scrubbing can wash ugly off an ugly dame. Joe grunted at that and went out to the porch and hovered there, till finally he hiked down to the highway and stared at headlights as they passed him by. Then he come back and took a chair onto the porch and kept a vigil.

I told him he was off his nut to mope out there like that. Hell, if she meant to come she'd be here by now. Joe give me a sour mouth and went right on sitting in his gloom, waiting on his Rose Allen. I didn't much want to join his misery so I went to bed and I don't know when he did the same, but in the morning he lay in his bed, eyes open to the ceiling.

I asked him, "Did you sleep any?"

"A little, here and there."

I sat up and rubbed my face. "Ain't no dame worth losing sleep over."

He turned his head to bleak eye me. "Something could have happened."

"I suppose."

"Or maybe it's me. Maybe I said something that got under her skin."

I scratched my balls.

"Or maybe I disappointed her somehow."

"Maybe you did, at that." Since he was not susceptible to bawdy humor none, Joe give me more bleak eye. "Aw, for crissake, Joe, it was only one night. Get ahold of yourself."

Which was what he done, so that by noon I about convinced myself his gloomy vigil the night before was but a deviance and too rare to be counted.

We didn't go to the studios that day, but to a farm in Pomona, where an actual barn was set to be burnt down. Guffey had us rig up a stunt involving pulleys and lines. He told us to be careful and get the details right. Since Dix was doing the stunt his own self and since we had only one barn to burn, Guffey had us checking and re-checking every piece of equipment so nothing went haywire. At noon, we got frisky, me and Joe, and Albert included, and we took to hollering and whooping while we jumped from the loft into a pile of hay underneath, like we was school kids and full of sauce. It was gratifying to see Joe throw back his head and laugh from the belly like he done.

But that night, soon as we got to Sunset Haven, he was right back at it, sweeping the porch and scrubbing the floors and washing the windows. Along about nine, Rose Allen still hadn't arrived, which didn't surprise me none, and Joe once more did what he done the night before. He dragged that chair onto the porch and plopped hisself in it and picked up his vigil.

I turned on the radio, thinking to interest him in music, or maybe getting him to practice dancing. But it wasn't no use. He had found the gloom again and no matter how spright or jazzy, he wasn't going to participate in no pagan rites, no sir. So I took the cards and peg board out to the porch and managed to get him to play some cribbage, though he was pretty much distracted the whole time staring at headlights on the highway more often than he did the cards.

Sometime after ten, headlights dipped from the highway, and an automobile pulled up to our bungalow. It was Albert's Chrysler.

"Boys," he said from his window, the engine grumbling under him, vibrating him so his voice wobbled. "It was inspiring, tonight's meeting was."

I dropped my cards and stood but Joe stayed right where he was. Albert, got from his automobile, the engine still grumbling, and rotated his neck back and forth.

"We had a speaker from the Wobblies. Some guy called Vincent Saint John."

"Who's he?" I piped up.

"Some big shot who knew Bill Haywood before he ran off to Russia, and he knew Debs, too, before he got sent to prison."

A union man what got sent to prison? That perked me up some, with me saying, "Is that right?"

"You should have heard him."

Pulling his leg, I said, "Who? Debs?"

"No, Saint John. He give me an idea and it's a beaut; an idea what I can do to unionize at Empire."

"Oh boy," Joe said from his throat. "Albert, don't try it. Please don't you try whatever it is."

But Albert was too inspired to admit any warnings, saying, "Saint John said the wage system is evil, and it's undemocratic. He said it's evil so much of the wealth belongs to only a few greedy individuals who don't care any about the workers who make their money for them. It's obscene cause they wind up with more money than they can ever hope to spend in three lifetimes, even if they eat sirloin and oysters every night and sleep on silk sheets. That being the case, he said, there has to be a revolution in the workplace, where the worker becomes his own class, a class to equal those greedy few who have all the wealth. And that's what got me to thinking."

Oh Jesus, here we go. Another of his tirades, but as it developed it did have a new twist.

"So I raised my hand and Saint John seen it and nodded at me. I told him I worked at Empire, that I was a wage slave who was fed up with it. And I told him I took his words to mean the guys like me at Empire, the wage slaves, we could band together and make our own photo plays and split the profits even-steven. We could make these photo plays without no big shots telling us what to do. Saint John grinned when I said that, fellas. He grinned and he said, and these are his exact words, he said, 'That's the spirit, young man. That's the kind of thinking the I.W.W. means to inspire.' How about that?"

"That's about the craziest damn thing I ever heard," I told him.

But Joe sat up and focused on Albert, saying, "You know, you might have something there."

"You bet I do. I can see it now. We pool our money to rent us our own cameras and sets, whatever we need."

"We don't have enough money to make no flicker," I told him.

"So we get us some investors."

"From where?"

But Albert didn't answer me, going off instead to say, "We can be our own actors. I've got half a dozen photo plays already written."

"It could work," Joe said, thinking hard about what he was hearing.

I held back on my doubts, but least Joe had roused from his funk and before I knew it he and Albert went to Albert's bungalow in Albert's Chrysler to work on the details. Me, I sat in Joe's chair, but I wasn't taking up his vigil. I was too agitated for that and nowhere near as gloomy.

Now I ain't so naïve as Joe and Albert, or them Wobblies neither. I know the workings of this sorry old world better than most, and I know about the getting of money. I know them greedy few Albert was talking about stole most of their money, them stealing it fancy-like and with lawyers and politicians helping so they can get away with it. And I know they sit tight on that money, guarding it. Won't be any of them investing in no moving picture made by guys like Joe and me and Albert.

Still—

I had to admit it. The idea of making a moving picture got my blood churning, it surely did. Could guys like Joe and me and Albert pull it off? Could we make our own moving pictures? Why the hell not? We didn't have nothing to lose.

Hell, wouldn't that be something, if we could?

The next day, fate and fire proved the folly of such speculating.

CHAPTER 22

" **A** lbert," Guffey said, "Have you checked out that pulley again, like I told you an hour ago."

Albert and Joe was sitting, feet dangling, on the back of a truck what brought some cameras and other equipment. They was working on a production plan, or so Albert called it, for the making of their very own moving picture. Joe and him had been confabulating off and on all morning when Guffey, him being a fella what got nervous easy, come stomping up and asked his question.

Albert looked up from his scribbling to say, "I'll get to it, Guff."

Guffey frowned. "I don't trust that pulley's lock."

"Don't worry none, I checked. The lock's okay."

"What the hell are you up to?"

"We're planning our futures," Albert told him. "We're planning on being our own bosses, that's what."

Guffey wasn't happy with that answer, his mouth showing it, but there wasn't more for him to say. From the moment we had got to that farm in Pomona just after dawn, we done checked and triple-checked the rigging and tested it till the sun was flat burning at noon. Even Guffey, nervous as he was, had to admit there wasn't nothing more we could do but wait while the camera folks finished setting up their gear and framed their shots. They had four cameras to make certain they got it right the first and only time. And Dix hovered over them camera guys, talking, always talking and running the show in grand style. Wasn't nothing for us to do till Dix told them to fire up the barn and crank up those cameras.

Guffey headed for the barn, disappearing into its doors. Albert said, "The sad thing about Guff, he don't even know he's a wage slave. Joe, what do you think, should we invite him to join our moving-picture company?"

I wasn't so eager to know the answer to that, so I wandered off to watch Dix walk around the front of the barn, checking to see if the charges was set proper. He stopped to look up at the mouth of the loft, which was probly thirty feet or so from the ground, that barn being as tall a narrow barn as I had ever seen. Hell, it was going to burn fast, that was certain enough, the boards of it stained that gray and wood-rot dry. He took ahold of the rope what was meant to save him from a fire and tugged it few times, but not so hard as to lift the bale of hay tied on the other end, it being a counterweight.

Now that rope ran straight up to a derrick arm—a 4x8 jutting off the roof and where the pulley was mounted—then running back down to the bale of hay. The idea was this: Dix was going to jump from the burning loft and catch the rope what was then going to lower him slow and safe to the ground while the bale rose to the pulley. It sounds risky in that a slip or a miscalculation could break a few bones, but back then some moving-picture stars did most of their own stunts—Dix specially so. Realism, that was his bread and butter, and he wanted the camera to show it was he escaping the fire and not no ordinary five-buck-a-stunt guy like me or Joe or Albert. It was what his audience expected of him.

Now he pulled hard on the rope, pulling on it till he crouched on his heels and the bale lifted a foot and dangled, while Dix held it so, the rope creaking from the weight of it.

"It'll hold," I told him.

Letting go of the rope, he smacked his hands together and rubbed them. He give me a look meant to drill a hole in my forehead, saying, "It better."

Dix looked back up at the rigging and tugged at the rope again. He said, "I want to see it again."

"Okay, I'll do her," I said, heading for the barn.

"No, not you—Albert," He called out, "You and Pooch go test that rigging again. I want *you* riding it down, not Pooch."

I could see the sense of it, why he wanted Albert to make the jump. Of the three of us, he was closest to Dix's weight and build. Still, it stung.

Albert give his pencil and book to Joe and slid from the truck and followed me into the barn, where Guffey blinked at us, saying, "It's about time."

He hustled out to talk to Dix, the both of them looking up at the mouth of the loft.

Now inside, that barn was stripped empty, livestock included, cept for some spiders and such. Wasn't no need to burn up animals of consequence, nor alfalfa neither, since we was shooting only the outside of the barn to get Dix making his perilous leap from flames. Course how he got in that barn and tied up and near scorched before he got free was set to be filmed at Empire in one of them studios, where they got a machine to vomit out smoke without no flames, it being non-inflammatory that way and not so deadly for moving-picture stars.

I climbed up the ladder to the hay loft, and Albert come right after me. The two of us stepped up to the mouth of the loft and looked down on Dix and Guffey, and seen Joe had moved to the bale of hay to check its drop after we let go of the rope. Dix waved an arm to tell us to get on with it.

"I think he's scared," Albert said.

Probly, that was so. Hell, I didn't blame Dix none. If it was me, I wouldn't do it, not with them flames licking my backside before I could make the jump. But that wasn't my lookout. I didn't have no public what expected me to risk life and limb.

Anyway, Albert leaned out and caught the derrick arm and monkey-walked his hands to the pulley, hollering down after he checked it over, "It's ready, dammit!"

He hand-walked back and I helped him to land in the loft. I give his ugly mug a grin and without a by-your-leave I jumped out the loft, catching the rope and sailed out a couple feet before the rope caught my weight and down I went, pretty as you please, the bale gliding right past me till I hit the ground and let the rope out slow so Joe could catch the bale.

I raised my eyebrows to Dix, daring him to bawl me out, and when he didn't, I stepped back and let go of the rope. Now it was Albert's turn.

He jumped onto the rope and rode her down gentle as falling snow, and when it was over, he bowed to Guffey and Dix. "It's a corker, Mr. Dix, a rip-snorting corker, guaranteed."

Dix only grunted and bustled off to talk to the fellas what was going to set off the charges.

Half an hour later, they was ready to crank the film. Dix and Guffey went into that barn and about thirty seconds after that Guffey come out, shouting, "Okay, fire away!"

The boys on the detonators set off the charges and through the smoke, flames began to creep up and write themselves on the walls of the barn. We couldn't see Dix yet. The idea was, he was going to fly sudden-like out of that loft, sort of like he was flying through flames and be a surprise to see. Each of the camera guys began to crank away.

After about four minutes, the fire had took solid hold and it was breathing and sucking up the air around us, so it was like water rushing by us and into that barn. "C'mon, c'mon," Albert started saying. "C'mon, dammit, jump."

You have give Dix credit. He is a showman. He planned on milking that fire for all the tension it was worth, when, wood cracking, he appeared in the loft, while behind him, gushing smoke, drapes of flame stirred—evil, terrifying drapes of flame.

He jumped for the rope.

Catching it, he sailed out, and kept sailing, till the rope couldn't sail no more but spun him around and left him stranded there for a moment, stuck in the sky, while he stared a godawful pathetic stare at us. Then the sky let go and the rope swung back, swinging Dix right back into the burning drapes. He was hidden now in the smoke and the rope come back out, but Dix wasn't on it. He had been swallowed by that fire.

"Goddammit, the lock!" Guffey said.

I knew what he meant, that the pulley's lock had somehow prevented the rope from passing through the groove, and that was the cause of this calamity.

All us folks on the ground was stunned, though the camera guys kept cranking.

But not Joe.

"Pooch! Albert! Grab hold!" He pushed the end of the rope with the bale tied to it in our hands. "Hold it down in case that lock slips!"

With that, he grabbed the other end and commenced to shinnying his way up. Once he was clear from the ground, Guffey took his end, holding it down so it didn't sway as much.

Joe climbed.

And he climbed, smoke pouring around him.

The heat of the fire began to singe my face, or so it felt.

When he got level to the loft, Joe started to swing hisself, swinging wide until he threw hisself into the mouth of fire and smoke.

Now we waited, and the heat throbbed on my skin. But I wasn't backing off. You better believe I wasn't backing off.

Joe appeared in the loft with Dix hanging onto his neck for dear life, retching up smoke, the whole of him black from smoke, cept where his eyes were jumping from panic. Behind, them drapes of flame was swollen and billowing full. Joe and Dix threw themselves out and grabbed the line, Dix being under Joe, the fire flapping out of that loft right after, snapping hard at where they was.

After Dix and Joe shinnied down, choking and gagging the whole way, both of them collapsed to the ground, coughing and retching some more, till the lot us, with Guffey shouting to hurry up, pulled them far enough from the fire wouldn't none of us burn.

Somehow canvas sacks of water appeared and both Joe and Dix washed the smoke from their mouths and splashed it all over them, cooling their skin.

Guffey said, "C'mon, boys, let's get them in the truck so we can take them to a hospital."

But Dix, coughing, said, "No! No hospital!"

Joe stood, saying, "I don't need no hospital." He chugged down a long drink of water, then poured more over his head, shaking the drops from his hair. "Damn near got broiled, though, didn't I?" he said to me personal.

Dix wallowed some more, gagging on fresh air and lifted his head so I could see tears smeared around his eyes. Damn, he stank of smoke and flame. So did Joe. With the help of Guffey and others, Dix finally managed to stand. He gasped some more and found his weight, shrugging off the others. He looked at Joe and croaked out, "Thanks for— "

I don't think he much wanted to thank Joe, specially with all of us guys standing around watching, but it wasn't till we got to Lone Pine that I seen into him more and found out why he didn't finish his thanks.

Not that Joe seemed to want any thanks, him not saying nothing back but staring careful into the scowl Dix put on, a scowl what warned Joe to keep what happened in that burning loft private and unexplained. Joe nodded once and looked at the rigging. The ropes was burning and the derrick arm and pulley, too. The barn whooshed and the walls cracked and groaned and sagged before collapsing.

All of us watched the burning for a time.

Finally Dix walked up to Albert and glared into him, saying soft but treacherous, "You're fired."

He walked toward his automobile, and Albert ran after him. "No! Mr. Dix, it wasn't my fault. It worked all right when I did it. You seen that."

I wanted to tell Albert to knock it off, to stop pleading. It wasn't manly to sound so weak as that. I ran and grabbed for his arm to hold him back, but he slipped through and reached for Dix, turning him by the shoulder, "Please, Mr. Dix. You can't blame me for what happened. It wasn't my fault."

Dix give him a brutal stare and shoved him away, so that Albert stumbled into me and both of us went down. He got in his automobile and drove off, with us choking on the dust he left behind.

Albert looked at me, and he was close to crying, "This isn't how it's supposed to happen! This isn't it at all!"

CHAPTER 23

Back at Sunset Haven that night, Albert and Joe rode the surf on their bellies for a time, but it didn't work none, Albert coming from the waves hangdog dismal and suffering. I was worried for him, and so was Joe, so we sat, the three of us, on the sand and rock to watch the sun drown itself in the ocean.

Albert said, "It wasn't my fault. You know it wasn't."

"I know," Joe said

"I don't understand what happened. It don't make sense."

"The lock must have slipped," I told him.

"Yeah," said Joe.

"He could have got killed," Albert said, giving both me an Joe a panicked look. "If he had—"

In the breathing to follow, a picture of Dix's face, while he was stuck in the sky on that rope, come to mind. It was comical, how his face looked, the horror in it absolute and therefore comical. Not that nobody laughed cause it was gruesome, too, when that rope started carrying him back into those drapes of flame.

"Why didn't he let go?" Joe said.

"He couldn't," I said.

"Better to fall than land in fire."

"He froze up, Joe. That's how some fellas do, come life or death. They freeze up. They lose the ability to reason."

Course I didn't know if that was true with Dix, but it sounded good and seemed to agree with what Joe said next. "When I got to him, he was standing there coated in smoke, like he was hypnotized, staring into those flames."

In my head I saw Dix standing before that fire. It didn't make much sense, why he didn't turn and run and jump out of that loft. Unless he couldn't cause he was snared by a trap of the mind, a trap he set hisself. I mean, he was a master of celluloid, a guy what thought up stories in images and melodrama, and so in the face of them flames, his imagination flared up and took its rule. Could be he believed a devil-god had hypnotized him, a devil-god what wanted him for a sacrifice. Hell, maybe that wasn't so, that sounding pretty nuts, but it could have been, and he'd have died if Joe hadn't come to get him.

Nowadays, I sometimes think about Dix dying in that loft of fire. Sure would have made things easier for me and Joe and Albert if he had. But that's the way of the world, ain't it? I mean by that, in real life the villains mostly get away; they mostly win it all. While guys like Joe and Albert and me—well, let's just say we wind up holding onto the short end of luck.

Albert asked, "Why'd he fire me? He had to see it wasn't my fault."

"Mostly, he's a bastard," I answered.

Joe laughed. I figured he saw the humor of it, that he had rescued a genuine bastard and it was too late now to throw him back.

Albert said, "I haven't told Astoria yet."

I said, "She knows already."

"I suppose that's so."

Empire was a rumor mill and it must have had a fine old time with what had happened at that farm. Astoria had to have known by now, which left me wondering, why wasn't she here? Why wasn't she nursing Albert's grief along with us?

Albert said, "I got unfinished business at Empire. Dix, he's still got my photo play."

Joe said, "Albert, give it a few days. He'll get over it. Me and Pooch, we'll talk to him in a few days."

Albert perked up at that, saying, "Yeah, he'll see it wasn't my fault."

"He only did it, fired you, because he was scared."

"That's so," I said.

Albert said, "He was distressed. That can make a guy do funny things."

I said, "The smoke probly addled him some."

Joe laughed again.

Albert said, him trying on a bright voice, "Yeah, in a couple days, you guys talk to him. He'll take me back. He's got to."

Joe said, "It's good, you having this vacation. Gives you time to work out our production plan."

"That's true," Albert said. And he smiled some. "I'll just tell Astoria I took some time off to get my moving picture planned out. She'll see it's smart of me to do that. She'll see I'm a guy who can't miss. Some day I'm going to be as big a director as Mr. Dix."

I didn't bother to tell him contrary, seeing as how me and Joe without no Astoria had spent the past hour trying to rouse him from his despair.

After a few minutes we stood up and climbed the stairs to the top of the bluff, and stopped, the three of us seeing Rose Allen standing beside her Cadillac coupe, the last of the sun in her face and making it glow. She smiled her relief when she seen Joe and stepped away from her car.

Without giving me a glance, Joe said, "Pooch, you don't mind, do you?"

Actually I did, but Joe wouldn't have heard me none, him trotting along to meet her, leaving Albert and me behind to see her open her arms and hold him close when he got to her. The two of them stood that way for a long while, and her eyes was open but did not see Albert nor me, nor even the sun. I suppose she wasn't seeing nothing but only intent on knowing Joe again, knowing that he were unburned and alive for her.

They turned and walked back to our bungalow and disappeared inside.

Albert asked, "Do you think Mr. Dix knows about them?"

"Probly not."

"If he finds out—"

"You gonna tell him?"

Albert worried on that before saying, "Ain't my business, is it?"

He had that right. But it was mine, as Joe's genuine and only friend. And it bothered me plenty, specially cause Rose Allen done lied to me. She said she'd never come back here. But now, this—

Hell, the woman betrayed Joe in Missouri. It wasn't nothing for her to lie to me. And there wasn't nothing I could do about it. Not now anyway.

"C'mon, Pooch, I got some wine. Let's go to my place and I'll tell you about how Dix made that woman a moving-picture star."

CHAPTER 24

I don't know if what Albert told me that night was accurate. Some of it echoed of the moving-picture magazines, and don't nobody take much of what they say for truth, but all of it was filtered through Albert, him being undependable and a guy what thought like Dix did, in grand images meant to stir an audience and complete only cause they do stir. So, I don't know what to say about her history, cept this: can't much of it be actual.

Dix rode his horse among dunes only to stop when he seen her, she but a figure atop a dune against the darkening sky. But as she neared, stepping from the desert into his knowing, walking into the dying sun, he held his breath. She was magnificent. And he spoke to her and learned she was lost, but that's all he learned, she unable then and ever since—it was amnesia, or so she and the magazines claimed—claimed to say how she come into this desert, she an eternal mystery to him and the world.

Dix took her to his camp, and there she bathed, with the help of other women, at a nearby oasis, the Joshua trees and cactus standing guard. And so she emerged, glistening and pure from the waters, and clothed herself in a robe and went to the campfire above, where Dix saw the glory of an original woman, seeing Eve fresh risen and nubile from the waters of Eden. At that very moment, while her eyes read his face, he decided to give her to the world. He decided to make a moving-picture actress of her.

And in the days what followed, as *SCIMITAR NIGHTS* was filmed among the dunes, he versed her in the art of celluloid storytelling. Course Albert didn't know if they was lovers during all this, but I ain't one to deny the proclivities of human nature. They must have shared a tent on those desert nights, with him weaving his spell and she open to the magic of a guy what could build new and exotic worlds never seen before by any of us.

They returned to Hollywood, and he took her to Empire Studios where she was brought to the cameras, them being merciless and the only judges what matter. She stood before them and played the scenes Dix had trained her to play. And the cameras, they recorded a woman complete in her soul, a woman designed to be captured on film, her slightest thought rising to her face and trembling before the lens. Thus she was elected to become a star of the screen.

But a new star needs a moniker for the ages. Rose Allen Frazier was ordinary and not true to the myth of this woman with no past what come out of a desert. Dix ruminated on this and watched her on celluloid till he heard the music from all instruments, hearing the music of the sun and desert, and so he come to designate her as Symphony.

After this, her first moving picture began. *A NEW TOMORROW* it was called, and in it she had but a few minutes to convince us she was magical and a nymph. I say nymph cause in that flicker that's what she was mostly. Course some of you know what I'm saying, having seen it for yourself, but if you haven't what you see is this: you see her in a fountain at a mansion with the water splashing over her. Around her a party's in full swing, with booze aplenty and no regrets by any. Now the camera watches as she, this nymph, sees Dix and walks through the water, the whole of her parts moving like women do in their private knowing of sex, till she reaches Dix, him playing a gentleman gambler. She lifts her arm to him, the water dancing a halo around her, and he takes it and pulls her from the fountain. And so they dance the tango, with drops of water getting flung from her hair. And after, the music done, she returns to the fountain, looking back over her shoulder at him, her face teasing him, asking him if he meant to join her.

Probly it was that one look over her shoulder what made her a star of the screen. That's what Albert said and I agree, cause that look had in it the promise any man hungers to know at least once in his life.

But it was a lie, that look, if Albert was to be believed. And since he was there to see it happen, I ain't got no reason to doubt this part of his story none. It was really a look of desperation, he told me. You see, that water was cold and they had done the scene a dozen times, mostly doing it cause of her, cause she was new to the camera and too aware of being wet in a flimsy gown what hinted at her secret parts. And she was shivering. Not that this stopped her any, she never complaining nor letting on she was miserable. They kept cranking the cameras till she got it right, she hiding the awful of it in that last look what promised so much to the man brave enough to follow her into that cold, cold fountain.

When *A NEW TOMORROW* got played, she was a sensation. The studio got flooded with fan letters for weeks after. Seemed like the whole country wanted to know her story, the news rags quick to follow this up. So, Dix and Symphony told the myth of her being lost in the desert and coming to him by magic, a myth what got adopted as actual and undeniable in the months to follow.

When I asked Albert if he believed the myth, he said of course he did. It would be wrong not to. It would be a desecration against all Hollywood yearns to become. I didn't know what to make of this, and I didn't know what to make of what he said next, neither.

"It's peculiar, though," he said, "how Symphony disappears every so often. She disappears for days, three or four days at a time. Not even Dix knows where she goes. In the magazines and at Empire, folks speculate on why she does this, but if you ask her why, she won't say nothing but walk away and forget you. And she don't tell nobody, neither, when she means to disappear. She just goes away, vanishes, leaving us all to wonder. She don't even answer the newshounds when they ask her about it.

"But I got me a theory; I think she returns to the desert. I think she has a secret oasis where she bathes and renews herself before God."

I didn't think much of this theory, but I wasn't one to cast doubt on Albert's beliefs. Hell, it didn't any of it matter, anyway. Still, it was entertaining, the myth of how she got discovered by Dix.

But that night while wine heavy and trying to sleep on Albert's sofa, his story nagged at me. Hell, I didn't blame Rose Allen for denying her past and claiming amnesia; nor Dix neither, since building lies was this world's oldest and most profitable profession. What nagged at me was the folks what watched their antics on screen and read about them in magazines and such. I couldn't figure why they was fool enough to buy sorry lies and myths. I guess they just ain't satisfied being what they are born to be, and somehow that's sad cause that ain't much of a way to know life. But, like I done said before, I ain't no philosopher and don't nobody want to hear this anyhow, it being too critical of what moving pictures can do to harm a body.

But something else nagged at me about that story, and come the morning I decided to get an answer.

With the dawn I waited beside Rose Allen's Cadillac. When she come out of mine and Joe's bungalow, her fresh from a good sleep in Joe's bed, I stepped up to her and glared at her. "Well, if it ain't the desert princess."

She looked to Joe who was on the porch, and I seen an apology on her face. Then she stepped past me and opened the Cadillac's door.

I said to her back, "What I want to know is, what happened in them two years between Joe going to prison and Dix finding you in the desert? Can you tell me that?"

From the porch Joe said, "Pooch—"

Rose Allen looked over her shoulder at me, though this look wasn't like the one she give Dix before returning to her fountain. This one was confused and maybe hurt some, but it settled after that and become resigned. She said, "Life happened."

With that, she got in her automobile and drove off, a few of the pebbles under her tires kicking up and bouncing off my legs.

I glared now at Joe, saying, "So did she tell you about them two years?"

"No."

"Did you ask her?"

"Of course I did," he said going back into our bungalow.

I could tell he didn't want to talk about it, so that left me kicking at the gravel and cursing Rose Allen for breaking her promise to me, her saying she would never come to Sunset Haven again, though I don't know why I expected different. That woman don't keep promises, she keeping only secrets.

So, I let it go and went into the bungalow to pack up for the trip to Lone Pine and the desert beyond.

CHAPTER 25

It took near four hours to drive from Hollywood to Lone Pine, and thirty minutes more headed east before we come over a hill and I seen the camp what got set up for the cast and crew of *WESTWARD, THE WAGONS*.

This camp took up sixteen, maybe seventeen acres with a couple adobe buildings fifty yards from the road. Further along, fixed tall among a dozen or more corrals full of horses and oxen and cows, an old windmill creaked. To the south a pond, fed by water that windmill dredged up, shone green-gray and looked to be deep and cool, shaded like it was by juniper and a tower of rock what had a tree growing in it. I swear, it was a tree growing from a rock. Tents had been pitched in rows to the north, them being for the crew mostly, though a separate circle of tents was pitched near the pond, them being for Dix and Symphony and Rooney June and the other actors.

Cept for that tree, the camp looked about like I expected. What surprised me, though, was the Conestoga wagons – pioneers called them prairie schooners, I do believe – lined up by the corrals. I counted ten of them, and damn, standing near them I seen they was huge, the lumber of them thick and scarred and the wheels taller than me and their spokes thicker than my arms. Jesus, the sight of them near shook my bones, but I didn't let nobody see that, climbing like I done up into the seat of one. I took up the whip and cracked it few times, showing I was ready to drive that wagon like I was expected to in the days to come, even if I had serious doubts I could do it.

Anyway, folks scattered getting themselves squared away. Joe and me found our tent at the end of a row, its backside facing a blue line of mountains, most of them crumbled stones. Wind nipped at the tent's canvas, blowing in snatches and spurts, and flurries of sand got lifted up and scurried for a few feet. After we got settled, Joe lying in his cot, I wandered off to get a feel for this place what seemed wind-scrubbed and bare. I seen a guy wrapping cameras in oilcloth. I asked him why and he said it was to keep sand from the innards.

I headed for the adobe buildings and who should I see coming from one but Astoria Starr herself, wearing dungarees and a man's flannel shirt and looking sweet enough to be served on a cake. Her face looked keen to see the adventure happening in this desert in the mountains.

"What are you doing here?" I asked, surprised to see her.

She said, "Pooch, I'm an assistant. That's what I am. A production assistant. I got promoted special by Mr. Dix himself yesterday afternoon."

"How about that?" I said, thinking of the night before and of Albert drunk on wine and crying cause his Astoria wasn't there with him. But that's how this sorry old world works. While he was pining for the loss of his job, she done got promoted by the man what fired him. Ain't that a hoot?

"That's my office," she said, pointing at one of the adobe buildings. Then she pointed to another building. "And that's Mr. Dix's office and he don't share it with nobody, like I got to. His office is really nice. Have you seen it yet?"

I shook my head. I didn't care none about them offices, not when I had something to get off my chest, so I piped up, "Albert missed you last night. He needed you."

The smile fell from her face but she clamped it back on, saying, "Oh, he'll be all right. The silly boy, he shouldn't have done what he did to Mr. Dix."

"He didn't do nothing to Dix."

"Really? Oh, well, I'm sure it will work itself out."

I looked at the ring on her finger, and when she seen me looking at it, she hollered out, sudden-like, "Barbara, oh, Barbara," and minced off to get away from my glare, joining another dame what was dressed similar to her, she another production assistant, or so I took it.

What a piece that Astoria was. A real gold digger. Well, Albert didn't know it yet, but he was lucky to be rid of her. Still, it galled me, her not having the decency to give him back the ring. I stared after her like a constipated snake till I had enough and headed to the pond cause I wanted to see that tree growing out of a rock.

It was mostly dead. Limbs stripped bare of bark stabbed into the sky and wore grooves like stone what had been eroded. But on the tips of some of them, bristles grew. The damn thing looked like the kind of art I heard them frogs do—you know who I mean, that Picasso guy and his pals—art full of twists and angles don't nobody expect. But that tree wasn't made by no artist, it being a sculpted by wind alone.

The rock and tree leaned over the pond and the reflection of them shook in the water. I tossed a stone in the pool and the reflection broke apart.

Hearing steps, I turned and seen Yancey Dix coming toward me. He smoked a heater, one of them skinny kind, and the smell of it was strong and clean. "Well, Pooch, you've invaded my secluded bower, I see."

I took his meaning, but I wasn't going to leave. Not just yet. I pointed at the tree, "Is that the tree what this place got named for?"

Dix chuckled. "Hardly. No, that tree is miles from here. But it's the same kind, a bristlecone pine. It looks rather tortured, doesn't it?"

"Don't see how it can grow in rock."

"Things do have a habit of growing in the most unexpected places."

He puffed on his heater, I could tell he wanted me to leave, but I planted myself firm and let it rip, thinking that was the only way to get it said, "You shouldn't have fired Albert."

"Albert?"

"Yesterday, at the barn, it wasn't his fault none."

"Oh, you mean Alfred."

"Hell, he wasn't the one what froze up."

Dix pulled the heater from his mouth and scowled at me, saying as treacherous as he sounded when he fired Albert, "Froze up?"

"Yeah. Just that."

"Did Joe tell you that?"

"He didn't have to."

Dix took this in and I swear I could hear his brain clicking while he sorted what I said. "If he told you that, he's lying."

More like, you are, but I didn't say as much, just staring at him. His face eased off the menace and he put the heater back in his mug and said, "It isn't always easy being a public figure."

What the hell was he talking about?

"I must maintain a certain persona, one that doesn't involve freezing up."

I looked at the tree, seeing the limbs of it stabbing the sky. "How old do you think it is?"

"The tree? I've heard more than a thousand years."

"And it's still alive, growing in stone – ain't that something?"

"I suppose it is."

I looked to see Dix's profile, him looking up to see the tree. It was then I got the truth of it. Like the tree, a lie had rooted now in the stone of his head. And them roots was digging deep. Wouldn't nobody tear down that lie, not even Albert, nor Joe, nor me. And the lie? It was simple: he did not freeze up. Public figures like him don't freeze up. It was impossible for that to happen, in spite of the lies Joe could offer.

What do you say to guy what could trick hisself like that? I was at a loss, so I went back to how I started, "It wasn't Albert's fault."

Dix dropped his eyes and fixed them on the water. "Pooch, neither Hollywood nor I appreciate a red who agitates for a union."

"Albert ain't no red."

Dix scowled at me just like he had the day before after failing to thank Joe proper. "He is if I say he is."

What could I do? There wasn't no reasoning with the man. So, I give the tree a last gander, and that's when I heard a gun go off in the distance. The wind stretched its echo and made it frail. The gun went off again. Dix said, "It must be Minerva."

A few minutes later I found her in a canyon east of camp. Standing behind her, I watched as she clicked back the hammer of her pistol and took aim and fired. Thirty yards further on, a knob of cactus flew off its plant, bleeding fragments in the air. She did this again. And again. Doing it until both guns was empty.

As she re-loaded, I stepped up to her and asked, my admiration in the asking, "Don't you never miss?"

"Never when it counts," she answered back.

CHAPTER 26

That night the wind died off, and the desert smelled of sage and smoke from the campfires what got lit hours before, with the coming of dark. Six of them fires was dotted along the camp, but the dark was indifferent to them, it being definite and with no moon to ease it. Them campfires wasn't much good for nothing but holding back the cold some. For a while Joe and me sat around one ourselves, sitting with the old-time wranglers and cowboys, listening to them swap tales of the Old West. A few of them had rid with Buffalo Bill Cody's Wild West Show, and they told tales about Sure-Shot Minnie, the Belle of the Plains.

One of them stories was a corker.

Seems back in '01, while in France, a mountain lion what traveled with the show got loose from its cage and run up into the seats, causing a great commotion. Them frogs scrambled every which way, gabbling their jumble of a language as if they could hide in it somehow. But this one girl on the top row, her but fifteen or so and a pretty slip of a doll, wasn't versed in matters of escape. She tripped and fell and rolled, bang-bang-bang, down each riser and, splat, landed into sawdust near the cage. The lion watched the whole of her bouncing along, and from his perch on a seat above, he roared his intent to tear out her throat. Darned if that ain't when Sure-Shot Minnie, Winchester carbine in hand, stepped between that cat and that slip of a doll. Now you'd think she do what a man would in this situation; you'd think she'd plug the cat between the eyes. But not Sure-Shot Minnie. No sir! Instead, she raised her voice, scolding like a schoolmarm and used the carbine as a prod. That cat roared and batted at the gun and the pretty slip of a doll screamed and gabbled French didn't nobody in that tent need translated. But Sure-Shot Minnie wasn't one to wilt. She kept prodding till that lion got her message and like a school kid what got caught stealing pennies, it slunk back into its cage, Sure-Shot Minnie prodding him the whole way. After, the lion locked up, nobody else daring to move, she lifted up that slip of a doll and got her standing. Well, sir, having witnessed a genuine scrape with death, all them frogs applauded Sure-Shot Minnie, who done swept off her hat and bowed just like a man.

At the story's end, I looked around: in the faces of those veteran gents of the Wild West resided pure admiration. I figured they was grateful to be working alongside Minerva Masterson.

But entertained as I was by this tale, Joe wasn't. Instead, he couldn't sit still, him squirming and looking into the dark toward where the actors had their campfire, till finally after a few more minutes of this, he walked off, with me tagging along, into the sand and stones.

Wasn't too long before we wound up forty yards from the actor's campfire. We dared get no closer. Even if there wasn't no sign to say it, this fire was off limits to Joe and me and the extras and technical folk. It was a fire reserved for principal actors, them what made the big bucks. Rose Allen was there, as was Dix beside her, the two of them facing us, while the other actors sat in a circle around their fire, all of them sitting in actual chairs.

They drank coffee what got poured by an actual butler from a big enameled coffee pot, and while he did this, they talked, though we wasn't close enough to make out the words, us snug in the dark and invisible. Now Rooney June stood and held up a bottle, reading off the label aloud, it looking to be a bottle of booze. He poured some in each actor's cup; pouring extra in Dix's when Dix told him to. Koko the monkey jumped onto Dix's shoulder and stuck his nose in the cup before backing off, his lips folding on themselves. Might be, he didn't much approve of alcoholic spirits nor breaking the law.

Dix quieted him and raised his cup and said something, till the others raised their cups and saluted him and they all drank, Koko again squawking his disapproval. Dix handed off Koko to the butler who took the monkey into a tent. The actors returned to their talk, and soon enough a laugh lifted up and carried to us, it dying away. Rose Allen, finishing her laugh, leaned into Dix's shoulder and she took his arm and wrapped it around her. She grinned, and the fire's light caught on her face and in her eyes. It tangled in her hair. She seemed most happy.

Joe hunched up and shoved his hands in his pocket, though I couldn't tell if this was cause of the cold or cause of her familiarity with Dix. After a while of watching her smiling and speaking and laying her head on Dix's chest, Joe said, "I never believed it could happen, Pooch. Back in Missouri when she talked of being an actress, I thought it was just talk. I did the same, too, me talking about sailing the seven seas and finding treasure in sunken ships. That's all I thought it was—just talk."

We watched them more, seeing Rose Allen stand and talk, while the others, Dix included, looked up at her, the light flickering on their faces. Leaning down to Dix, she kissed him and went into the same tent where the butler had taken Koko. Dix said something now and stood and he went into that same tent.

"C'mon," Joe said, him sounding sad, and we moved deeper into the night.

They next day I was dressed as a pioneer and sitting in one of them prairie schooners, with a big old woman beside me, she wearing a bucket bonnet big as an umbrella. The two of us was husband and wife, but we didn't say much to each other, both of us just sitting and sweating on that wagon and being nothing more but part of the scenery, while a scene got acted out near another wagon further down the line.

In this scene Rose was supposed to come from a wagon where she'd been up the night, helping another woman to birth her child. So, she come out of that wagon, carrying the child, meaning to present him to Rooney June, who was the new father, she telling him they couldn't save his wife, though the child was just fine, and a healthy bawling brat of a boy.

But as soon as she stepped off the last step of the wagon and headed for Rooney June, Dix shouted out, "Cut! Cut the cameras!"

He stepped up to Rose Allen and glowered at her. "What have you done to your hair?"

It hung limp and unfurled after a long night of birthing a baby.

"It seemed right, given the circumstances," she told Dix.

"You look like a washerwoman. You look worse than that."

"I look how I should look. For God's sake, I'm a pioneer and not a motion-picture star."

Dix looked out at the crowd of us and hollered, "Where's that damn hair-dresser?"

"Yancey," Rose Allen said, her voice giving off a warning, "you want this movie to be authentic, don't you? Isn't that what you promised the newspaper hounds?"

"Are you throwing my words back at me? Are you?"

He stood back to let us all see how he suffered at the impudence of this woman. But Rose Allen wasn't backing off none, even as he waved at the hair-dresser to join them. "Now I want her hair pinned up and I want more rouge on her cheeks. She looks like a ghost, she's that white."

"I am an actress, Yancey Dix, and I know how my character should look after a night without any sleep. She wouldn't wear make-up nor be concerned with her hair falling down."

Dix, sarcastic now, and threatening, said, "My dear, you really must get over this absurd idea that you are an actress. Bernhardt is an actress. Pickford is an actress. So is Lillian Gish. But you? Believe me, you have a long way to go before you'll be an actress."

Dix couldn't have slapped her any harder, and she give him a look meant to fill him with poison. But when that didn't work none, him playing the wounded victim for us all, she took a swipe at him with the baby. Course it wasn't a real baby and only a doll, but its head flew off and rolled in the sand, which was pretty funny, the gal beside me laughing as much as I did.

Rose Allen turned away and marched off, disappearing into one of the adobe buildings. Dix hollered after her to come back. He even hollered an apology, but I didn't believe its sincerity. Soon enough he tramped after her and went into the same building.

I climbed from the wagon to stretch my legs and wandered over to get a drink from the trough under the windmill. Minerva was there dressed up like a lady pioneer in one of them bucket bonnets. She squinted at the building where Dix and Rose Allen had gone. She said, "Good for her."

"I don't know much about play acting, but it seems to me she's got a point," I said.

Minerva eyeballed me. "Of course she does."

Joe come up to us and took another cup from the table and filled it from the trough. He winked at me and grinned, saying, "Damn shame, ain't it? Us standing here with nothing to do."

I could tell he didn't mean a word of it; I could tell he was perfectly delighted by what had just happened and ready for more.

Minerva said, "After this, I'm done with motion pictures. I'm tired of this, and I'm tired of the shenanigans and drama of it all. I've got me a nice little house down on the beach south of L.A. A place called

Carlsbad. It's as pretty a place as I have ever seen. That's where I will go, dammit, and all the Yancey Dixes of the world can hang, for all I care."

With that, she walked off.

Joe laughed and said, "Pooch, things is getting quite interesting, ain't they?"

CHAPTER 27

That night I couldn't get comfortable no matter how I put my pillow on that cot, probly cause the desert outside the tent had shoveled a grave in my soul, a grave what waited for a customer. Jesus, ain't it funny, how a fella's head works in the dark of a desert as ancient as time?

Across the tent on his cot, Joe read a newspaper by the light of a lantern what hissed. I said, using words to shove aside my morbid musings, "Joe, what you reading about?"

"About this fella in Tennessee, a teacher named Scopes. Seems he's set to go on trial soon for teaching something called evolution."

"What's evolution?"

"I don't know exactly. Mostly it's got something to do with where man comes from. It says here it's a new science, one that 'challenges a belief in God and the divine order of things'."

"Bet preachers ain't too happy about that new science."

"I suppose so."

"I never cared for what preachers say."

"They sure do raise holy hell if you cross them, like this Scopes fella did."

I couldn't have said it better. Hell, I never did trust a preacher. All of them is full of lies. They read from a book full of lies, a book which no god done writ, but a book writ by preachers themselves. They was running a sting, it was that simple. And in running it, they done twisted this old planet into a sorry mess. It looked like this Scopes fella was the next egg to be crucified.

I stood up, agitated now, and ready to belt a preacher in the chops. I said, "I bet Dix loves them preachers. I bet he loves everything about them."

With that said, I walked out of that tent and into the night.

Now, right here, I want to explain about what just happened. I don't want you getting the wrong idea. I ain't suggesting I'm a blasphemer nor a body what denies god. But, you've got to know this, a preacher ain't no different than Dix. All either of them do is make up stories to please an audience. There ain't nothing noble in telling stories, neither, it being mostly trickery and gimmicks. You better keep that in mind, cause when you are in a desert like I was just then, stories won't keep you warm none, and they won't make you safe from calamities, neither.

Now the dark of that night near choked off my eyes, till they adjusted enough for me to see the shadows of folks clustered around each of the campfires. I skirted them and headed toward some dunes, when I seen Rose Allen and Minerva strolling along, Minerva carrying a lantern. They was talking, and I caught a piece of it, hearing Rose Allen say, "Yancey's in trouble. He's spending a lot of money, and the studio—"

Before I could follow them to hear more, I smelled tobacco from a heater and turned to see Dix watching me watch them ladies. It unnerved me, how he snuck up like he done, but I didn't let on I was bothered.

"Eavesdropping, are we, Pooch?"

"It wasn't intentional."

Dix laughed. He stuck his heater back in his face and the tip of it flared up. "Well, it was on my part. You know, it's not easy working with an actress as sensitive as Symphony. She does have her moods."

Rose Allen and Minerva climbed a dune, the orange halo from their lantern swaying.

Dix said, "But she needs me more than she thinks, if only to keep her from making bad choices."

"You mean like today? About her hair?"

"Ah, yes, the artistic choices—But I wasn't speaking of them; no, I was speaking of other choices."

"What choices?"

"Her seeing Joe again. That's not such a good choice, is it?"

"How did you find out?"

He puffed at his cigar and took it from his mouth and used it to point at Rose Allen atop the dune. "Sometimes, to accommodate her moods, I let her have her way. But never when it matters."

I faced him square and planted my feet. "What did you do? Hire a private dick?"

Dix laughed. "Nothing that dramatic; no, Symphony told me. She tells me everything, in time. "

"When did she tell you?"

"Last night. In our tent."

"Hell, it don't—"

Dix puffed at his cigar, his face reading stone certain under the smile.

"Why'd she do it? Why'd she tell you?"

"For love, Pooch. Tell Joe, why don't you? Tell him she did it for love."

"What do I look like? Western Union? Tell him yourself."

"I can do that. Yes, I can."

An hour later, me stranded on my cot, tired from trying to sleep, I thought about waking up Joe. Maybe I should warn him about what Dix said. Maybe if I did, the two of them could duke it out. Now I ain't one for fisticuffs, finding such antics primitive and risky, in that a guy could get maimed. But maybe this one time it was necessary, just so Dix would back off and let Joe find for hisself he was on the short end of a fling. Soon enough Rose Allen would dump him. Hell, I should have told Dix that. Or maybe I didn't have to. Maybe he knew that already. Maybe that's what she told him in their tent, telling him that it was only a fling. If she did –

I danced away from that idea, but it returned; and I knew fisticuffs was unavoidable. Joe would fight, guaranteed, if only to prove Rose Allen loved him and not Dix. Joe would shove Dix's lie back down his throat, which wasn't such a good idea for a reformed thug what had sworn off prison. After a dust-up with Dix, no holds barred, fair as it might be, he'd be the guy what sat in a cell. A judge would see to that. Hell, maybe that's what Dix wanted. Maybe the bruises and scrapes was worth it, if Joe got incarcerated again. Damn, if that was the case—

I didn't wake Joe.

And the next morning I kept my mouth shut. Like I told Dix, I ain't Western Union. But all day I kept an anxious lookout. Dix never come near Joe. Probly cause he was too busy.

First thing that morning, Dix had us shoot that scene from yesterday, the one where Symphony handed a baby to Rooney June. She didn't squawk none when the hair-dresser pinned up her hair, nor did she squawk at getting rouge on her face. And she took Dix's direction without no words back. That scene only got filmed twice before Dix was satisfied and told her so. She didn't say nothing back, and she never did let her hair unfurl the rest of the day. I guess she wasn't being moody no more.

After that, till near twilight, he shot three more scenes, him working fast and definite and driving the herd of us to be quick about each set up.

But come the dark, I got anxious again, thinking now was the time for Dix to find Joe and have his say. That being the case, I left Joe sitting around the fire with the wranglers and searched the camp for Dix.

When I couldn't find him, I asked a camera guy who told me Dix was working late in his office, so I headed that way, seeing light in the window. I stared at that light a while, rehearsing in my head the words I'd use to explain about Rose Allen's fling with Joe, thinking I could render it harmless and of no consequence, when the door to his office opened and who should come out but Astoria Starr.

She stepped along, headed for a nearby campfire, when she near collided with me before catching herself and asking a startled, "Who is that?"

"Just me."

"Oh. I thought you were somebody—"

I waited.

She said, "But you're not."

I waited.

"Mr. Dix and me, we just finished up some re-writes. That's all it was."

I waited.

I guess she give up on whatever she couldn't quite get said, cause she brushed past me in a sudden spurt. I waited more, reflecting on my new discovery.

It didn't surprise me none, Dix having congress with Astoria, it mostly verifying he didn't have no morals. Fact was, he was a thief—the worst kind of thief, cause he didn't steal cabbage nor ice nor what a decent thief steals, but stealing people instead—stealing them with promises and stories of fame and wealth and adventure and love. It didn't scare him none, neither, this stealing, cause ain't nobody dares to stop a gent what dresses hisself elegant and talks fancy from stealing whatever he hungers after. And what Dix hungered after was simple: he hungered for the world's soul. If he could steal that, he could be the equal of any god, or so he supposed.

Least that's what I decided as the light moved from the window and the door opened to show Dix holding a lantern. He shut the door and I ducked deeper into the dark while he passed by, headed for his tent.

I couldn't help but smile. Maybe, just maybe, I'd have to have to have a little talk with Rose Allen. A little talk about morals.

CHAPTER 28

But I couldn't get near her. That next day Dix kept the whole production company hopping, us working right up till dark. And the day after, a big shot from Empire Studios showed up. Rumor had it Dix was on the outs with the studios, something about cost overruns. I didn't know if it was true or not, but after the big shot spent a morning watching us shoot a scene or two, with his flunky scribbling down everything the big shot told him to scribble, he and Dix and the flunky went into Dix's office. An hour or so later they come out, and the big shot and his flunky headed back for Hollywood, while Dix set us back to work.

Didn't any of us know what it all meant, cept to spit the same rumors back and forth. Later that day, near dusk, after meeting with the main actors first, Dix called a meeting of the whole company. He stood on a wagon and, with sun at his back putting him in its halo, he said this, or nearly this as best I can remember, him saying, "Now I've heard the rumors. I know some of you think Empire means to shut us down. But that isn't the case. Not at all. But they have shortened our schedule. We've only twelve more days to get our location shots. Twelve days, people. It seems even artistic integrity must pay heed to the calendar. And what does that mean for you? Just this. I pay all of you a fair wage, and dammit, I mean to see you earn that money. We will finish all our location shots in those twelve days, and I expect each and every one of you to stay on your toes and give me what I need to make *WESTWARD, THE WAGONS* the masterpiece I know it can be. That's all, until seven tomorrow morning."

So there you have it; the big shot had put an edge on him, and the next day there wasn't nothing jake about his mood, it being irascible and his words more curt and bristly than usual. And that's how he stayed in the days to follow, while he rode us roughshod and spurred us on till we couldn't hardly breathe, till the company was hangdog tired and prone to mistakes—what only got Dix more agitated.

No wonder them campfires got pretty dreary after the first couple days, what with most everyone nursing their grievances, though didn't none of them speak up when Dix come near, them just choking down the sourness of his mood like the foul medicine it was. I figured Dix heard them complaints, him not being deaf nor an idiot, but he paid them no mind. He couldn't afford anymore worries, not if he was going to satisfy them big shots at Empire.

Anyway, that's how it went day after day, with Rose Allen secure in her secluded circle of tents near the pond when not working; or if not there, she and Rooney June and other actors drove to a place called Bishop to eat in restaurants and spend the night in a hotel. So you can see I couldn't get to her, much less talk personal with her.

As for Dix, I stopped worrying about him telling Joe anything. He was a man of bluster and bold airs, and a womanizer to boot, but not after that big shot's visit. No, he transformed after that into a bitter drudge what held tight to his schedule, and demanded we all do the same. Truth be told, and this ain't easy to admit, he worked harder than any of us, and longer, him working late into the night in his office. And before you think it, I'm telling you, Astoria wasn't with him. I know that for a fact cause I seen it for myself, and Joe did, too, we both seeing just how hard Dix worked.

We seen it cause didn't neither of us sleep much at nights. I figured it was that damn desert. It breathed, seemed like, and made us both restless and melancholy. So, without saying much, we rose from our cots and prowled the camp. We prowled on cat feet and kept ourselves invisible. Not that there was much need for that. We wasn't looking to steal nothing, and nobody could see us anyway, them all asleep on their cots—cept for Dix. Each night our prowl took us near his office where we sneaked to the window to see him inside, me verifying it was him and only him, Astoria being elsewhere and not a part of this man as he worked, him writing mostly, or reading aloud words which I figured he writ hisself.

Just so you know, I never did tell Joe about Dix and Astoria, but I thought about it each time we looked in that window. Only reason I didn't tell was cause I couldn't depend on him keeping it secret, him being likely to shout it out, which could only serve to embarrass Dix. And Dix was not a man to be embarrassed, even if troubled. He'd rage at us or anybody else what called him a pervert, him claiming he done been appointed a moving-picture star and therefore exempt from ordinary matters of morality. So, it had to stay secret, till I got a chance to talk to Rose Allen in private. Not that I wanted to anymore, but it was necessary. I had to talk with her not only about them morals but about how best to dump Joe, if only to stop him from swimming to Japan again to soothe his broken heart. Not that any of this mattered while we stared into that window and seen Dix alone at his work—the whole of him edging toward haggard.

After we left Dix, we prowled more, ending up each night near that pond. By that hour the dark was lit some with a big slice of moon, and the shadow of that lone pine fell across the water, pointing straight to Rose Allen's tent.

We'd stop there and feel the dank cool and smell minerals rising off the pond. And so we'd watch Rose Allen's tent, till after a few minutes Joe did a curious thing—he got to his knees. He did this every night, kneeling like a hayseed boy what offered a dead toad to the gods above. Even on them nights Rose Allen was in Bishop, he did this. And one night, this the seventh one, he did something more mystifying. He used a stick he was carrying to hit hisself on the shoulders. Hold on now, he didn't hit hisself so it could hurt, it being more of a tapping, and he tapped hisself regular, like beating out music, him doing this ten or twelve minutes. I whispered out and asked why he did that to hisself, and he told me to shut up and went right on hitting hisself. Damn strange, the whole of it. Even now I can't figure why he did that.

The next day went like all the ones before, us driven by Dix and sick of this desert and its wind; and with the sun near gone, the cold of the night sharp and getting sharper, Joe and me headed for the showers. We always took our showers in the near dark, mornings and evenings, it being the times when nobody else bathed, probly cause the water the windmill pulled from the bowels of the earth was cold enough to shrivel a nun's titties. But that's how we liked it; not the temperature, mind, but bathing in private.

A canvas stall had got erected, big enough to hold four guys. You pulled on a rope and the barrel above tipped and water drizzled down through a trough with holes in it. Cept for an occasional shout at the cold on our skin, didn't neither of us talk while we scrubbed and soaped and rinsed. Mostly we kept our thoughts to ourselves. But this time, Joe broke our reverie to say, "I can't get her alone. Rose Allen."

I told him, "If she wants to see you, she will."

"No, I mean, it's important I get her alone."

"Why's that?"

"Cuz I been thinking, Pooch. I been thinking about the future. I been thinking how I can make things right between us. Each night we go to her tent, that's what I think about."

I gasped while more cold water ran over my skull.

He said, "It's funny, but you know what I'm doing while we're looking at her tent? I'm trying to convince her to come outside to talk."

"You're gonna have to get louder, if that's what you want. You're gonna have to shout out her name."

"I can't do that. It's gotta be a secret, her coming out of that tent and finding me there."

I didn't see no point in suggesting that involved mind reading, which neither of us was much good at, specially with Joe on his knees and tapping his shoulders with a stick. Instead, I asked, "What do you want to say to her?"

Joe stepped from the shower and used a towel to rub hisself hard. "I want to ask her to marry me."

I warned you: Joe was love-loopy. And now you got the proof of it.

"Suppose," I said," she don't want to marry you?"

"Damn, Pooch, there you go again. I swear you must have been born sucking on a teat of vinegar."

That may be so, but I still thought my question was valid, since I had Rose Allen pegged different than him, me pegging her as someone what had no time nor inclination for love nor marriage. "Hell, if she does say no, could you give her up? Could you?"

I seen his face worry over that idea for a while, the towel dangling in his hands, before he bucked hisself up and said, "I won't have to."

"You ain't got much to offer. She's rich and you ain't. She's famous and you ain't. She don't need a man. Not even Dix, though she probly don't know that yet."

"I—I—none of that means anything."

"But what if she says no?"

Joe wadded up the towel and threw it on the wood slats what was the floor, saying, "Then I gotta try harder, that's what. I gotta try harder."

I didn't know what to say. Joe's persistence baffled me. Sides, I didn't know what he meant by trying harder, but before I could ask, he picked up his towel and marched out of that shower stall.

Damn, love-loopy—I ain't going to explain about that no more, cept to say human nature and human reason ain't never in tune. Else wouldn't none of us be unhappy. Now ain't that the case?

That night, the camp asleep, we went on the prowl again. We stopped like usual to watch Dix work in his office, and ten minutes later we wound up by the pond, the moon's light more definite, making the shadow of that lone pine in the rock more definite.

Weren't too long before Joe got to his knees again, him crying out a silent Rose Allen, silent crying for her to come to him; and then he commenced to tapping his shoulders with that stick like he done the night before, which angered me some, so I left him to his vigil and prowled by myself, prowling further from camp, prowling in the dunes to the south.

That's when I heard my name called out, which had me jumping for the moon, I was that startled.

"C'mon up!" I heard and looked at the top of a rocky dune to see Albert B. Kothe waving his arm at me to do just that.

So I climbed up to him. "What the hell are you doing up here?" I asked him.

He held up binoculars, saying, "Looking for Astoria."

Oh, jeez, how do you tell a fella his fiancée has stepped out on him? And why did it have to be me what did the telling? I poked a foot at the edge of the blanket he had spread out. "This ain't no way to get Dix to hire you back."

"I know that, Pooch, but I—I miss her."

"She's asleep by now."

"Which is her tent?"

"I don't really know, cept it's at the other end of the camp. That's where us wage slaves got put."

"I gotta see her, Pooch. Will you help me?"

"No, and if I was you, I'd forget about it—head back to Hollywood."

Now I didn't say this to be mean-hearted, nor did I care if he saw Astoria or not, but I did know if he trespassed into camp and got found there, Dix would never have nothing to do with him again. Nor would anybody else what mattered, after Dix warned them. Hell, Albert would have writ his own obituary in the moving-picture business.

But Albert, as love-loopy as Joe, didn't have no time for me to explain the danger in seeing her, cause he started to scramble from rock to rock, headed down the dune. I called after him and finally caught up to him when we both got to the floor of the desert.

"All right, all right. I'll help you out. But we gotta do it my way."

"Whatever you say, Pooch."

"You come back tomorrow night and hide up there like you been. I'll bring Astoria out to you. How's that?"

"Pooch, I—thanks."

"Now get out of here till tomorrow night. Make it around ten or so."

"Sure, that's fine. That's real good, Pooch."

With that, he climbed back up that hill till I seen the blackness of him up there pulling up his blanket and throwing it over his shoulders. Then he disappeared down the other side of the dune.

Christ, I had to laugh. I was a pretty sorry excuse for cupid. But damn, if that wasn't the role I done just took on. Ain't that a hoot? And me not even believing in love.

CHAPTER 29

Rooney June was born with greasepaint in his veins, or so a wrangler told me and Joe on that first night in Lone Pine. Ever since a tyke, he'd been trodding the boards, to hear the wrangler tell it. And when the flickers come along, Rooney June was johnny-on-the-spot. Course he wasn't no big star like Dix or Symphony, but he'd been around so long folks just naturally had a fondness for him, probly cause he was a sport and a gadabout, and a fella what relied on pranks to keep a company laughing. As to that greasepaint in his veins, I figure he had washed most of it away by then, him being a devout dipsomaniac what ignored the ban on spirits.

I say this cause that next morning at dawn, me fresh from the shower, I seen a strange automobile pull up to the adobe buildings, where Rooney June stepped out to meet the driver at his window. Wasn't long after that he fisted over some cabbage and a box was handed to him. The automobile swung a loop and took off, while Rooney June walked along, the glass in that box clinking. When he seen I had witnessed the exchange, he winked and said, "Just a personal delivery of mother's milk," and carried off the box to his tent.

Mostly Rooney June amused me. He'd tipple through the day and laugh off Dix's bullying and bluster, pulling a prank or two for the kicks of it, what didn't help Dix's disposition none, it being near humorless since that meeting with the big shot from Empire. But he tolerated Rooney June's clowning to a point, them being drinking buddies of long standing, though when he got exasperated enough, he'd bark. Rooney June backed off then and kept hisself in check for a time, nursing at his flask.

But on this morning he went too far. I don't know why he did it, made Dix the butt of a prank, but I figured he worried for his drinking buddy and meant to ease the coils what had got wrapped too tight for too long in Dix's gut. Almost like an act of kindness, not that Dix seen it as such.

Right here, I got to confess—I was a silent partner in Rooney June's prank. Now don't get me wrong. The prank was purely Rooney June's idea. But I went along with it, seeing as how I was the one set to play a dead Indian thief. That's right—me, a dead thief on screen. It's the only time I made an honest buck from thieving, and I got kick out of it, specially after Rooney June revealed what he wanted me to do.

So, there I was, dressed in Indian duds in the morning sun. Dix stepped up to direct me, saying me it was deepest night. Well, I looked at that sun and I looked at him and he told me not to worry, they could doctor the film to make it night. Though I didn't see how, I took his word for it.

Anyway, the cameras rolled and I, a blood-thirsty savage carrying a knife, snuck into the wagon train what had bedded down for the night. The fires was burning low with some fellas sleeping around them and other folk sleeping under the wagons. I snuck close to the back of a wagon and reached up to grab a woman's Sunday-go-to-meeting hat what had flowers on its brim. I had no idea why Dix wanted me to steal that hat, nor why any savage would even want such frippery, but I didn't raise no objection, figuring the sooner I acted it out, the sooner we could get to Rooney June's prank. After planting that hat on my head and moving on, a woman near the wagon waked to see me and screamed out to the world that a savage horde had invaded. So, my face full of menace, I waved my knife to show I meant to cut her throat, when Yancey Dix took action.

He rolled up in a crouch, pulling up his rifle, and took quick aim and got off a shot what hit me square in the chest, driving me back. I fell and landed in a fire—that earned me five quick and easy bucks—before I rolled free of the flames, leaving the hat behind to burn. And then I died.

Now the next scene happened hours later in the morning. They wouldn't have to doctor the film for this scene none. Yancey Dix had gathered the wagon-train folk into a burial party. Since he was a Christian man, it was his duty to see that any savages shot by his own hand got a decent send-off in a white man's coffin. He prayed and the folk prayed with him. Then he bent to the coffin and opened the lid, meaning to put a bible on my corpse, that being the Christian thing to do. And when he did, he said so all could hear, saying it formal like they did in silent flickers, "Is this the face of a villain I see before me?" Only this time, instead of my corpse, what he seen was his own face staring back at him—his face in a mirror.

Most of the company was in on the joke, them howling and braying and generally busting a gut after he said them words about being a villain and looked down to see his own face. I figured it was healthy, that laughing, specially with the duress of the past week. And I didn't feel bad about it none, neither, being complicit in Rooney June's prank, me hiding in a wagon and peeping out to see Dix's face.

And that face had exploded, while the rest of him blowed up and up, and finally he roared out in that Shakespeare voice of his, "Rooney June, you bastard, I've had it with you and your drinking. You, sir, are a drunk, and as far as I'm concerned you're finished in this business. Finished, do you hear?"

Rooney June swallowed the cud of his laugh, and his face said, "Oh-oh!"

The company froze up, the laughter dying out quick, while Dix glowered at them all. "As for the rest of you, you should be ashamed. We haven't the time for this sort of—"

"Stop it, Yancey," Rose Allen said from her seat on a wagon.

Dix turned to her.

"They've done everything you've asked of them."

"And this—this stunt, just what is that?"

"They're having fun, Yancey. Something you seem to have forgotten about lately."

"Fun?" He waved at the mirror, "Is it fun to mock Yancey Dix?"

"Yes, when he deserves it."

Dix stepped back at that and glowered at the whole company. And the company, it wilted, though remaining at a kind of ragged attention. "Rooney June, get some java in you and sober up. Do it now, dammit."

Rooney June backed away.

Dix said, "We'll shoot the scene again in fifteen. Where's that damn half-pint who's supposed to be in the coffin?"

But before I could stir, Rose Allen jumped from her wagon and walked to Dix and said straight to his face, "I'm taking the rest of the day off."

Everybody froze up again.

Rose Allen stalked off and mounted a horse and said, "If you're smart, Yancey Dix, you'll give everybody the rest of the day off." Tugging at the reins and kicking her heels into the horse's ribs, she galloped off, into the desert.

Didn't anybody move, till Dix said, "Where's that damn half-pint? Where's Pooch?"

I showed myself.

"All right," Dix said to everyone, "in fifteen we shoot the scene again without Rose Allen or Rooney June."

As I climbed to the ground and headed for the coffin, I seen Joe sidle away and get on a horse. He rode off in the desert, following Rose Allen.

Dix seen that, too, him standing stolid and unmoving, as he watched Joe disappear. When he turned to me, I seen his face was sad, though I couldn't see the reason for that. He said to me, brusque now, "Get in the coffin."

Which I done, after I took out the mirror. But after I laid back I looked up at Dix and winked. He slammed the lid on me. Some people just ain't got no sense of humor.

Well, the day stretched on and neither Rose Allen nor Joe returned from the desert. But that didn't stop Dix none. He kept right on filming. In one scene Rooney June ate a slice of pie. Dix shot that scene six times; though even I could see it didn't need to be shot more than once. I figured Dix was punishing Rooney June. And it seemed to work, cause Rooney June was green after the sixth time and run off behind a wagon where I could hear him puke.

Wasn't long after that, I seen Astoria sitting on a stone nearby. She had a copy of the photo play and was making notes in it. I went to her and said, "Why you doing that?"

"I have to keep track of things, since we're not shooting in sequence."

I only had a vague idea what she meant, but I kept my ignorance to myself, saying, "I saw Albert last night."

"Did you? Where?"

"Up there?" I pointed to the rocky dune, and she frowned. "He wants to see you up there. Tonight. About ten."

"Oh." That's the simplest word, ain't it? Oh. But she put a lot into that word, putting in mostly her reluctance to consider Albert at all.

"I'll take you up there if you want."

Shaking her head no, she wriggled the ring from her finger and handed it to me. "Give him this. Tell him it's over."

She stood up and walked off, joining the camera guys.

Seems I ain't much good at playing Cupid.

Anyway, I scanned the desert for a time but didn't see Joe nor Rose Allen.

As dusk settled the wind some, I went to the shower stall and was scrubbing away when Joe come in and stood beside me, tipping the barrel and shaking his head at the drizzle what come down.

"What did she say?" I asked him.

Joe scrubbed at his face for a moment before looking at the cloth in his hands and saying, "Damn, sand burns your skin when you rub it."

"Did you ask her?"

"I did."

"What did she say?"

Joe shrugged and grinned. "I gotta try harder."

CHAPTER 30

I left Joe to the wrangler's campfire as soon as it got dark and hiked past that rocky dune, not seeing no sign of Albert. I hiked to the road beyond and sat on a stone slab, it facing the way he had to come if he meant to keep our meeting. Around me the desert breathed, it breathing like a beast, with me riding on its spine and huddled up, hands jammed in my coat's pockets.

Could be, it was the cold, it was that miserable, but right then I cursed Albert and Joe both. And I cursed any other sap what thought love could be permanent or a refuge from trouble. Hell, from what I've seen, love—if it exists, which ain't saying it does—is the only trouble what can never be corrected. Sure, when it's new, it's shiny and a joy to behold, but after time it gets broke and winds up like glass what can't get swept away. Ain't nobody wants broken glass in their heart.

I know it sounds grim, but what the hell, I didn't much appreciate playing Cupid. I mean, there I was, a fella what lived by his wits and a quick hand, but since I met Joe and Albert, I had wound up abetting them in crimes of the heart. And I don't much believe in that kind of crime cause there ain't no profit in it. Least, the coppers and judges couldn't jug me for playing Cupid, though that didn't console me much. I ain't one what wants to admit he's been a dupe in the name of love.

After a while, head lamps jumped along the road, and I figured it was Albert, so I stood up and went to the road and waited there. The lights jumped more and in time I could see the black hump of his automobile making the last swing around the curve and ease along till the head lamps bathed me in their white.

Albert got from his automobile and said, "Pooch?"

The engine grumbled and chugged, and around us the desert breathed.

He come toward me. "Where's Astoria?"

I shook my head.

"Where is she?"

I took the ring from my pocket and handed it to him. He give it a gander then looked at me, confused. I nodded at it, saying nothing. He stared at it more and when he looked at me again, his face white in the head lamps, it looking stark, he said, "What's this mean?"

"She—she told me to give it to you."

"Oh."

Ain't it funny, him saying the same word Astoria did, him saying that simple oh? And like her, it meant so much more, it meaning sorrow for him and broken glass grinding in his heart.

With that, he hauled off and flung that ring into the night. He turned and got into his automobile and the head lamps shivered while he put her in gear and swung around, heading for Lone Pine proper.

I didn't go to look for that ring. Sometimes it's best to let the desert take its tribute and leave it be. Still, I did ache some for Albert, that poor ugly sap.

It had to be after five in the morning, with me sleeping on my cot, when I heard the sound of an automobile's horn, it coming closer and closer, with an engine growling under it, so I jumped up and Joe said from our dark, "What the hell?"

Head lamps swept past our tent, the horn still bleating, bleating, and now I heard Albert's voice "Astoria! Astoria! C'mon on out, Astoria!"

Me and Joe hustled from our tent, and we wasn't the only ones. A regular crowd poured from the tents, while Albert drove past them, sounding his horn and crying out for Astoria.

Minerva appeared, her wearing nothing but a slip and her hair in pigtails, and marched into the automobile's path, planting herself there and daring Albert to run over her.

The brakes creaked and the automobile rocked, while its head lamps washed onto Minerva. Albert hopped out and shouted at her. "Where's Astoria!? I have to see her!"

Joe said to me, "He's polluted."

And that he was. He must have found a watering hole in Lone Pine somehow, and now he was full of the derring-do only alcohol provides.

Minerva said, "Albert, you're a sorry sight to god and man."

Albert wavered at that, floating on fumes, or so it seemed, till he seen Astoria and Barbara come from their tent, Astoria wrapping her arms across her chest. "Astoria, baby," he said and lurched toward her, till somehow his balance got tangled up, and he toppled into the light of his head lamps, toppling at Minerva's feet.

Some folks laughed, and others shuffled about, while one called out, "Get him some training wheels."

Astoria laughed loudest—a great cruel laugh.

Albert give up trying to stand and looked into her laugh, till his throat strained and he swallowed a few times, and then vomit gushed from his gut and splashed into the sand, it splashing on Minerva's legs and on her slip. The stink of it near burned my nostrils. But that didn't stop Minerva none, she being a lady of mercy, and she crouched beside him and used a hand to rub his back while he went on vomiting.

Some in the crowd was disgusted and ducked back into their tents, but others laughed again and joked about Albert's sorry state. As for Astoria, she talked to Barbara, the two of them confabulating in whispers.

Soon enough, Dix and Rose Allen arrived and stood above Albert and Minerva, Rose Allen wrapped in a shawl and Dix bare-chested and immune to the morning cold.

Albert retched some more, but only thin strings come from his mouth; till he retched a last time and nothing come up but what had to be rancid air.

Dix said to Minerva, "Take him over to the kitchen. Get him some java."

Minerva, still rubbing Albert's back, said, "He needs a shower first."

Dix nodded and walked to Albert's automobile. Reaching in the open door, he shut off the engine and cut off the head lamps, not that we needed them to see anymore, cause the sun was close to rising, the band of its coming wide in the mountains behind our tents. Dix walked back and towered over Albert.

Albert looked up, his eyes watering, and said, choking to say it, "I only wanted to see Astoria."

Dix shook his head, and when he spoke he sounded sad, him saying. "Get some sleep, Alfred. And a shower. Then I want you gone. You're not welcome here."

Albert said, "It's Albert."

But Dix probly didn't hear this, he already walking off with Rose Allen walking beside him.

Minerva got Albert to his feet and guided him toward the shower, though he balked when seeing Astoria, and veered toward her.

Astoria whispered something more at Barbara and the two of them turned and went back into their tent, tying the flaps closed after them.

Albert stopped to see this and said, him whining, ""Astoria, baby, I need to see you."

But didn't nobody in the tent answer him back.

"Astoria —"

Minerva folded an arm over his shoulders and maneuvered him along, herding him toward the shower stall, with me and Joe tagging along, seeing as how somebody had to tip the barrel for poor Albert and make certain he did not drown.

Albert slept most of the day on my cot, with me or Joe or Minerva checking on him now and again. After the day's shooting, he roused and sat up and took the bowl of soup I handed him. He crumbled a soda cracker into the soup and scooped out a bite, and another, his hand shaking at the effort of it.

"I guess it's over, ain't it, Pooch?" he croaked out.

"Dames ain't worth the trouble they put us through."

Albert nodded bleakly and scooped up another bite. He swallowed it and said, "I meant Dix. But you're right; it's over with Astoria, too."

"Forget about that slut."

Albert didn't like me saying that, if I read his face right, his wounds being that raw, but he give it up to stare out the tent, his voice sounding thin as he said, "Could you do me a favor? Could you talk to Dix about my photo play?"

I told him I would, and when he finished his soup, he stood up and went to his automobile. Joe was coming to the tent just then and he called out, "See you in a couple days, Albert."

Albert waved at him and cranked up his automobile and set the gears and took off, raising up a thin tail of sand.

Joe said, "It's sad, ain't it, how a woman can hurt a guy?"

I didn't have no argument with that, specially considering the source.

"When we get back to Sunset Haven, I gotta have a talk with him."

"About dames?"

"No, about our own motion-picture plans. I got some good ideas for our movie."

"You mean that western flicker you two been palavering over?"

"I do," he said, ducking into our tent.

A gust of wind roused and sand flew in my mouth. I spat it out and headed for the shower. I didn't know about this moving-picture business, and I sure didn't believe Albert and Joe was ever going to make one, but I did know I had had enough of this desert and its nasty nature. Even if they did make their western, I wasn't going to be a part of it, not if it meant I had to suffer this desert again, it not being a fit place for a thief to be.

CHAPTER 31

That night sleep caught up early with Joe, but I wasn't so lucky. I sat for a time at the wranglers' campfire slow drinking a cup of java and hearing more of their stories and tales. When the moon finally rose, it having grown mostly full orange in the nights since we got to this godforsaken desert, I headed for Dix's office. Since there was no light in the window, I opened the door and called his name into the dark of that room but didn't nobody answer back.

The moon's light was enough for me to see the lantern on a table by the door. I lit it and looked around. Tacked on the walls was pencil drawings, dozens of them. Sketches Dix drew of shots from *WESTWARD, THE WAGONS*. I even found a couple of me as the dead Indian thief. In one I wore that silly woman's hat, and I had to admit Dix got right these jug-handle ears of mine. A couple more of them drawings lay on the desk. I studied them. That's when I come across the one with Joe hanging from that lone pine growing out of rock. That picture set me back a step, and I folded it up and stashed it in my pocket. Joe had to see it; he had to know what Dix thought of him.

I went through the desk and in one of the drawers I come across a brass money clip. Probly had got discarded. Wasn't all that valuable, but I pocketed it. I didn't consider it theft. Hell, if it had any value, it wouldn't be in that drawer in the first place. Ain't no thievery in lifting an empty money clip nobody wants.

After blowing out the lantern, I left the office and prowled about till I got to the actors' campfire. Rooney June sat alone staring into the flames. He lifted his flask and drank. After that, he wiped his mouth with his forearm and stared more into the flames, him looking sad and unnatural, in that I had never seen him like that before, as alone as that. I thought about going to talk to him, but stopped myself. He looked like he didn't want nor need no company.

Then I heard a splash with another one to follow. Sneaking past

Rooney June and using the boulders to keep hidden I got close to the pond, close enough so I could see Rose Allen and Dix climbing to the top of that rock with the tree growing out of it. And as they stood now with the tree between then, I seen they was naked. The moon and water had turned them silver. I took out the drawing of Joe hanging from that tree and realized Dix must have penciled it while standing right on this spot where I stood, or very close to it.

Now Dix reached a silver arm across the tree and she took it, clinging to it, and the two of them jumped to the black water below. And as they slid under its shine, silver sheets flew up and tattered quick, falling back over them. Rose Allen surfaced first, wiping hair from her face, when Dix come up and pulled at her, the two of them a silver tangle on black.

They both laughed and she swam to the pond's edge and stood there, the water lapping at her knees. Slivers of water ran from her hair and down her breasts, that water more white than the rest of her. Then she done a peculiar thing: she cupped her breasts and lifted, as if offering them to the moon. Dix moved up behind her, and he put his hands over hers, the two of them cupping her breasts. She leaned back her head to include him.

Real careful, I backed away, keeping the sound of me small, till I couldn't see them more. I ain't no pervert. But seeing what I did convinced me of one thing. I had to talk to Rose Allen about them damn morals, and I better talk about them before we head back to Hollywood.

As I stretched on my cot, Joe piped up, "Damn, Pooch, don't you ever sleep no more?"

"I can't. Not in this damn desert."

Reaching into my pocket, I pulled out the drawing of Joe hanging from the tree. "Have you seen this?"

I handed it to him. He took it and tilted the paper to catch the bar of moonlight what come into our tent, saying finally, "I seen it." Giving me back the paper, he said, "You oughta put it back," and rolled over, settling into sleep.

Now that left me scratching my head. Didn't he see Dix wanted him to hang, even if only in a moving picture? Sometimes it was disheartening, how he neglected to see things for what they was.

The next morning I put the drawing of Joe on Dix's desk and waited by studying his other sketches till he showed up, making a face what told me I didn't belong there.

I didn't bother to mention he didn't scare me none. Funny, ain't it, how when you see a guy naked, he don't bother you so much no more?

I said, "Albert wants his photo play back."

"Albert?"

"You know who I mean."

Dix went to the desk and seeing the drawing of Joe, picked it up. He tested the creases in it and then tried to smooth them out by pressing the paper between his palms, saying, "That isn't your business, that photo play of his."

"Hell, I know that. But I'm doing a pal a favor."

"Are you?"

He tried to stretch out the creases, till the paper tore, and he dropped the torn drawing on his desk. Dix tried to stare me down, but I wasn't playing. I just hung there, waiting on him, till he said, "I'm busy, Pooch."

"So, what do I tell Albert?"

"Tell him what you want."

He took up some papers on a clipboard and walked out of that office, leaving me flat and unsatisfied.

Since this was the last day of shooting, Dix rushed us along and in the afternoon the company gathered on the cliff what hung over the pond, the cliff what had the rock with the tree growing out of it.

Time had come to film Joe hanging from the tree.

Us extras, all dressed as pioneers, stood in a crowd and waited, solemn-like. The reason Joe had to be hung was biblical—an eye for an eye. The night before while drunk he shot a man in the back. It was an act of meanness and booze, and now he had to die for his crime.

So, now, the cameras got cranked—Joe, unshaven with his hands tied behind his back and his eyes painted red and dabbed with grease to look like tears, walked up to that tree. A hangman's noose hung from a limb, the other end running to a man what sat a horse. Joe hung his head in shame and looked to be sobbing, his shoulders heaving.

Rooney June come up to Joe, his face dead to pity. It had been his brother what Joe had shot the night before. He delivered a sermon to us in the crowd, him pronouncing the rightness of bringing justice to a lawless desert. With that he placed the noose around Joe's neck, while Joe pleaded for mercy, his eyes shining with them tears. But Rooney June had no mercy. He tightened the noose.

"Cut!" Dix hollered out from behind a camera.

He come up now to Joe and asked, "Are you ready?"

Joe said he was, and the noose was took from his neck and another rope was thrown over the tree's limb. This new rope clipped onto the harness what Joe's shirt covered, clipping just behind Joe's neck. The man on the horse eased the animal along, and Joe raised like a side of beef getting hung to cure. He must have thought it hilarious, cause he took to kicking up his legs as good as a showgirl, what got the rest of us to giggling till Dix told him to knock it off.

Joe hung there, swinging, and rested his head on his shoulder and stuck out his tongue, and he made other silly faces, him being a kid playing at the end of his rope. But when Dix called out, "Roll 'em!" Joe stopped his clowning and did his dance in air, his dance of hanging, the camera shooting only his legs and no higher, till Dix hollered up to slow it down, and then hollered to let his feet twitch a time or two and then stop, with them feet swinging there, and us extras a blur beyond them, staring up at a coward what deserved to die.

Dix arrived on his horse a moment later, but it was too late to save Joe from Rooney June's barbaric justice. Course they got into a fistfight under Joe's dead feet, Joe looking on and laughing the while and cheering on Rooney June, who finally got tossed by Dix off that cliff and into the water.

Well, that was it, the last shot, but right then there was a terrible crack. I looked up to see Joe's grin shrink into a sick knowing. Another crack come and the limb of that tree collapsed, taking Joe with it, both tumbling off that cliff, the rope trailing after till it caught up short. I hollered at the horseman to let it go, and right after he did, we heard splashing.

I didn't wait none, and Dix didn't, neither, the both of us heroes what jumped off that cliff, but when I sank into that water and the ice of it sucked off my skin, I forgot to be heroic. Panicking, I clawed for the sky, and when I come up, I seen Dix scowling at me. But before either of us could do more, Joe bobbed up, and seeing Dix, shot a rope of water in his face. Dix wasn't so happy about that, neither, but Joe only laughed and said, "Fellas, I appreciate the concern," before he flung hisself out and kicked for shore, him swimming like a mermaid and without no arms, the rope and harness trailing after, where Rooney June helped him out and commenced to untie his hands.

I grinned at Dix, a grin what said, How about that Joe? Ain't he something?

Dix just paddled for shore. I guess he didn't like to be thwarted in performing heroic rescues.

But I do have to admit, that man did have a streak of decency, for that night—after we done packed up as much gear as we could on the trucks—Dix visited each campfire to thank his company by delivering flats of bottled Pabst packed in ice. Pabst from Canada, or so read the label. I drank three bottles, it tasting pure golden. By the time the moon rose an hour later, I could hear shouts and laughter coming from all the campfires, along with some singing, and even a Victrola scratching out Tin-Pan Alley tunes. After twelve days of bitter tribulation, the company had let down its hair.

At our campfire, the wranglers and Joe staged a drinking contest what Joe won, him downing five bottles of beer in seven minutes. After, to celebrate, he give a ripe belch and grinned at me. The wrangler's laughed and started a new contest. Soon enough a guitar appeared and Joe took up singing along with the wranglers. That's when I left them to it. I ain't no warbler, specially when it comes to cowboy ditties. Sides, I had unfinished business to conduct.

I threaded my way past each of them campfires, refusing an offer to sit with Minerva and have a bottle of beer. I congratulated most everybody what called my name but I didn't stop. When I got to the actor's campfire, I walked right on up, not paying no attention to that invisible no trespassing sign.

"Pooch!" Rooney June called out and saluted me with a bottle of champagne.

The other actors all smiled at me. They was looped. And Dix was, too, him wearing the sloppy face only booze can make. He said, "Pooch, my half-pint compadre, sit down. Have yourself a glass of bubbly."

"No thanks."

Rooney June hopped up and handed me a bell-shaped glass and filled it with champagne from his bottle, "Go on, now, drink up."

"I ain't got a taste for fancy spirits."

"I don't blame you," Dix said, standing. He laid an arm over my shoulders and offered me to his actor buddies, him saying, the ridicule winking in his voice, "Liquid refreshment should be reserved for adults only."

While he and the other actors laughed, I poured the wine on his shoes, not that he noticed, nor even seemed to care. I wriggled from under his arm and handed the glass to Rooney June, asking him, "Where's Rose Allen?"

"Who?"

"He means Symphony," Dix said, him saying it like it was a secret to be whispered loud enough for everybody to hear.

One of the actors, an old woman with a hawk's nose, pointed and said, "I saw her go that way."

"Little man, what could you have to say to our Symphony?" Dix asked, him sounding sour with his ridicule.

"That's my business."

Dix backed off, throwing his hand to his heart, as if I stuck a knife into it. "Pooch, how can you speak to me so, and I, the man who butters your bread?"

Didn't nobody laugh at that but Dix. I stepped off, meaning to leave, when Dix caught my arm and pulled me away from the others. "Pooch, I apologize," he said, breathing fumes at me. "I apologize for my unseemly behavior just now."

Using a finger to tap his head, he said, "Sometimes I forget myself. I forget others haven't been as lucky as I."

I kept glowering at him.

"But I have to know, I really do, what business could you possibly have with Symphony?"

"It's personal."

"About your friend, Joe, I take it."

"You know that."

"Yes, so I do. So I do." He fought the booze in his blood and righted hisself before saying. "You're acting as his intermediary, is that it?"

"No, I ain't no cupid. Not no more."

"Ah, that's fine. That's—"

"She's gotta leave him alone."

Dix blinked at that, surprised. "I couldn't agree more."

"So I gotta tell her that."

Dix thought about this, his face getting sad. "It won't change anything, but I won't stop you. So, fly away little bird, and drop your seed in her ears."

He made an elaborate bow and nearly fell over before catching hisself.

As I stepped away, he said, "Pooch, that woman—she could break any man's heart."

The broken limb floated at her feet. She looked to see it was me and then she prodded the limb with her foot and watched it bounce. Silver lines rippled along its edges. Water lapped.

She said, "Is—is he all right?"

"He's drunk and singing cowboy songs."

"Did—did he send you?"

"No. This is my idea."

Her face got curious. "You don't like me, do you? Most men do, but you—you don't."

After seeing I wasn't going to say nothing about that, she walked a ways along the bank, pulling her shawl tighter around her shoulders. The beads what got sown into it glittered. She said then, her back to me but her voice riding light, "Don't worry, Pooch, I'm not going to marry him."

"It ain't right," I said to the back of her head. "It ain't right, you stringing two men along at the same time like you're doing."

She turned, and her eyes glittered as much as the beads on her shoulders. "Stringing along? Are you saying a—a woman can't love two men at the same time?"

"It ain't moral, and it ain't healthy."

Rose Allen laughed. "I'll have to take your word for that."

"I ain't joking, lady. You could hurt him, stringing him along like this."

"Pooch, he's stringing himself along. He doesn't love me. Not really. He—he only loves the idea of me."

I didn't know what to make of this, her saying what I knew was true. Did she mean it, or was she stringing me along? Hell, maybe that's what she did to every guy she met, strung him along.

"Soon enough," she said, "we'll get tired of each other."

As I walked off, I hoped that was true. I surely did. But something else about what she said nibbled at me, that being the idea a woman could love more than one man. That didn't seem normal, nor nothing like what the books and poems and moving pictures say. Hell, if it was true—

I couldn't figure what it meant, this being foreign to me and the kind of French thinking what could corrupt a guy.

Aw, let it go, Pooch. Just let it go. That's what I told myself. But I couldn't cause in Rose Allen, in her thinking, I saw myself. I mean, she saw love like I did, seeing it for what it is, it being nothing more but sex gussied up by romance. But that was the pity of it, least in Joe's case, cause it meant Rose Allen couldn't be true of heart.

A few hours later, Joe shook me awake.

What is it?" I asked.

Joe had turned on the bull's-eye lantern and he shot its light into my face. I shoved it aside, cursing him. Here I had finally eased into some sleep and he had to cut it off. There ain't no justice in this world.

"I just realized something," he said.

"What?"

"That scene with me hanging, and some of the others, Dix didn't write them. He only changed them and made them different, that's all."

"What are you saying?"

"This motion picture, Dix's picture, he didn't write all of it. Albert did. He wrote it."

CHAPTER 32

By late afternoon, we got to Sunset Haven, and Joe went to Albert's bungalow. He figured the best way to break the bad news was on the beach after they rode the waves on their bellies for a while.

As for me, I aired out the place and marched across the gravel. I was in sore need of consolation, what I soon got in Mrs. Edward Beneke's tired old arms. The next thing I knew, I awoke in her bed, the sun painting gold on the sheets.

I went back to my bungalow and Joe was lying on his bed, staring patterns into the ceiling. I said, "Did you tell him?"

"I did."

"How'd he take it?"

"He's gonna sue."

"You mean in a court?"

Joe oozed out a sigh from his soul and said, "Pooch, am I a fool? Am I?"

"Only when it comes to dames."

Sitting up on his elbow, he said, "Somehow I gotta convince her, Pooch. Somehow I—I don't know. Somehow I got to be bigger than Dix. That's what I got to be—bigger than Dix."

His eyes burned desperate hard at me, waiting for me to agree, but I couldn't do that. I said, hearing her words by that pond, "She's tired of you, Joe. And I think she's getting tired of Dix, too."

"No, Pooch, that ain't so. Oh, she's tired, all right; she's tired of being trapped. And I got to be the guy to free her."

I didn't see how she was trapped, but you can't argue with a victim of romance. All you can do is shrug.

I picked up from the dresser the money clip I got from Dix's office and left Joe to his sorry delusions. I went to Albert's place, hearing the sound of the ocean and feeling the cool of its wind. I thanked the stars I wasn't in no desert no more. Albert's automobile wasn't there, but I knocked anyway. When he didn't answer, I opened the door and went in. I put the money clip next to his radio on the table, right where Albert could see it easy.

Now I can tell, you think that was a damn strange thing to do, and maybe it was, but I'm glad I done it. Albert deserved to get something out of Dix, since he never did get a chance to sue him in a court.

The next morning, Joe shaved twice and splashed on enough bay rum and Vitalis to make a skunk sing. After, he dressed hisself ritzy as a tycoon and even topped it off with his short-brim fedora. I didn't ask him why he done this, it being but part of some scheme to be bigger than Dix, I figured.

When we got to Empire, me still parking my Ford, Joe said, "Pooch, tell Guffey I'll be along later. I got plans I have to actuate just now."

With that, he put on his fedora and tilted it just so, and hopped from the automobile, not even shutting the door after him, he was in that much a hurry. I didn't see him again for three more hours, that being when the hounds from hell busted free from the chains what held them.

Course I never expected to see no hounds on that western street where we first seen Dix, remember? That street where him and Minerva had the shooting contest for the reporters? The whole company was involved, us being citizens of that town. Me, I was a storekeeper sweeping my porch, what give me a grand view of the shenanigans to follow.

Now in this one scene, Dix and Symphony was riding horses down the main street, talking about the ranch they was going to buy. She rode side saddle in a striped dress with a little plate of a straw hat stuck to her head. And Dix was dressed as a gent—vest, pocket watch, and all to go with it, revolvers included under his coat. And as they rode down the street, wagons passed and actors strolled and other people on horses passed them by, and down from my porch three kids was playing marbles in the dirt—the lot of us striving to recreate a morning in the history of Redemption, Arizona, in 1855 or thereabouts, though I never did know if such a town was actual.

Well, we run through the scene a half dozen times to get the pace of it, so them cameras could crank the whole of it without stopping none. Dix ticked off some adjustments here and there, though he didn't say nothing to me or them boys in the dirt, before he mounted up and rode to join Symphony down at the end of the street. "Roll 'em!" an assistant hollered out, and I took to sweeping like I'd druther be fishing, and rest of the town come alive along with me, while Dix and Rose Allen begun to prance along on their horses. That's when Joe appeared at the other end of the street, down by the stable.

Now when I say appeared, you got see it for the grand entrance it was. For leading the way, on leashes, was these two mastiffs—them being the hounds from hell, or so we was about to see for ourselves—with Joe coming after, the short-brim fedora riding swell over his brow; and he was leaning back to slow them mastiffs down, the lines of their leashes straight enough to hang laundry. And behind him come a boy, a coon, of eight or nine years what carried a sign what read MERRY ME, ROSE ALLEN—JOE. After that come three more coons blowing on trumpets, and a skinny white boy banging a drum, the lot of them playing passing poor *I WANNA BE LOVED BY YOU/ BY YOU AND NOBODY ELSE BUT YOU.* And last come a girl of fifteen or so, a wisp of a girl, dressed all in white, including white gloves, and she carried a basket of flowers.

The whole town stuttered to a standstill, everybody turning to see the spectacle.

As for Dix and Symphony, they stopped dead in the middle of the street, near as wordless as the rest of us.

Them mastiffs pulled and Joe strutted along, leaning back, with his parade marching behind. Now I don't know how he got them mastiffs, nor why he thought to have them lead the way, but Joe could be unpredictable. You have to admit as much. I figure he wanted to be magnificent, like a general returning from a war to strut the streets of Rome back in the days of Caesar. And that's sure how he acted, walking slow along that street and dipping his head at faces he knew or even risking a wave of a hand till he had to set it back on them reins so them mastiffs couldn't break for hell.

"Cut! Cut!" I heard the assistant yell.

Now I don't know where he come from, but sudden-like, Koko appeared, him dressed in a cowboy hat and vest. He scampered down the porch right past me and jumped over them boys in the dirt and scampered in front of Symphony and Dix. I ain't one to read a monkey's mind, but maybe he thought to protect Dix from a beastly mangling, cause them mastiffs set up a terrible howling upon seeing that monkey and lunged out, ripping them leashes from Joe's grip.

Seeing threat to life and limb, Koko forgot his intention to be a hero and run between the horse's legs, what set them horses to bucking and whinnying and acting as if Satan had come a-calling. Which maybe he had, cause them dogs yapped and snapped at hoofs flying about their heads, till Koko, what had climbed onto a balcony, shrieked at them hounds from hell and even threw a flower pot at one.

Couldn't no rider stand up to that. Rose Allen—she no longer acting and not Symphony—tumbled from her saddle in no time, and Dix come down moments after, while both them horses took off, the mastiffs from hell chasing after them. Koko, shrieked some more and waved his fists from the railing of that balcony, him proving the winner after all and crowing about it.

By now Joe had run ahead of his parade, which was still playing its song, though it sounded ragged by then and out of tune. He ran right past Dix and swept up Rose Allen, whose straw hat was hanging from the side of her head. He set her down gentle-like and plucked the hat from her hair and tried to set it back where it belonged, till she slapped at his hand and took the hat and threw it away. Damn, she was flustered and angry and I could tell she was fed up with Joe's tomfoolery.

Joe said, "It wasn't supposed to go like that."

From his balcony, Koko chattered an answer, though I didn't have no idea what he meant. Them musicians finally got the sense of things and stopped the noise.

Joe waved at the girl in white, the girl with the basket of flowers to come on up. She did; she was scared, but she come on up and Joe took the basket from her and she took off running back to the stable.

Joe put the basket in Rose Allen's arms, and turned to point at the sign the boy carried. But Rose Allen wasn't having nothing to do with Joe's spectacle. Instead, disgusted and fuming, she dropped the basket of flowers at his feet and stalked off, people quick to get from her way.

"Rose Allen!" Joe called out, trying to pull her back with the anguish of his voice, but she never hesitated in her leave-taking. Joe took a step and said her name again, it sounding weak and not how a respectable thug should sound.

Could be, it was that sound, the brokenness of it, encouraged Dix— him being a natural-born fool underneath his winsome ways. I say a fool cause after getting to his feet, he pulled at Joe's shoulder, turning him into a target as he reared back and took a swing, clobbering Joe a good one on the jaw.

As Joe went down, the whole town gasped and one them boys at my feet said, "Key-rist!"

But I wasn't so shocked as they. I knew Joe for what he was—a genuine tough guy didn't nobody knock on his ass, less he was a fool and didn't believe in retribution.

Now Joe looked up from the dirt at Dix, and his eyes got bleak like they did in Joliet. One guy in the crowd across the street laughed, probly cause he was scared. Joe stared into that guy for moment, him staring to say he wasn't a love-loopy sap no more, a message the guy got, him choking off the laugh. Everybody else forgot to breathe, or at least I did.

Joe stood up real slow and turned his Joliet face on Dix, it a merciless and frightening face to see.

Dix backed off a step and looked around, but there wasn't no rescue in sight. So, he set hisself up like a pugilist, a regular Jack Dempsey, with his fists raised. But Joe was a thug what didn't heed no rules of the ring. Didn't no fancy pugilist moves bother him. He stepped inside Dix's next swing, taking it on the shoulder and drove his fists, one after the other, a dozen times it seemed, into Dix's gut.

Dix folded up and landed on his knees, trying to suck down air what couldn't get past his throat, while Joe glowered down at him, saying, "She's my woman, pal, and that's the end of it."

His face white now and sweating, Dix looked a sick and twisted look at Joe. It was plain, what he meant that look to say, but Joe was a tough guy what had handled worse than this sorry excuse of a dope gasping on his knees in the dirt. Probly Dix knew that, cause after a moment more that twisted look fell apart and he was spooked, though he put on his bluster and squeaked out, "You're fired. And so is your little friend over there."

"That don't change what I said, pal. Rose Allen's mine, and I'll be coming for her."

Joe scooped up his short-brim fedora and walked off. Dix stood up and began to straighten his clothes, until Koko climbed down from the balcony and jumped into Dix's arms. Dix petted the animal and when he seen I was watching him, his eyes threw knives into my skull.

I dropped my broom, and while my eyes threw them knives back at him, I followed after Joe.

CHAPTER 33

To this day, Joe's spectacle seems preposterous, like something you'd see in one them foreign pictures from Germany, with everything stretched out and running against the grain of common sense, but hell, it did get reported in *TRUE STORIES* and *PHOTOPLAY*, them each dishing the scoop on it. Maybe you read about it, and maybe you thought it was a lot of hooey cause you ain't never been sold on Hollywood and its excesses. I can't blame you, if that's the case, cause I ain't been blinded by its glitter, neither. But Joe was, and that's my point. He was blinded and a thug what wasn't versed in the intricacies of designing an opus to challenge his rival and charm the eye of his lady love. But that don't make it less authentic, for his intentions come from the heart and sang of his desire for Rose Allen.

At sunset Joe and me and Albert got a fire burning on the beach. While it burned to coals, we drunk dago red from the jug Albert brought and talked of the day's doings.

Albert got a kick out of Joe's spectacle, and in no time the two of them was laughing at Dix being terrorized by a pair of devil hounds before I put a damper on their hilarity, suggesting we was now without jobs and near penniless to boot. "Don't worry about it," Albert said. "You can come work with me."

So, now you know, after he got back from Lone Pine, Albert put aside his grief and found a job working for a moving-picture company called American Eagle, it being a company what ran things on the cheap, churning out serial westerns and spy stories and comedy shorts. It rented a studio in some place called Poverty Row, down near Sunset and Gower.

"Tomorrow, fellas," Albert said, "I'll ask Vanderhoff to hire you. Won't pay much but it's enough to get by."

I wasn't so eager to hear that, me being fed up with the workings of them studios, but Joe perked up and they got to confabulating again about making their own flicker. Albert had him another western he could adapt into a serial, with Joe playing the lead and me as his sidekick. At the time I had no idea what that word meant, so I piped up, "What's this sidekick do?"

"He's the comic relief, that's what."

"Hell, I ain't no clown, nor funny to boot. And I sure ain't going to piss in front of a camera just be funny."

With that, both Albert and Joe took to howling. I didn't see what was so hilarious about what I said, but I figured it was the wine. It can make a fool out of any guy, if he ain't careful with it.

Albert finally got a hold of hisself and said, "Pooch, a sidekick rides aside the hero and helps him. Only thing is, he's eccentric, see?"

"Eccentric how?"

"Well, all you gotta be is yourself. You're a natural sidekick."

"I don't see how. I ain't eccentric, I can tell you that."

That got Joe and Albert howling again, and I took the jug from Joe and held on tight. I didn't much appreciate them laughing at my expense, and I sure wasn't going to give them that jug back, not till they stopped and got proper with me.

But Albert didn't read my mood so good, him saying, "You don't gotta do nothing, Pooch. Why, you're naturally endowed to be a sidekick."

"What's that mean?"

"Damn, he's feisty," he said to Joe.

"As touchy as they come."

"We could use that." Now to me: "Pooch, I'm referring to you being a bantam in a world of heavyweights."

So that was it: my height again. I looked at the wine in that jug and shook my head. I couldn't decide whether or not to clock him with it, but Joe interrupted my debate by plucking the jug from me. He took a pull and passed it on to Albert, saying, "You know, it might be best, us moving on to American Eagle. We'd really get to see how pictures get made."

He and Albert took to speculating about our futures at Poverty Row. Albert even said this, what sounded odd to me, him saying, "Ain't no big shots on Poverty Row. No, the fellas there are regular eggs like you or me; fellas who ain't afraid to give a guy a break and show him the ropes. I'm telling you, boys, they'll put us on the right path and we'll have a motion-picture company up and running in no time."

I didn't believe that for damn minute. Big shots or not, them fellas on Poverty Row wasn't in business to teach us the ropes, least not for free. But I didn't say as much cause I was brooding. Now most times, it don't bother me much, them sorry jabs at my height, but every now and then somebody says something what gets under my skin, and I got to worry at it for a time—which I did, while the two of them went on talking big about Poverty Row.

Anyway, after a while Joe poked the fire with a stick, and I set the micks we had wrapped in tin foil in the coals, while Albert put the steak on the hand grill. And later, when I got some of that food in me, I forgive Albert. I can't hold no grudge against a guy as ugly as he, a guy what had his own endowments to be a sidekick.

Now I want to talk about this sidekick business. I figure by now that's how you've pegged me. But it ain't right, you doing that. Sure, this is Joe's story, but I'm the guy telling it, ain't I? It's my language you're getting, and it's through my eyes you're seeing what happened. Hell, think of me as the director Joe and Albert wanted to be. Think of me like Dix. I'm giving you the best seat in the house, and I ain't gussied it up with lies and sentiment, neither. So, dammit, don't you go characterizing me as no sidekick. I'm a storytelling artist, that's what I am, an artist what won't be characterized as eccentric cause of his height.

After we ate, we talked more, talking now of Dix and Rose Allen, and some about Astoria.

"Have you seen her yet?" Joe asked Albert.

"No, I don't care if I ever do. She's a tramp and a party girl, and she ain't got my heart anymore. So that's it."

Joe said, softly, "You're lucky. I wish I could root Rose Allen from my heart. But I can't. She's got a good hold on me."

"What are you going to do?"

"I don't know – my spectacle today, I guess it was wrong, but I was only trying—"

"Trying what?" I asked.

"To prove I was worthy, I guess."

We watched the foam running onto shore, and Joe poked at the embers with his stick. "Thing of it is, I can't just carry her off like they did in the old days. So I don't know what to do now."

"Give her up, Joe." That's what I said to him. "Give her up and let's go to Frisco for a while. Albert, you can come, too. After that, we can come back here, if you want, and start up a moving-picture company, though I ain't playing no sidekick to nobody."

"I can't do that, Pooch. Not yet anyway."

Now right then I got a good idea, knowing Joe was a guy what believed in symbols and signs and fate. I took his hand and Albert's, too, figuring both of them needed a ceremony, if only to beat back the blues in the night. "C'mon," I told them, pulling them up and leading them down the sand to a wave what washed up to their waists. "Hold it right here," I said, pulling down on their arms till they stopped.

"What are you up to, Pooch?" Joe asked.

I held up their arms, with me in the middle and I shouted out to god and every one of them stars above, "Hey, you up there, god or whatever you are, you see these two guys. These are good guys, you hear me? They got good hearts, and they don't deserve the recent suffering you done brought on them. So, I'm telling you now, give em a break. Wash Rose Allen and Astoria from their minds and souls. Wash em clean so they can find women what are better suited to their needs. And while you're at it, help them get this moving-picture company up and running. I figure you owe them that much, after how you treated them."

Course nothing much happened, cept another wave rolled in. Hell, I didn't expect anything would happen. I done told you, there ain't no god what cares about us, but that didn't matter. It was the ceremony what mattered. Neither Joe nor Albert objected to what I was doing, both of them looking up to the sky like they expected any second to see a burning chariot racing across the moon or some other miracle.

I suppose that tells you how desperate they was, both of them willing to buy into my ritual. Even Albert, him being mostly parlor pink, seemed taken by my prayer and shuddered at what I done next, which was this: I scooped up some water and dribbled it over his head and then I done the same to Joe. And as I did this, I said, "Now there you are, god, the two of these guys has been washed in the waters of the world. They been washed in the tears of the world, and now they is whole again, and like boys what ain't got no grief in their hearts. So you do your part now, dammit. You do what you're supposed to do."

"Is that it?" Joe whispered.

"That's it."

"Damn," Albert said, "I do feel better. A lot better."

Joe grinned and slapped at the water, sending a gout of it in my face, which got the two of them laughing once more and it wasn't long till I was laughing right along with them, the three of us splashing ourselves and sporting about ducking each other and generally raising a ruckus in them waves, till Joe broke it off to say, "You know something, fellas, I think it's gonna work, this washing Rose Allen from my heart. I think it's going to work just fine."

Now I ask you, given it was my idea to do this ceremony, am I any kind of a sidekick? Ha. Not hardly.

Anyway, we trooped out of the water and up the bluff and we didn't get far before the head lamps from two cars bounced along the gravel and pulled up to us. Didn't take but a moment more for me to realize the devil's goons had come a-calling.

CHAPTER 34

Actually they was eight goons, four from each automobile. And they was huge, bigger than Joe and some of them twice as heavy, the kind of goons what had muscles in their ears.

They spread themselves out circling around us, cutting us off. One of them stood up to Joe and said, "You gotta be Joe Holder."

"What of it?" Joe said back at him.

But the goon wasn't interested in conversation. He threw a punch at Joe, but Joe slipped under it and used his head to butt the goon's belly. The goon "oofed" and fell to his ass, but the other goons didn't hesitate. Four of them plowed into Joe from all sides. Joe couldn't do much but collapse and fold himself up, while fists and legs thudded into him. Damn, they was like machines, them goons, kicking and pounding without no hitch, the slabs of their faces wearing nothing but grim duty. Albert wasn't no better off, him being lambasted in a like manner by the other three.

I didn't know why they didn't jump me right off, like they did Joe and Albert, but I wasn't going to stand there, neither. So, I jumped on the back of one of the goons what was kicking Joe and stuck my fingers in his nostrils; I pulled for all I was worth, and the guy roared and backed away, trying to throw me off, but I kept tearing at his nostrils, till he slammed hisself to the ground, slamming hisself mostly on me.

That stunned me some, and the arm and shoulder he fell on went numb. After the goon tore hisself free, he kicked me three or four good ones and then jumped back into the machine what was pounding on Joe.

I struggled to sit up, feeling cold fire in my shoulder, knowing it was probly separated. I hoisted myself to my knees and looked up. That's when I seen in one of the goon's automobiles another person. I stood up and, cradling my arm in the other, I shuffled closer to see it was Astoria, who must have rode along to identify us, though from the glitter in her eyes I seen a sadist residing in her heart. Least that's how I figured it.

She was chewing gum and watched me back, before she turned her head to watch what happened to Joe and Albert.

But there wasn't more to see, cause the goons had done their job and now they filed past me. The last one brushed into my shoulder what got that cold fire to flare up again. He sat beside Astoria, who looked past him at me and chewed her gum until she smiled and took it from her mouth and tossed it at me. The goon pulled the door closed and them two automobiles roared off, kicking gravel in my face.

Now getting assaulted by trained goons ain't like it is in the moving pictures. It hurts, dammit. The three of us was hurting. It took us ten minutes before we could drag ourselves to Albert's automobile and make a miserable drive to a hospital.

The doc patched us up one after the other, like he was working at Henry Ford's assembly line. Albert took seven stitches for a gash over his eye and Joe got his chest wrapped in a body bandage. He had some bruised ribs, and one of them was maybe cracked. The doc told them the damage wasn't permanent, but they'd wear the marks a long while. Best thing they could do was rest up a few days. As for me, the doc said some muscles was tore in my shoulder, and while he packed my arm in a sling, he said again, him having said it earlier, "Gentlemen, you really should let me call the police. Don't you want to make a report?"

Joe said, him quiet now and back to the tough guy he had been in Joliet, "We ain't calling in the coppers."

The doc give him a funny look, confused, "I don't see why not."

Albert piped up, "We don't need em."

"But," the doc said, him still confused, "the police can investigate and arrest the guys who did this to you. Don't you want justice?"

Joe said, "This ain't none of the coppers' business."

The doc's eyes got big, him understanding now. Tying off my sling he said in a near whisper, "You boys could be making a mistake."

I didn't think that was so. Justice don't always come from a copper or a judge. Sometimes justice has got to be more personal to be satisfying and this was one of them times.

"Doc, the courts have never been much good to me," I told him. "Fact is, they ain't so sensitive to me. Nor the coppers neither."

"But you boys could get in trouble. After all, this isn't a jungle without a rule of law."

"That's where you're wrong, Doc," Joe said. "It's more of a jungle than you think."

"And we're the proof of it," I said, while I hopped off that table and swaggered out of that hospital with Joe and Albert tagging after me.

We was banged up pretty good and didn't do nothing but sleep mostly for four days. Albert and Joe raised up a crop of ripe bruises in no time, them matching the scrapes and cuts and such what scabbed over but looked ugly enough. Albert's bandage over his eye made him a pirate. As for me, after the second day, I took off the sling. I couldn't sleep so good with it on, me rolling onto my side and the pain of it jolting me awake. So, I slept sitting up on the sofa in the front room. Sides, I didn't want to be no invalid longer than I had to be. Hell, I didn't even medicate myself none, cept for a few aspirin. And neither did Joe. Albert mostly pulled at jugs of dago red, him claiming it was the best medicine in the world. That's how it went for us them four days. We was restoring ourselves, that's what we was doing. We didn't talk serious about what them goons did to us till on the fourth night after it happened.

Joe and me was playing cribbage on our porch. Now and then, automobile head lamps flickered through the weeds as they passed us. Sometimes a truck or two grumbled along. But mostly all we heard was the ocean calling to us, asking us how we was feeling, it worried about our wounds and such. Now I know an ocean don't get worried but that's how it sounded, it sounding sad cause we suffered so.

I seen Albert first, him coming out of his bungalow carrying his jug. He marched along the gravel until he got to Joe and me, where he stopped and said, "What do you fellas think about a gun?"

"No guns," Joe said.

"I think we should have one, in case Mr. Dix sends those goons back here."

Joe shook his head. "Albert, do what you have to. But I'm telling you, I ain't using no guns."

I couldn't blame him. Wasn't neither of us any good with guns. Nor Albert neither. Hell, you got no business using a gun lest you're ready to get arrested for murder, cause that's all a gun is good for—murder. And even if we was hard-boiled cons, wasn't neither of us willing to commit one.

But Albert seen it different, him seeing it as necessity, I suppose, him saying, "There's too many of them."

Joe nodded at that. "That's so, but I ain't using no gun."

"A guy's gotta protect himself."

"That's so. But me, I'll do that another way."

"How?" Albert asked.

"I ain't decided yet."

"Well, I'm getting a gun."

Albert glared at us. Then he said, his voice breaking some, "Astoria was with them goons. I saw her."

The ocean kept calling to us, and I realized all our wounds wasn't on the outside.

"She threw gum at me," I said.

Albert nodded, saying, "Dix probably made her do it."

"Probly."

"He had no right to do that. No right at all. But that's how they are, those privileged guys. They don't care about regular guys like us."

Albert slumped and said, "Tomorrow I'm getting a gun." He walked off, shoulders hunched, back to his bungalow.

Joe said, "Pooch, we gotta keep an eye on him. Something ain't right with him. We gotta keep an eye on him."

The next afternoon Albert got his gun, a rifle. He took me up in the hills to try it out. Joe refused to come along, him headed to the ocean where he was going to ride the waves on his belly. He told Albert he should forget about trying out his gun and ride the waves, but Albert paid him no mind, stalking off for the hills across the highway, with me coming after him. We hiked up a hill and I looked back to see the blue of that ocean stretching out wide beyond Sunset Haven. But Albert wasn't interested in no scenery. He took to shooting at birds and lizards and a jack rabbit. He didn't hit nothing. Either he didn't know much about how to work a rifle or his eyes was bad, I couldn't decide. But watching him, seeing how desperate and fierce he was to hit what he aimed at, I realized Joe was right. Albert had slipped from his center some, and that we'd better keep an eye on him.

After half an hour of shooting, we hiked down the trail to Sunset Haven, and without no words, Albert hiked with his gun over his shoulder to his bungalow while I went into mine. Wasn't long after that that I heard an automobile pulling up outside and I come out the door to see Rose Allen in her green Cadillac.

CHAPTER 35

Opening her door, she got from her automobile and walked around it, walking careful like she didn't want to offend me none.

Now I done told you: I didn't much approve of Rose Allen's morals, and when she stopped and poured a haggard look at me what said sleep had done abandoned her, that pleased me some. Guess it appealed to my sense of justice.

"Is he all right?" she asked.

"We'll live."

"Is he in there?"

I shook my head before saying, "Tell me, Rose Allen, was you a part of what Dix done to us? Was you in on it?"

Her eyes got big while a slow wind rippled in her dress. "No—I couldn't—no, I swear—"

I believed her. But I wasn't so forgiving as to tell her that, me saying instead, "I don't get it, why you carry on with that Dix character. He sure don't measure up to Joe."

"It's—it's complicated, Pooch."

Wind gusted up and her dress rippled again, before I said, "It ain't complicated for Joe. With him it's simple."

"I know."

"And he wouldn't send no goons out to take care of his own business."

"I—I know, Pooch."

"Joe ain't that mean nor heartless."

She jerked up her head, and I could see she was angry now and maybe hurt some. "I didn't ask him to come out here, Pooch. I didn't ask him to complicate my life."

I didn't have to answer, cause Joe come up the bluff and she saw him and waited while he walked past them other bungalows, walking straight for her.

"Hello, Rose Allen," he said.

Her hand raised to touch his face, the bruises on it, but he turned his head to stop it. All she could manage to say was, "Oh, Joe."

Joe said, him stiff with the saying, "Why are you here, Rose Allen?"

"I—" Tears swum in her eyes. I couldn't tell if they was real or not.

"Did you come to say you'd marry me? Is that why you're here?"

She shook her head and somehow them tears disappeared. She looked into Joe while the wind come up and pulled at us. "I just don't—"

After he waited, Joe said, him not so hard now, "Rose Allen, answer me. Is it over between you and me? Is it?"

She raised her hand again, and this time he let her touch his face. Her fingers smoothed the cuts and scabs, and she said, breathing it mostly, "I don't know. I just don't know."

She'll never know, I wanted to scream at Joe. She's just stringing you on more, I wanted to say. Don't let them fingers fool you or them tears what come up again and swum in her eyes. Just tell her to get lost.

But Joe didn't need no advice, him saying, "If we go on, you've got to dump Dix. Can you do that?"

Her hand fell away; and even though she wasn't a woman for wrinkles, a crease come between her eyes, it being like a thorn what sprouted on a face full of trouble, with her saying, "I don't know how—"

"You just tell him, that's how. You tell him to drop dead."

"I—can—do that."

I didn't believe her. I thought she was just trying out them words and did not mean them.

Joe said, "If you tell him, I'll be here, I promise you that. But you have to tell him before you can come here again. You have to do that."

Without looking at her more or showing any affection, he stepped up on the porch and went into the bungalow and then into the bedroom.

Rose Allen looked at me, before she said, her being more definite, "I can do that. I can."

She got into her Cadillac and took off.

When I got into the bedroom, Joe was wrapping hisself in the body bandage. He said, "Do you think she'll tell him?"

I shrugged.

"I think she'll tell him. I really think she will."

Joe sounded like she had, both of them saying words they knew wasn't true, but saying them anyway. Guess they thought if they said them words enough times, they'd get true—which seemed a pretty slim notion to me, and not so dependable.

The dark come along and Joe listened to the radio, the bluesy sound of its music riding on a trumpet, a sound what made me ache for the pain of it, a sound I didn't want to hear more if I meant to sleep that night. Sides, I was restless and tired of that bungalow. Without no words, even as Joe asked what was wrong, I walked into the dark and got in my Ford and headed south down the highway, just motoring for the motion of it, I suppose, and to fill time. While the miles ticked off, I considered more what Joe had said to Rose Allen. I considered the rightness of it. Love-loopy or not, a guy has got to set down rules, and I ain't talking about the law; I'm talking about how you got to stand up to a dame and let her know what you expect. Those kind of rules, I'm talking. The kind of rules what matter. If a guy has them, can't no dame make a fool out of him.

Wasn't much traffic on the highway, and most of it headed north, but in time I come up on a Ford like mine parked at the side of the road, its head lamps blaring at the night. The door was open and a man was vomiting. I pulled past the automobile and parked in the wash of its lamps.

I ain't a guy what acts from charity often, but now and again I see an egg suffering and I got to ask him the why of it. So, I got from my Ford. The beach wasn't that far off, the white of water crawling along its face. I walked up to the other Ford like mine and smelled the stink of sour booze and gasoline fumes—his engine was running—and rotten kelp what sat in a clump under the automobile. "You okay, buddy?" I asked.

Groaning, he laid his noggin on his seat and didn't even look at me.

I prodded at him, and he groaned again, but his eyes stayed closed, and the sour stink poured off him. The ocean wasn't that far off; maybe I could drag him down there, throw him in and wash off the stink. But he was fat and I wasn't so charitable as that, not with my shoulder aching like it was. So, I prodded again but it didn't do no good, him having passed out. That's when I seen the wallet on the seat beside him.

Well, I said it before, I was a born a thief, and I ain't one to pass up an easy opportunity when it comes knocking; and I sure didn't have no apologies nor regret for breaking my promise to Joe. I mean, when you're near broke and too beat up to get hired by most any boss; necessity, hungry for its due, rears its head and shows its big teeth. Necessity scares the hell out of some guys, but not me, not then, not now—no, sir. I spat into them teeth; I denied them their due by leaning across the man, leaning into the stink of him, and I took up that wallet and checked to see a wad of bills, which I done pulled out and stuffed in my shirt pocket real quick. I put the wallet back on the seat cause I ain't so bad a thief as to steal a guy's papers and pictures and such. I'm a cash-and-carry thief, it being decent that way. Standing up, I did what a charitable soul should. I shut off his engine and head lamps, and I found a blanket in the back seat and draped it over that poor sap. What the hell, I owed him as much, after the donation he done made to Pooch's Survival Plan.

Back in my car, I counted out that donation, it coming in at ninety-four smackers. Wasn't a fortune, but it would do us for a few weeks.

Feeling at peace with the world, I made my way back to Sunset Haven and seen the light in Albert's bungalow. After parking, I walked over to his place and looked in the door, doing like Joe said: keeping an eye on him.

He slept on his sofa, the rifle laying across his lap and at his feet a half-empty jug of dago red. In one of his hands was Dix's money clip.

Just like I done for the drunk at the side of the road, I laid a blanket over him and shut the door after I left to keep out the damp air.

Like I told you, sometimes I get an inclination to be charitable.

CHAPTER 36

Fact was, them ninety-four clams come in handy cause Albert couldn't get us no jobs at American Eagle, least not right away. He told us Vanderhoff wouldn't hire us till the newest serial was ready for the cameras, that being in a week or maybe two. So, me and Joe bided our time, and it was pleasant, the air rich with summer and the ocean calling to us. We both sported for hours in the waves and on the beach. We dug up abalones and clams and ate them raw on the shell after squirting some lime on them and washing them down with beer. On two of them nights we went to a restaurant and a flicker after, though never one with Dix nor Symphony. We even went to a dance hall one night, and Joe danced—which got me to dancing alongside him, the two of us dancing with one skirt after another, skirts without no names, and that was fine by me. I guess you could say them ninety-four clams had bought us a genuine vacation.

Course, after a week of this, both of us baking side by side on the sand, Joe said, "How we doin' on jack?"

"We got around eighty bucks."

Joe sat up, looking at me funny, "Where'd all that dough come from?"

"I been saving it."

He slapped my arm, though it didn't hurt none and said, "I can't afford to lose you, Pooch. Not to no prison."

"They gotta catch me first, and that ain't likely cause I'm too slick for these California coppers."

"I ain't kiddin, Pooch. I don't want to find your sorry ass in a jail. It ain't worth it, wherever you got that jack. I just ain't worth it."

He jumped up and threw hisself into the waves and swum for Japan.

Hell, this dictionary I got says a cockle is a shellfish—sort of like a clam, I guess—and I don't know what that's got to do with warming a human heart, but that's what mine was. It was warmed to the cockles by what Joe had said. Well, he didn't have to worry; I only returned to my criminal ways to deny necessity, and since we was going to report to American Eagle on the next day, it looked like necessity had put away its teeth for the time being.

But I don't want you to get the wrong idea and think we was healed and at peace in paradise. Any healing by Joe and Albert was only on the outside. I say this cause both of them took up peculiar habits. Every night before he slept, Joe went into the weeds and looked south down that highway, him standing there and looking for a good half hour before he'd give it up and come to bed. And Albert was just as peculiar, him prowling through the bungalows and along the shore every night, with that rifle over his shoulder and the jug of wine hanging from his hand. I didn't think to disturb either of them. Sometimes a guy has got to wrestle on his own with his demons, and there's the truth of it.

The next morning Albert drove us to American Eagle, it being a converted feed store down on Gower. Only had two rooms to it and a storage shed used as a garage out back. The bigger room was crowded with saddles and other horse gear, and along one wall was racks of cowboy outfits, with some furniture stacked along another. In between was piles of crates and sawhorses and trunks and even a hat tree. The camera equipment and lights, what there was of them, was clustered in a corner, looking as shabby as everything else in that room. I was used to Empire's operation, and didn't see how there was enough equipment to shoot a moving picture, and I said as much aloud. Albert set me straight, him saying, "American Eagle rents its cameras and lights and what all for the day. Rents it from Empire mostly. It's cheaper than owning the whole outfit."

"But where's the studio?" I asked.

"Right here," Albert said.

"But you can't do no acting in here."

"Vanderhoff doesn't shoot pictures in here. They get shot, most of them, out in Thousand Oaks. When interiors need to get shot, Vanderhoff rents a studio from Empire for a day or two."

That surprised me. Damn, I thought, ain't that clever, how a guy could run a studio on the cheap? Ain't nothing wrong with that, long as folks still come to see your picture show. Damn, could be, I was wrong. Could be, Joe and Albert could set up their own moving-picture company, if they had the clams it took to get such an operation up and running. Curious, I asked Albert, "What do you figure it costs Vanderhoff to make a serial?"

"Probably about six, maybe seven thousand."

"And do them serials make any money?"

"They have so far. Of course that's because Empire distributes Vanderhoff's films. If it didn't, those films couldn't get into the theatres. But Empire makes money off independents like Vanderhoff."

Before I could ask more, the door slammed open and Vanderhoff bustled into the room, carrying a camera and tripod over her shoulder. She was wearing an aviator's skull cap and a scarf, along with these cheaters what magnified her eyes to near twice their size. Truth be told, everything about her looked magnified—which was curious cause she wasn't much bigger than me. But she filled up a room just by how she stood and how she cocked her head, it being huge, the head of a man twice her size, and her hands being the same way. As if somebody mismatched her parts but screwed them on her torso anyhow. When she seen us standing by her office door, she set down the camera and said, "C'mon."

Wasn't no kind of greeting in her nor a need to know our names, for she went over to the costume racks and sorted through a few sets of cowboy duds and pulled one down and held it up to Albert, checking the size, before she said, "Put that on." Which Albert did, him stripping to his skivvies without even blushing. Not that she seemed to notice, her handing other duds to Joe and then to me, saying, "C'mon, boys, hurry it up."

Now I ain't never changed clothes in front of a strange dame. Nor did Joe. But she wasn't putting up with our bashful natures, her saying, "You haven't got anything I haven't seen before."

Albert laughed at that.

So, Joe and me got to swapping our clothes for them cowboy duds, and while we did Vanderhoff said, her clipping out the words without hardly breathing between. "Three bucks a day. That's what I'm paying. Ten hours a day. That's what I expect, and I use every minute of them, so be on time. Now I got a truck out there needs loading. Let's get to it."

She started throwing saddles and horse gear in a heap, and when we was dressed the three of us carried it out the door and loaded up a truck, while Vanderhoff went into her office and slammed file drawers and yelled into her telephone for a time, startling my baby ears by yelling, "Shit!" to whoever was on the other end of that telephone line. Ten minutes later Albert sat up front with Vanderhoff while me and Joe sat with the horse gear in back. While the truck banged its way to Thousand Oaks, I shouted out to Joe, "I didn't expect Vanderhoff for a woman."

"It is unusual," Joe said, grinning.

"She must be one of them new women I heard about. One of them emancipated women."

"I don't know; but what the hell, I'd rather work for her than Dix."

He had that right. But I found it curious, a woman what could cuss like her, me hearing that "Shit!" again. It didn't seem normal to my ears. I didn't quite know what to make of that, but I figured I'd keep my mouth shut, it not being practical to offend the dame what handed you three bucks a day.

One thing I got to say about Vanderhoff: she worked fast. At Empire, Dix and Cardwell took their time. They'd shoot three, maybe four set ups a day. But Vanderhoff shot nine or ten. She wasn't so concerned about lighting nor where to put the camera. And she cranked that camera her own self. I don't know if this was to economize or cause she was an artist, but that was what she done.

And through all of that first day and the four what come after, she cussed at us, cussing from a mouth to match the foulest to be found in Joliet.

After that last day, it near dark, Albert turned his Chrysler into Sunset Haven, and in front of our bungalow there she was, Rose Allen standing by her green Cadillac.

CHAPTER 37

Joe hopped out of Albert's automobile before it stopped, with me coming right after him. He trotted up to Rose Allen and the two of them stared into each other for a moment before she said, "I told him it was over."

Joe put a hand to her cheek and said, "I've been waiting, like I said I would."

"You look better than the last time I saw you."

"I heal fast. I always have."

Nodding, she said, "Good." Gently she took his hand and held it to say, "Can you come with me?"

"Where we going?"

"It's—it's a surprise," she said, her eyes smiling for him.

"Give me a minute to clean up." Joe stepped past her and went to our door and unlocked it.

She hollered up to him, "Change into your dancing shoes, Cinderella."

Joe grinned and said, "Should I take a shower?"

"Be quick about it, mister, because I'm hungry and can't wait much longer."

After he went into our bungalow, I eyeballed Rose Allen before saying, "Does Dix know you're here?"

The smile ran from her face and she said, "I—don't think so."

"But if he does, will we be seeing more of them goons later tonight?"

"I—that—that should never have happened."

"But it did," I said, wagging my arm up and down and still feeling the hurt in it.

"Yes, it did."

"So where are you taking Joe?"

"To the Biltmore."

"Ain't that where all the picture stars go to drink and dance? Guess that means you don't care none if folks see you and Joe together."

"Of course not."

"But I wonder, don't some of them folks run with Dix?"

"What are you saying, Pooch?"

"Just this: could be, you're taking Joe to the Biltmore to rile Dix."

"And if I am?"

I didn't know how to answer that. Hell, so what if Dix got riled? Ain't no skin off my teeth how nasty Rose Allen got in dumping him—if that's what she was doing. But did she have to use Joe to do this riling? Was it worth the risk of more goons piling out of cars and looking to crack open our heads? Damn, this appearance at the Biltmore could surely be a detriment to Joe's and my general health and well being. So I said, "You better not be lying about dumping Dix, cause if you are—"

"I'm not lying," she shot back, her eyes daring me to say different.

I didn't. Instead, I took her at her words and said, "Well, don't stay out so late. Joe's got to work tomorrow."

With that, I walked down to Albert's bungalow. In a few more minutes Joe come out looking swank and as grand as any picture star. Though I couldn't hear them none, Rose Allen clapped her hands, and I could tell from her face she was pleased to see Joe looking so elegant. Wasn't but a moment more and the two them got into her Cadillac and drove off.

Albert said, "It's a shame we can't all be as beautiful as they are."

Once dark got a good hold on Sunset Haven, I sat reading a newspaper on our porch and hearing the moths bumble against the light over my head. That's when a fancy automobile bumped through the weeds and onto the gravel and growled to a stop with its head lamps aiming right at me, near blinding me, they was that bright.

The door opened and a black figure got out and said from over the door, "Where are they, Pooch?"

It was Dix's voice.

I used the paper to shield my eyes, saying, "Not here."

Dix, the blackness of him, just stood there, while his automobile rumbled between us.

Now a gun cracked out and echoed. I got no idea where the bullet went, but I turned to see Albert on the porch of his bungalow cocking his rifle for another shot. A snap of my head showed Dix, if I read his blackness right, shifting his weight and looking ready to run. Back to Albert, I seen him aim and the gun cracked again and this time I heard the bullet in the weeds beyond us.

I guess Dix wasn't so eager to find Rose Allen and Joe no more, cause he disappeared into his automobile and backed it up fast and took off, while the gun cracked again and a bullet chased after it.

Scant moments later, Albert pulled up in his Chrysler and shouted out, "C'mon, dammit, before he gets away!"

I jumped into the automobile and Albert handed me his jug of dago red. "Here! Hold on to that!" He slammed his gear into place and let up the brake lever and off we spurted, weeds whipping past us. Wasn't but a moment more and we hit the highway running hard after Dix.

Now the only reason I jumped into Albert's Chrysler was to stop him from hurting hisself or others, Dix included. But the laugh was on me—literally, as it turned out—cause I couldn't get him to slow up none. And I tried, believe me. I hollered for him to stop a half dozen times, and when I reached to pull on his brake, he knocked my hand away and swung the Chrysler to the right so we was riding on the shoulder and not no pavement. Rocks clattered under us and right next me, close enough so I could touch them, telephone poles flicked past one after the other. I shrunk up in my seat and held onto that jug and stiffened myself. Damn, this wasn't no way for decent thief to die. No way at all.

Albert hauled his Chrysler back on the road and honked his horn at the produce truck in front of us, and when nothing happened, he veered into the other lane and roared to pass that truck, cept now head lamps was coming straight at us. Albert yanked his Chrysler right, somehow squeezing us between that produce truck and the other truck what roared past us so close I could feel the heat of it rushing past Albert and into me. Albert pushed on the throttle harder and the truck at my shoulder fell away. That's when I dared to say, "Albert, I ain't no Keystone Kop. I can't get up and walk away from a crack up. I ain't that comical."

Albert slid his eyes from the road to see me, and that set him to laughing, him laughing so hard I thought we was doomed, till he eased off on the throttle and let the Chrysler bump along the side of the road and stop. The truck we near clipped honked at us while it rumbled by. Albert laughed some more, saying between fits of that laughter, "You should see your face, Pooch. I really did scare the billy bejesus out of you."

"Dammit, Albert! What's wrong with you?"

"I'm broken, Pooch, and I don't know how to fix myself," he said, and as he did sadness come into his face. "That's all I'm trying to do—fix myself."

"Well, you can't do that by near killing me in your automobile."

He nodded at the rightness of that.

"And you can't go shooting a picture star. A judge'd crucify you."

Taking the jug from me, he uncorked it and took a swallow and handed it back for me to cork up. "I couldn't hit him anyway. You've seen how I shoot."

I had to admit it; he had a point there, but you never know—he was the kind what could get unlucky even if he didn't aim and wind up riding the electric chair into damnation.

Albert put the gear in place and nudged on the throttle and as we drove off again, he said, "I got somewhere I want you to see."

An hour later, Albert pulled us up to this old Victorian house in the middle of farm country. Light spilled from every door and window, and music spilled out, too—music what wailed Chicago jazz into the night. Didn't take no genius to see this was a brothel, though more stylish than the ones I visited back in Illinois.

Albert parked his Chrysler under a pepper tree and separate from the automobiles sitting at every which angle in the dirt around that house.

Albert looked over at me and said, "It's a regular gentleman's club in there. Bankers, lawyers, even a moving-picture actor now and then. "

"Dix ain't in there," I said, looking at the house close from my window.

"I know that," Albert said, opening his door.

We went inside.

It was plush and full of furniture and drapes and carpets from the turn of the century. There was a bar in there serving pots of booze disguised as tea. And it wasn't no bathtub gin nor flavored wood alcohol, neither, but bonded whiskey what come in on a boat from Mexico, or so the fella behind the bar said.

And there was girls.

And they was beautiful, most of them.

And they was moving-picture stars, for all I could tell.

Now I ain't fooling you none. I recognized Mary Pickford, Pola Negri,

Mabel Normand, Vilma Banky, and even a Clara Bow what looked more luscious than the real "It Girl." I mean, she was genuine peaches and cream. Course I couldn't name them all, those girls what pretended to be actresses from the flickers. Not that I was inclined to give them names, me being too bowled over by the very cleverness of their imitations. Clever, that's what I said, and I still got to admire what they done to get along in life.

Funny thing, though, that house closed down about the time talkies took hold. I don't know why. But could be, them silent actresses was more gratifying, if you get my meaning, than the crop they got now. What do you think? That is a good question, ain't it? Whether one generation of skirts is more sexually desirable than the generation what comes after it. Sure wish somebody would write a movie article on that topic. I surely do.

But that's not what you want to hear from me, is it? So—

After a pot of bonded "tea" we drunk from these cups what had flowers in the bottoms, Albert took Mary Pickford up the stairs, and I, having contracted with Clara Bow, followed after him. Albert tripped in the process, he was that spifficated, but Mary Pickford righted him while giggling and led him up the last stair and into the room on the right, the "It Girl" conducting me into the next room.

Now I ain't going to dwell on details here; I ain't so salacious as that. But I got to say, Clara Bow lived up to her reputation and then some, and I was having a high old time discovering how the parts of her worked, when the door banged open and Mary Pickford swarmed into the room and slapped my bare ass.

CHAPTER 38

I looked up from my doings to see she was angry—and it was plain to see why; vomit was stuck in her hair and on her face and shoulders. She said, "Get that friend of yours out of my bed." Then to Clara, who looked over her shoulder at the two of us, she said, "Look what he did to me, Mae. Just look what that yaboo did to me."

Mae? What happened to Clara?

Hell, she waggled her rump and scooted away from me, saying, "Ida, honey, let me," and cradled Mary Pickford, not including me none in her comforting.

I dressed quick and give Mary Pickford an extra ten, thinking to soothe her sobs, which she took and held to her bosom, while Clara who was Mae got a cloth wet in a wash basin on a stand near the bed and used it to scrub at Ida's face. I dressed quick and slunk from the room and went to claim Albert.

Naked, he sat on the bed of the other room, and he was sobbing as loud as Mary Pickford, sobbing so loud you'd think he was about to cough up his actual lungs. And he stunk. So, just as Mae done to Ida, I scrubbed him up, using the cloth from the wash basin what was near the bed. As I did, his sobs drifted off, ending with a few rancid hiccups.

"Damn," I said, "We got to get you home."

"Pooch," he said, the ugly of him spread limp on his face, "I'm shamed of m'self."

"Don't be no crybaby," I told him.

"But, it ain't right, what happened. It ain't manly. I should have finished. That's what a man does. He finishes what he's started. Aw, I ain't but a big stinking flop, Pooch. And all cuz of Dix, that bastard."

I yanked on his pants and his shirt, manhandling him to shut him up. I don't got no patience with a guy what pities hisself. But when it come to his shoes, I wasn't going to help. I don't get on my knees to any man, and since he was too drunk to tie his own shoes, I carried them in one hand, while I used the other to get him off that bed and out of the room.

I drove us toward the ocean, till Albert roused hisself and told me to swing by Empire Studios, which I done. He told me to circle round to the back, and I done that, bumping along a dirt alley, till he told me to stop. I did just that.

Now the night was dense, there being clouds blotting out the moon; and I could smell oranges. I suppose that's cause part of Empire had once been a citrus orchard, and some of the trees was still standing back there, standing in one-legged humps against the mountains behind them.

A coyote yipped. It sounded close. And another coyote, farther off, answered him, its yip running into a thin yowl.

Albert said, "You see that door, there?"

I did. It was a slit of a door set in a stretch of sheet-metal wall, the corrugated kind. "It ain't got no lock on it," he said.

With that he got from the car and went to the door and opened it, showing me dark space on the other side of that corrugated wall. "I got to piss," he said and stepped through that door.

I had no idea why he couldn't take his piss against that wall, but what could I do? I got from his car and run after him, trying to stay quiet the whole while. That's all we needed, to get arrested for trespass by some studio bull.

I couldn't find him at first, till I run past a warehouse and seen him plugging along a road between other warehouses. Catching up to him, I told him this wasn't such a good idea, but he just said, "I got to piss."

"So, piss already, and let's get out of here."

"No, I can't piss here."

"Then where?"

"Right there," he said, pointing at the back of a billboard, the face of it open to the front gate at Empire and the road beyond, it standing a good twenty feet above the ground so the walls didn't block it none. Approaching it from the back, we was in its shadow cause lights on a rail shot up at that sign so any passerby what drove his way past Empire couldn't miss it. As Albert rounded that sign, stepping from the shadow, I pulled him back, hissing, "Are you nuts?!"

I waved my arm at the guard shack what we could see on an angle through the gates.

Albert blinked at me. Then he went to one of the legs of that billboard and unzipped hisself and took to pissing.

Curiosity got the better of me, so I edged around that sign, hugging what shadow there was and looked up and seen in its lights Yancey Dix and Symphony standing side by side before a Conestoga wagon what had other wagons behind it, stretching in a curve across a prairie. Above in old-time lettering it read *COMING SOON—YANCEY DIX & SYMPHONY—WESTWARD, THE WAGONS.*

Albert spattered his piss at the foot of that sign. And just when I thought he was done, he spattered some more. It was near about the longest piss a man ever took; and I couldn't help myself, I grinned. Hell, it was better than shooting Dix, if you ask me. It was poetic, that piss was—poetic justice.

CHAPTER 39

The next morning, Joe, Albert and me rode in an outlaw bunch getting chased by a posse. Along with five other guys, we rode down a hill and straight at Vanderhoff who was cranking her camera; then we rode through a tract of trees—and after that along a dirt road what wound up the face of a rock mountain. And while we rode, we shot off our pistols at the posse behind, shooting by twisting in the saddle and banging away without no aiming. Not that it mattered if we did cause there wasn't no bullets in our pistols but only gunpowder what spat out smoke and grit—the smell of sulfur hanging heavy and sticking to our outlaw duds.

That smoke burned my nostrils and didn't help my disposition none, neither, cause I was suffering after my night of carousing. Albert suffered worse, him looking near pale green like he done swallowed poison. Joe, amused by our collective discomfort, said, "Boys, take my advice, don't ride in an outlaw gang if you can't hold your liquor."

I didn't much appreciate his humor.

About noon, Vanderhoff had us break for lunch. We was under a stand of scrub oaks. From the back of a truck, she handed each of us a brown bag. Inside was a ham and Swiss on rye and an apple. Wasn't nothing but canteens full of warm water to drink. "Fellas," she said, "eat up damn quick. In a half hour, I want your butts back in the saddle."

Wasn't no muss or frills to that woman, and I kind of admired that.

Anyway, Joe and me found us a rock to sit on and got to eating, but Albert drifted away to sit by hisself twenty feet off, with his back to a tree. He give us a sullen look once he was settled, and then didn't pay us no mind. "What's a matter with him?" Joe asked.

"He had a rough night."

"He looks kind of droopy."

Hell, cept for Joe, so did the whole of our outlaw gang, the lot of us coated in sweat and droopy with riding hard through the morning. But even as Joe rode and sweated beside us, he wasn't droopy, but sat up bold and pert and ready to converse about his night at the Biltmore.

"Pooch," he said, "it was a sight to behold. I ain't kidding you, Charlie Chaplin was there. And Douglas Fairbanks and some guy Rose Allen called Ramon Navarro. I couldn't recognize some of those actors, but it didn't matter. Rose Allen knew them all. And she knew the big shots—the producers and directors. And she introduced me to some. She introduced to two directors called Ford and Fleming, and they told me I had a face for western films. That's exactly what they said—a face for western films. Ford even said he'd keep me in mind. How about that?"

"That's something, all right."

"Got me to thinking, I gotta get Rose Allen to take me to more of them shindigs where the big shots go. I gotta get to know those guys like Ford and Fleming better. I gotta talk to them about Albert's motion picture. I bet they'd love to hear about it."

Joe looked over to Albert and raised his voice, "What d'you think, Albert? Maybe we can even get those big shots to pony up some dough. Maybe we could get them to produce our movie."

Albert shouted back, "What big shots?"

"The ones I met last night."

"You mean Symphony and Dix's crowd? Hah, not likely. They ain't giving us no money to make a picture. They don't give a fart for guys like us. All they'll do is what Dix did—steal our work and claim it for their own."

"Now don't be like that, Albert."

"Aw, Christ, when are you going to wake up, Joe? When are you going to see they're using us?"

"They can't all be like Dix."

But Albert, disgusted, waved Joe off and stood up and stalked away.

"Damn," Joe said, "he's hurting, ain't he, Pooch?"

I nodded.

"Well, let's give him some time. But, you know, I got an idea. I gotta talk to Rose Allen. What d'you think, Pooch? Maybe she'd want to invest in our picture. Hell, that's what I'll do. I'll talk to her.

"Last night she told me she wasn't going to work with Dix anymore, that WAGONS was her last film with him. So, she's got to be looking for new opportunities. Besides, producing Albert's picture would give us a chance to work together. That's what we talked about last night, working together.

"I can see it now. The two of us—along with Albert and you of course—could take Hollywood by storm. Why, we'd be a golden couple, like Fairbanks and Pickford. Yeah, why not? She'd love to produce a film. I know she would.

"Just wait till I tell Albert about this. It'll cheer him right up."

Damn, it was remarkable, how his mind ran off and got Rose Allen to produce Albert's photo play. I was left with no words, but could only stare at him. I decided right then and there, Joe wore rose-tinted cheaters and had tricked hisself so he couldn't see his Rose Allen proper no more. Ain't it something, how a woman can ruin a guy's perspective and get him to speculate on a world what can never be?

After lunch, Vanderhoff had us change our hats and shirts, and she had us pin on badges. Now we was the posse what chased after the outlaw bunch we had been all morning. We rode down that hill and right into that camera Vanderhoff cranked, and we rode through the same trees and up that road against the face of that rock mountain; and we shot off our pistols the whole time. Only we shot them straight ahead, so the smoke rolled back and stung my eyes. Damn, this flirtation with the other side of law didn't improve my mood none, neither, not with the stink of them guns so deep in my nostrils. Funny thing, though, outlaw or posse, we had to be the worst shootists what ever rode a trail. Didn't none of us fall, nor even get nicked by all that flying lead. But ain't that the way of moving pictures, that they can defy the rules of a bullet?

About an hour into all this riding and shooting, an automobile pulled up to Vanderhoff. The driver got out, while Vanderhoff laid her arm across her camera like she meant to protect it—which might could be, from how this guy looked. I mean, he was a goon, only dressed up swank with a carnation in his buttonhole and two-toned shoes. But the clothes didn't hide his nature none, nor his intention to bully Vanderhoff. But she wasn't susceptible to being mistreated by this goon, her stepping from the camera to square up to him so she could bully him right back. They shouted at each other, but I was too far off to hear much more than fractions of what was said, and most of that profane. Pointing at us riders, he jawed some more, till whatever he said triggered Vanderhoff enough her face got red while her voice—I could hear the shrillness of it—got loud enough to say, "Get your sorry ass off my shoot and tell him to go to fuck off. Go on, tell him that."

Joe said, "Maybe we should go help her out."

One of the other posse guys said to stay out of it, and Albert added, "Vanderhoff can handle it. For now."

It looked as if he was right cause she grabbed the guy by the elbow and pulled him back to his automobile. The goon went along with it, too, him letting her manhandle him that way, though I could tell from his face it sore bothered him to hold back right then. She opened the door for him and then plunked him down in his seat and backed off, putting her hands on her hips and glaring at him while he said something more before he turned the wheel and the automobile rolled out a big circle, his tires kicking up a dust tail, and off he drove.

Joe said, "I wonder what that was all about."

Albert said, the sound of it bitter, "That asshole works for Empire. I've seen him."

Vanderhoff was fuming, and she marched back and forth behind her camera, cussing to herself, I was willing to bet.

Joe broke ranks and rode toward her, with me and Albert following. When she seen us coming, she hollered out, "What the fuck are you gawking at? Get back to where you belong."

"But—" Joe said.

"Go on, get back to where you belong."

The three of us ducked our heads and did just that.

With the sun near gone, while I drove my Ford the last few miles to Sunset Haven, Albert from the back seat piped up, "I bet Dix has something to do with it."

From beside me Joe said, "To do with what?"

"With that asshole from Empire showing up."

"Vanderhoff sure give him what for," I said.

"She's a pistol, right enough," Joe said and laughed.

"Don't nobody push her around."

"I believe she could have took his head off, if push come to shove." Joe and me laughed.

"It ain't funny, and she ain't so strong as that," Albert said, cutting off our humor. "She's just another wage slave with pretensions, like you and me. Sure, she's got her studio, but it only exists because Empire lets it exist. If Empire tells her to jump, she's got to jump."

"Sure didn't sound that way," Joe said.

"Doesn't matter how it sounded. If Dix sent that guy from Empire, she doesn't have any choice, not if she wants to stay in business," Albert said.

I figured all his talk was colored by his parlor-pink tendencies and his grievance with Dix. I didn't give him no credit for accuracy, not being so jaded as he and quick to find fault with a dame as feisty as Vanderhoff. Just goes to show: back then I didn't have no true grasp on how Hollywood's dark and dim machinery works. I only wish I did, cause maybe then I could have stopped Dix before he went too far.

CHAPTER 40

B y now you probly noticed Joe scrubbed and scraped hisself three or four times a day. Even in prison he done this, though I never did understand why, cept to believe Joe had a nose for soap and cologne and Vitalis. Guess he preferred them perfumes to how he smelled in the natural. Or could be, he wore being clean like it was a suit of armor. As if he wasn't going to yield to no dirt nor smudge, what meant he had to stay alert while armed with a cake of Castile and a wash cloth.

And sometimes—in this case the Sunday after a week of working for Vanderhoff—that meant he had to clean the world around him, or leastways my Ford automobile.

After borrowing a hose and bucket and sponge from Mrs. Edward Beneke, he worked an hour to get it gleaming bright. I joined in for the exercise of it, and for a time the two of us was throwing that sponge back and forth like a ball what exploded water in our hands. And we laughed at how good it felt to get soaked in that cold water under a clear hot sun.

But Joe broke from our play to take up a whisk broom and brushed at the floor under the driver's seat. In so doing, he discovered the ball and glove I done stashed there months before. "Where'd you get this?"

I had forgotten about that ball and glove, but since I've made it a habit never to confess to an act of theft, I said, "I found it."

Joe put the glove to his face and sniffed. "Damn, Pooch, I do love the smell of new leather." He tried to put on the glove, but it was too small, so he tossed up the ball instead and snatched it from the air; and as he tossed it up again, Rose Allen's Cadillac turned from the highway and bounced through the weeds.

Joe planted a big smile on his mug, but I frowned, while she drove in a circle and nosed up behind my Ford and shut down her engine. Handing me the ball and glove, Joe went to open her door, saying, "It's good to see you, honey."

The glove fit me just fine, and I tossed up the ball and caught it, smack, in the glove.

She seen me do this, and she seen me toss up that ball and catch it again. I was testing her, I admit as much, but she wasn't playing, she only turning from me and my antics and saying to Joe, "I have to talk to you—alone."

She give me a gander what told me to stay put, and marched into our bungalow with Joe following.

I threw up the ball a few more times, when it jumped away from me and rolled into the weeds. While I chased after it, I seen Albert coming down the hill with his rifle. Earlier, while we had been washing my automobile, we heard him shooting, the cracks of that gun running thin on their way to the ocean. He stopped to wait for the traffic to clear so he could cross the highway. That's when an automobile come up to him. It was one of them long gleaming automobiles from Germany, or so it looked. One of them expensive vehicles built for the rich.

Pushing my way through the weeds, I got close enough, even as I was on the other side of the highway, to see the driver was Dix. He talked to Albert, and Albert raised up his gun; but Dix said something more, and Albert lowered the rifle. Dix laughed, the laugh broad on his kisser, while Albert ducked his head and stepped around that automobile and trotted across the road.

He walked right past as if he couldn't see me and clomped through the weeds. By now Dix had made his turn and glided down the dirt rut what led to Sunset Haven. He seen me, right enough, and even dipped his head in greeting, while he sailed by in his fancy automobile.

I trotted after, seeing him pull up beside Rose Allen's Cadillac, before he got from his automobile and stomped into our bungalow.

Oh, Christ!

I hurried along till I got to the porch and looked in the door, where I seen Rose Allen sitting on our sofa, with Joe sitting aside her, the two of them looking up at Yancey Dix, what was saying, "—can only end one way—badly."

"You're not welcome here, Dix," Joe said.

"I have no intention of staying. I'm only here to for Symphony's sake. To stop her from ruining her career."

"Oh, please," Rose Allen said.

"I don't want her to throw it away like this."

Joe stood up.

Grabbing his arm, Rose Allen said, "Please, Joe—Don't—"

Dix went on, "She's misguided, dazzled, that's what she is, but believe me, Holder, she has no permanent ambitions concerning a future with you."

Joe pulled from Rose Allen. He circled to the right, and Dix did, too, keeping the distance constant between them. I seen both their faces now, and they was staring like guys do when they climb back into the jungle, though Dix smirked and Joe didn't.

Dix said, "Holder, you're a passing fancy. A bit of regrettable history. That's all you'll ever be to this woman."

"No, Yancey, please," Rose Allen said as she stood and got between them, using her body to block Dix from Joe; or maybe it was Joe she was blocking.

Joe said to her back. "Tell him again. Tell him you don't want him around you no more. Tell him again right now."

Dix looked puzzled and asked Rose Allen, "Again? What's he mean?"

Holding her hand up to stop Dix, she turned to Joe and spoke her words like they was stones she was stacking into a wall between Dix and Joe, saying, "I lied to you, Joe. I didn't—I didn't tell him like you wanted."

That set Joe back. He stared at her for a time and then at Dix, but his face couldn't find no reason for why she lied. "But—why would—"

"Joe," Rose Allen said, "it wasn't—I tried to. I did. But I just couldn't. That's why I'm here now—to tell you I couldn't. To tell you—"

"So tell him now. Tell him right here and now. Tell him it's over." His face was angry and wasn't giving her an edge. Nor Dix neither.

Dix stepped to the side, trying to dance his way around Rose Allen, but she grabbed his coat and pulled him to her, saying, her voice urgent with the saying, "No—not like this, Yancey."

He pushed her aside and she fell back onto the sofa. Joe jumped at Dix and shoved him, so that Dix back-pedaled and banged into the wall. A picture of a sunset over the ocean Mrs. Edward Beneke kept there, fell from its hook and clattered to the floor.

Bouncing back up, Rose Allen grabbed Joe and pulled him back, and when Dix came at Joe, doubling up a fist and getting ready to slug it out, she slapped him as brutal a slap as I have ever seen across the mouth.

That froze up everyone, and that slap kept ringing even after the sound of it was gone.

Dix broke down then, his voice a whisper and catching on itself, "Don't do this, Symphony. Don't turn me away."

She stared at him and her face flickered with thoughts what wasn't mine to know, before she looked at Joe and said, "I'm sorry."

"Sorry?" Joe said, stepping toward her, but she held up her hand to stop him and said to Dix, "I can't, Yancey; I just can't."

"Remember Mexico City?" Dix said to her. "Or the beach at Acapulco? What we said to each other."

"I—I don't—"

"I meant what I said."

Rose Allen picked up her hand bag from the sofa and opened its clasp and took out a cigarette case. Both Joe and Dix watched like boys after a fight, the both of them bruised and cowed and not knowing what do, cept to wait to see what choice she'd make—watching as she opened the case and took out a ciggy. Her hands trembled while she tapped it on the case. But she tapped too hard, and the ciggy broke and she dropped it to the floor, saying, "I—I remember. But—I can't—"

Dix straightened hisself and glowered at Joe. "He's not worth it, Symphony. No matter how pretty he is, he's only a thug and a con."

Joe looked at Rose Allen, his face stunned, "You told him? But you said you wouldn't—"

"No—he hired a detective."

"That's right," Dix said. "And he told me a pathetic history of a pathetic man—a strong-arm thug who received three years in Joliet for extortion and assault and mayhem. Why if this got out, the press could ruin her." He said to Rose Allen. "Don't you see that? The public won't forgive you for leaving me to go to a brute who consorted with gangsters and bootleggers and who knows what other bad characters."

Rose Allen said, while she put the ciggy case back in her hand bag, "You better leave, Yancey. I'll talk with you later."

Dix glowered, but I seen his face yield to her. He give Joe another glare what said he was dumping a truck full of bad luck on Joe, and stomped past me, brushing me aside, so I lost the ball I was holding and it rolled off the porch.

Albert stood by the fancy automobile like he was a guard, his rifle at his side. Dix marched right up to him, and when Albert didn't step aside, he snatched the rifle from Albert and slung it away so it clattered in the gravel by Mrs. Edward Beneke's place. Albert made a crow's sound, a squawk from the throat, and run after his gun, while Dix got in his car and motored off, his automobile slicing through them weeds, and his tires screeching when he got to the highway. The engine roared and whined as he shifted the gears.

Stepping from the porch, I picked up the ball, and watched Albert pick up his rifle. He turned it over, his fingers touching at the wood of its stock. After wetting his fingers in his mouth, he rubbed at the wood.

I walked up to him.

He held out the gun to me, showing some scrapes and gouges in the stock. "Look what he did," he said, and shook his head, rubbing again at the grain in that wood. He looked at me now, and his eyes had done deserted him and seemed not to know their obligation no more. He said, "He had no right to do this. Not to me."

He walked off now, taking his deserted eyes with him, headed back across the highway and up the hill again. I figured, from the look of his eyes, he done forgot he had already practiced his shooting. Damn, that didn't sit well with me, to see Albert acting like that. It near scared me, that's what it did.

After I watched him get small on that hill and disappear over its top, Rose Allen come from our bungalow, with Joe following her as far as the porch. When she looked at me, I tossed up the ball again and caught it in the glove. I smiled at her. But she didn't smile back. Instead, she got in her car without no more words for Joe; and as she drove off and passed me, I seen her face was bleak and kind of sad.

I stashed the ball and glove back under the Ford's seat, and after I did this I seen Joe was still standing on the porch and staring at the highway. I went to him and said, "Can we go to Frisco now? See them redwoods?"

He give me a slow eye before saying, "It ain't over, Pooch."

"Sounded like it to me."

"She owes Dix, that's why she couldn't dump him like I wanted."

"Owes him for what?"

"For how he helped her to be an actress. That's why she can't leave him to hang. That's why she has to dump him gradual-like. She doesn't want to hurt him. It wouldn't be right if she did."

He went back into our bungalow, leaving me to consider the sky which wasn't so pretty no more, though this had to be cause of my mood just then. Hunching up, I thought about not hurting Dix and decided Joe was more forgiving than me. Hell, I'd just as soon Dix died some sort of horrible, fiery death. As it turned out, I almost got my wish.

CHAPTER 41

L east that's what the news rags said on their front pages the next
morning. To this day I remember the headline on one of them; the
DAILY TELEGRAM, I think it was—DIX FROM PIX NEARLY NIXED.
Course Joe and me didn't read them till after another day of shooting
with Vanderhoff. Albert actually brought the rags, four of five of them,
to us when it was near dark. He laughed when he told us what they said.
It sounded cruel, that laugh did, but neither Joe nor me said nothing
about it. Instead we read them stories for ourselves, us trading the
papers to read the next one, with Albert sometimes reading aloud a
sentence or two and laughing more, though Joe finally told him to
knock it off. Albert looked hurt at that and threw down the rag he was
reading and stomped out of our bungalow.

I didn't see no reason for his tantrum, and Joe didn't neither. Hell, we
ain't ones to celebrate an accident where some kids got bad hurt, and I
thought I'd tell Albert that the next time I seen him. Joe said it must be
the dago red what was talking for Albert; and I agreed with him,
deciding that stuff could pickle a brain in its skull.

We went back to our reading.

Them rags pretty much reported the same details, almost as if the
same guy writ them all; and them details went like this: Yesterday, at
about one o'clock—that being a half hour after he left our bungalow—
Dix plowed into another automobile on the coast highway south of
here, in a place called San Pedro. Dix claimed it wasn't his fault none
cause he swerved to miss hitting a kid, a boy, chasing after a ball. Now
the automobile he hit, a roadster, had a couple of teenagers in it headed
for a picnic. They wound up with some broken bones, and the girl got
a concussion, but Dix only got some cuts and bruises, what didn't
surprise me none, him being one of them guys what finds luck in the
sorriest places. The coppers investigated and said they couldn't find no
kid chasing a ball, but they'd keep looking. They figured the kid done
got afraid at causing an accident and done scampered off, never to be

found. As for Dix, he told the newshounds he'd pay the doctor bills for the teenagers; and hell, he'd even buy them a new roadster, cause that's what a stand-up guy does. There even was a picture in one paper, I remember, it showing Dix signing the cast on the kid's leg while the kid raised up a thumb to the camera and the girl looked at Dix with these big cow eyes what said she couldn't believe how magical it was to be nearly killed at the hands of such a gorgeous man.

Now I ask you, do you really believe there was a boy chasing a ball? I didn't think so. Could be, he got the idea from me, from what I was doing when he left. What do you think? I think it's so—

In the days after reading about Dix's accident, Albert stayed away from Joe and me. He even took to driving hisself to Thousand Oaks while Joe and me went separate in my Ford. And at work he never hung with us no more, but ate his lunch by hisself, shunning the other guys and even Vanderhoff as much as us. Joe and me worried over this some and tried talking to Albert one night, back at Sunset Haven, but Albert just shut his door on the both of our faces and wouldn't come out when we banged on it. Couldn't neither of us figure why he acted this way, seeming to reject us so sudden-like and without no comment. Hell, he didn't even go to ride the waves on his belly no more like Joe still did, but instead climbed up his hill across the highway and potted away with his rifle. One night I looked from the bluff to see him small up there, standing like a stump with a rifle branching out of it in the dying sun, him painted near red, and Joe come up beside me, dripping with the ocean, a flap of hair swooping across his forehead, and said, "Looks like he's in hell, don't it?"

"Can't figure why he turned from us like he has."

"I don't think he knows why."

"Ain't nothing we can do for him, I suppose."

"Doesn't seem like it."

"Damn," I said, full of some kind of regret what was new to me, regret what made me uneasy.

Joe headed for the bungalow and I decided right then and there to go up that hill and give Albert a piece of my worry for him. So that's what I done, and the whole time I crossed the highway and climbed to him, he didn't move but just got more red as the sun bled out the last of its light.

When I finally got up there, I glared at him and said, "Albert, this ain't right, how you been acting recent."

Albert didn't stop looking into the sun and water, his eyes faded and not willing to see me none. He said, "Leave me be, can't you? Just leave me be."

Now I ain't a guy what appreciates a brush off, so I grabbed both of his arms, planting my mug in his face so he had to see me and I shook him, saying, "Dammit, I'm trying to be a pal."

Albert's eyes rolled over me, and they was lost to seeing this world, them seeing a dark and ghastly place I hope never to see for my own. He said then, "I don't need a pal—not anymore."

He lifted up his gun and stared into the barrel for a time. "I can see the grooves in there." He held the gun for me to see. "See them?"

I didn't bother to look. "C'mon, Albert, let me take you down to bed. You need some shuteye."

Albert nodded slowly. "Yes, I do."

So I stepped off, thinking to lead the way, but after I got a couple steps, I looked back to see him staring into the sun and ocean again. Well, I ask you, what could I do about that but what I done? I ain't a guy what calls on the coppers for any kind of help. That ain't in my nature. Sides, it wouldn't help none, anyway, him getting pinched for being peculiar. So, I left him there. I left him to his dying sun.

The next day Rose Allen showed up.

As for Joe, though he didn't say nothing, I could tell he had been anxious since that Sunday Dix barged in on him and Rose Allen. Every sunset since, he went to the highway to greet her; and as the dark settled permanent on the road, he'd return to our bungalow and, without saying nothing, read them news rags some more about the accident, reading the follow-up stories what got printed in the days after. Some of them quoted Rose Allen, she saying Dix was hard at work completing his masterpiece, *WESTWARD, THE WAGONS*, and not available for more comments on the accident. She also said she was sorry for both them teenagers what nearly got killed by Dix's Daimler, and that she had gone to visit each of them in the hospital. I couldn't see nothing in all this to inspire anxiety, but with Joe reading them stories over and over, that's what he had to be—anxious. Which explains, maybe, why his face, when he finally seen her, beamed. That's the only word I could find to use in this dictionary; it beamed.

The two of us had just climbed the stairs onto the bluff, both of us dripping and smelling of ocean, both of us strong cause our muscles had done been worked hard and throbbed with their certainty. As soon as he seen Rose Allen's Cadillac parked behind my Ford with her standing beside it, he broke into a run and took her into his arms and held her up in the air for a bit before he set her down and kissed her.

I drifted closer, seeing Mrs. Edward Beneke at her window. She nodded at me and kept on gaping at Joe and Rose Allen, who wore a feather on a band around her hair, that feather standing up persistent and pert enough to salute us all. And her face beamed near as much as Joe's.

Seeing me now, she called out, "Hello, Pooch!" like we was old buddies what had stirred the world in days past. I didn't holler back at her, but drifted closer, standing to the side, taking her greeting for an invite to watch them clutch at each other and beam.

But Rose Allen seen Mrs. Edward Beneke by now, and I guess that triggered what she did next, her taking Joe's hand and pulling him into our bungalow, away from a stranger's prying eyes and ears. I shrugged at Mrs. Edward Beneke and walked up to the porch and leaned on the wall, using it to hide me, and listened. This is what I heard—

"I—I left him—"

"My sweet Rose Allen, baby—"

"We had a fight—over you, and over the accident. He won't admit it, but he was driving too fast—driving recklessly, a lawyer told me. It— it was awful—what he could have done to those kids he hit. And he doesn't even seem to care. He thinks he can make it go away. But the kids—the kids have a lawyer. He won't let it go away."

Good, I thought, and Joe thought the same, him saying, "Serves him right, how he acts."

"But Joe—he's done something terrible."

"What did he do?"

"I only just found out. For the past few months Empire has wanted me to star in my own pictures, but Dix stopped them. He insisted I wasn't—ready."

"Why would he do that?"

"Because—under it all—he's afraid."

"Afraid of what?"

"Of getting older. Of losing his place at Empire."

There wasn't no voices for a time, and while I waited I seen Mrs. Edward Beneke in her window looking out at me, or maybe at Rose Allen's Cadillac, before she backed off and sat in a chair in a pool of yellow light and picked up a magazine to read.

Then: "I—I can't forgive him, Joe."

Joe didn't say nothing back, and after a time she said, "I—I moved out. I'm on my own now."

"Where to?"

"I can't tell you, Joe. Not—not yet, anyway."

"Why not?"

"Because I need to be on my own," she said, the sound of this defiant and definite. "I need to be—separate from Dix and from you."

"Oh, babe—"

"I don't mean to hurt you, but I must do this. Please let me do this."

Joe's voice released her, saying, "Of course, honey, you know I will."

"But I want to see a lot of you, you big lug. I want to see you as often as possible."

I couldn't hear more for a time, and I peeped around the edge of the door to see them in a serious lip-lock. I pulled back into my hiding and listened more, till I heard her say, "The premiere for *WESTWARD, THE WAGONS*—will you escort me, Joe?"

"What about Dix?"

"He wouldn't dare make a scene—not in public. Especially after his accident."

"Won't people talk? The reporters and them magazine hot shots?"

"Let them. I—I don't care."

But it sounded like she did.

Joe said, "I don't want to ruin your career none."

"You won't, Joe. I won't let that happen."

"Now you're talking, babe."

"It'll be our first time together on the red carpet, Joe. Our first—but not our last."

Could be, you've read about what happened at that premiere. Don't see how you could have missed it, what with the news rags and magazines telling the story from coast to coast. Hell, it could have got reported in Japan, for all I know, it being that big a story. Still—

I think about them words of hers about the red carpet, and I got to shake my head, even after all these years. Sure, it's ironic; ain't no doubt of that. But it's more. It's, I don't know, dreadful. I suppose, that's the word for it—dreadful. It's dreadful like it must be to wake up in a rescue boat alone in the sea. A rescue boat lost among a crowd of empty rescue boats. Dreadful because the sea is flat and the sky is vacant and without no sign of help, nor of anything but its own dreadful vacancy.

Two days later—Joe and Albert and me riding in a posse after rustlers this time – Vanderhoff stood in the middle of us to tell us what to do for the next shot. That's when an automobile pulled up to the camera and the goon with the carnation in his lapel—a red one this time—and two-toned shoes got out. He give Joe and me and Albert a smirk as he handed Vanderhoff an envelope. She opened it and took out a sheet of typed paper and read it. Then she looked at Joe and Albert and me, and her face was sad and told us she couldn't do nothing about it. She had to give in.

So, she fired us.

CHAPTER 42

I t shouldn't have surprised me, what Albert done next, what with the target practicing he had been doing so recent, but it did. And it surprised Vanderhoff and the posse, too—and even the goon, at first. What he done was draw the pistol from his holster and shoot the goon six times, the barrel of that gun spitting out flashes of orange what got washed away by white smoke. Since there wasn't no bullets in the gun, the goon didn't fall nor shudder with the limits of his mortality. What he done, after his surprise, was grimace, and I figured from that he didn't see no humor in all this.

But most everybody else did. Even Vanderhoff did. We was laughing at the silliness of Albert dressed in cowboy duds shooting a goon what tried to hide his animal self by sporting a red carnation and two-toned shoes like a swell born to silk. Only, it wasn't so sufficient cause the animal what resided in his soul roused up and in so doing killed our laughter, him roaring out and charging at Albert, who had pulled his other pistol by then, and readied to shoot it into the face of this beast coming for him. But before he could get off more than one shot, the goon grabbed the gun from his hand and hit poor Albert on the noggin with it, leaving a smear of blood above his ear. Albert sagged to his knees, and as the goon pulled back his hand to hit him again, Joe stepped up and grabbed that hand.

He and the goon glared into each other before Joe twisted his hand and made him drop the gun.

That goon wasn't smirking no more, but rubbing his wrist and I could see the animal under his skin was twitching, fighting to hold itself in. Joe set hisself there, the whole of him strong and not scared none to face no beast. But the goon righted hisself and pasted on his smirk and looked at Vanderhoff, saying, "I'll be out here every day from now on— to check that you ain't hired back these three miscreants."

Miscreant? That was a peculiar word for a goon to use, but I chalked it up to his pretensions and picked up Albert's gun, thinking I could get off the last five shots just to rub in my miscreant tendencies, good and proper. Which was what I done. I shot him five times in that smirk, daring his animal to come out.

Vanderhoff and the other eggs in the posse didn't laugh this time, even as it was still silly. I guess the appearance of that animal what lurked inside the goon was too ghastly for laughter.

But the animal kept itself reined to heel, though the goon's face showed the struggle it took to do this. When the animal was tight in its place, the goon looked at Joe, his eyes burning a hole into Joe's face, him shifting that look to Albert who was moaning and checking his fingers for blood, before looking at me to say, "Fucking miscreants."

He walked over to his automobile and opened the door and put an arm on it, waiting in this way for me and Joe and Albert to leave.

With me and Joe's help, Albert got to his feet and brushed us off. He give another check for the blood on his fingers then stepped up to Vanderhoff. "So, you're going to let them push you around."

Vanderhoff bowed her head.

"So, you're just another victim, ain't you?"

Vanderhoff raised her head, and she was angry now, saying, "I'm not a victim. I'm a realist, that's that the fuck I am."

Joe looked at all of us and bucked hisself up and said like he was on a stage behind a podium, "There's a war out there—a war between those who have and those who don't. And you sorry saps don't even know that. You don't even know you're losing that war. You don't even know you're nothing but disposable, nothing but—ah, to hell with you."

Albert marched past us, and he marched past the goon, and he got in his automobile and drove off.

The rest of us didn't say nothing till he was lost in the trees down the road, when Vanderhoff did, she saying, "Pooch, Joe, give it a month or two, till those assholes at Empire forget. Then I'll hire you back. Tell Albert that, will you? Just give it a month or two."

Well, I won't say I wasn't disappointed by this turn of event. Truth is, I enjoyed riding the outlaw trail in front of a camera; I enjoyed being on both sides of the law for the game of it. I knew I would miss the action, and I would miss Vanderhoff's profane practicality, she having etched herself in my mind as somebody worth her salt.

I don't know, though, if Joe missed it any, him being preoccupied with the upcoming premiere. Hell, the next day, Rose Allen even showed up and took him shopping to get some elegant duds to wear on the red carpet. He even got his short-brim fedora cleaned and scrubbed fresh. And when he put them on, I had to admit he had a flair for clothes, them hanging easy and natural to his frame. He certain did look like the moving-picture star he planned to become.

And that's what he and Rose Allen spent each day discussing, she offering to do for him what Dix done for her—to make him a star.

I don't know what else I can say about Joe and Rose Allen in them last few days before the premiere, cept that they was tender with each other and quick to laugh. And I suppose, I seen some of what they was as kids back in Missouri when they lived on farms and wasn't complicated with the choices they had made. I seen the joy they took in each other and how that joy was pure and added color to this tired old planet. Why, one afternoon, he took her into the ocean, and the two of them rode the waves, and it near took my breath away to see the sun glisten in their hair and on their flesh, like they was painted glossy and vivid in shades of light. As I seen them like this on the bluff, seeing the ocean stretch broad behind them, and they so genuine in its immensity, I realized they had discovered a new wholeness—or maybe it's the oldest wholeness, the wholeness of Adam and Eve re-invented in an ocean what was as much paradise as the garden where it all started. And even if Rose Allen still refused to tell Joe where she lived, keeping that part of her secret, it didn't seem to matter to Joe, him being happy to have her in these days and nights at Sunset Haven.

Yes, I said nights, and being a gracious fella, I surrendered my bed for Mrs. Edward Beneke's and slept sound enough.

And through all this Dix never returned. Nor did his goons. I kept my eye peeled for sign of them, but they as good as left us be, leaving me mostly to worry. I worried cause Albert hadn't returned, neither.

One night, while in her bed, I asked Mrs. Edward Beneke if she had heard from him, and she said, "I haven't seen Albert in days. He owes me rent. I don't know what to do. What if he doesn't come back?"

"He'll come back," I told her, and to prove it I got from her bed and claimed my wallet from my pants what was hanging on a chair. I dug out two tens and give them to her, figuring Albert could pay me back later. Mrs. Edward Beneke took them tens and folded them narrow and stuck them in a jewel box by her bed. She said then, her saying it in a wisp of a voice, "I won't spend them, Pooch. Even if he doesn't come back, I'll return them to you."

And when I settled beside her again, I felt her fingers, the coldness of them, run over my arm, leaving trails of coldness burning after them. I could tell them fingers was pleading with me to stay in that bed for the nights to come. Though Mrs. Edward Beneke never voiced this request, she didn't have to, it sang from the pores of her skin, it singing of a thirst for love I ain't never had. Cause of this, I mostly ignored this unspoken invitation of hers, and I suppose, that's why she never said the actual words of her heart, cause she knew I would never return to her bed if she did.

And as it happened, this was the last night I ever did sleep beside her.

The next night, the one before the premiere, I slept in my own bed, Rose Allen finally returning to her secret house. But it wasn't five minutes after I switched off the lamp between Joe's bed and mine, settling under my sheets, that Joe switched the lamp back on and went to the closet and opened its door. He stared some at the new clothes hanging in the closet and even separated a shirt from a vest before he took the pants from the hanger and refolded them over the wire.

"Why you doing that?"

"Wrinkles—they can't get wrinkled."

Oh.

He re-hung the pants and took up the shoes and adjusted the trees inside them. I could smell them shoes and the cedar of the trees—the newness of both. I said, "Don't even think about polishing them again. Not at this hour."

Joe grinned at me. "A fella's gotta look sharp at his first premiere, don't he?"

"Shuteye keeps you looking sharp, too."

Joe put down the shoes and shut the closet, shutting it careful, like he was afraid to let the air move around them duds. He got into his bed and I reached for the lamp, but he said, stopping me, "All night, Pooch, since Rose Allen left, I been thinking this better not be a mirage. That's what I been thinking."

I didn't know much about mirages, my knowing of them defined by our drive from Missouri over them desert highways. Didn't matter how far I drove nor how long, I couldn't never catch up to one. I couldn't even get close to one. But Joe had done it; he had caught up to his own mirage, the shining magic of a mirage. Somehow he had defied tricks of the eye and heart, and now he swam in waters of his mirage. Ain't that something? Ain't that a pure wonder?

Damn.

But I ain't a guy what can hold onto to magic for long. Could be, that's why I never caught up to them mirages. Nope, I ain't got the heart for such blind reckoning, not when someone dark and sinister could spoil it all. I'm speaking of a snake called Yancey Dix. So, I said, "What are you going to do about Dix?"

"Not a damn thing."

"He might try to knock you on your ass."

"No, he won't. Not when he's on a red carpet."

"I ain't so certain."

"Well, we'll see, won't we, Pooch?"

And we did, didn't we? We saw it in the movie newsreel what got shot at that premiere. And we saw it in the pictures the news rags had along with the stories what we read the next day and for days after; and we heard about it on our radios. We seen and heard all about that premiere for *WESTWARD, THE WAGONS*, didn't we?

Only, there was more to it than what we seen and heard. And that's what I'm going to tell right now.

CHAPTER 43

When I got to the moving-picture palace, searchlights already stabbed the sky. And there was other lights. Cameras in the hands of newshounds flashed. A newsreel truck parked on the sidewalk had a couple Kliegs on its roof aimed at the red carpet. Each of them fancy automobiles what pulled up to that carpet had head lamps what flared out more light. And the palace itself threw off light, the tower of it glowing gold—with a chandelier set over the door for the actors and such to pass under, a chandelier what had rainbows in it, rainbows what jumped up and disappeared so fast I near thought they wasn't real but another trick of the eye. Like more mirages.

I wormed my way through the crowd. That's one advantage I got over most folks: I can slide into crannies and slivers between bodies and shimmy my way through people what flock together and stink of sweat in the wool of their coats. And on this night, at this premiere, them people didn't pay me much mind, anyhow, being as how they was jumping up or standing on tiptoes to see the stars arrive in them long automobiles what had chauffeurs. Hell, not that I did, but I could have dipped wallets and purses from this crowd without no fear, they was that absorbed and full of bustle.

And they was full of talk too. Loud talk what sounded surprised; or if not that, rude and familiar as if they knew the stars deepest secrets and wasn't obliged to keep them secret no more. Or they sounded like in a church, with them crying out to lesser angels, crying out for a blessing they ain't never had.

"Oh, look," I heard; "it's Doug Cardwell. Gee, I thought he was taller somehow."

Or I heard, "There's Rene Adoree. Ain't she a beaut? A genuine doll—oh, Renee! Over here!"

Or, "That fella there, in the white hat, that's Buck Jones. He ain't so much of an actor, but damn, he sure looks swell on a horse."

Then a guy near me shouted and clapped and brayed out, "Buster—hey, Buster."

A girl, her face slack at the marvel of it, turned and snagged me in her arm, stopping me to say, sounding as if she had just run three miles, "That's Buster Keaton." More shouting had that girl craning near sideways, craning as if to climb on my shoulder, till she said, "It's Louise Brooks. Gosh, look at those freckles." She slid off me to say into my face, "I never knew she had freckles."

But I didn't have no time for freckles, what with breaking free of that skirt only to snake past a fat woman and some other fat ladies beside her, hearing them chatter on about stars I never heard of nor cared to see in the sudden gaps what opened before them.

Moments later, I wormed my way to a place near the steps of the theatre and against the rope meant to hold me back.

On the roof of the newsreel truck was a camera on a tripod, and a cameraman stood behind it cranking out his footage. Past him, across the street, was a white building what advertised furniture. It had three stories. A searchlight was on its roof and every now and then its beam swooped from the sky and poured white light into the crowd, it near blinding me, till it swooped away and left me to see a new automobile arrive. The door opened and out stepped Rooney June in a fancy cowboy get-up. Using his ten-gallon Stetson, he give a gallant wave to the crowd and then stepped aside and held out his arm to usher into the light Minerva Masterson.

The crowd vibrated, I'm telling you it did—and some in it "oohed," and others "awed;" while I said under my breath, "damn."

The reason we done this was simple: we was seeing a genuine American hero. We was seeing Sure-Shot Minnie what rode with Buffalo Bill Cody to entertain the kings and queens of Europe, this before the War to End All Wars when the world still nursed at the teat of incredulity, sucking at the spectacle of a woman what defied custom and could ride and shoot better than most any man. Hell, it was as if she stepped fresh from a poster of that time, she standing taller than usual in hand-tooled leather boots, the red of them a fine contrast beneath the whiteness of her white dress, it fringed and with spangles sown down the sides; and above that a tasseled vest glittered with beadwork and long pearl gloves what had more tassels; and on her head was a wide-brimmed cream hat with a red feather. And cradled in her arms was a rifle. But not just any rifle. No, this one had gold buttons pressed into the stock, them buttons glistening.

And now she and Rooney June, him looking smaller beside her, walked the carpet, and I swear, those closest to me, the fat women in particular, sighed. As she reached the steps, she stopped and frowned, and in the whiteness of her hair, it streaming down her back, I seen more rainbows jump up and disappear. She stepped away from Rooney June, stepping right toward me. "Pooch, what are doing behind that rope?"

The people around me shuffled and backed off a step, while Minerva said, "You should be standing right here, beside me, on this red carpet."

"I ain't dressed for it," I piped up.

"You're decent enough," she said and lifted the rope, but when a copper stepped over to stop me from passing under, she waved him off, so that I stood as she intended, grubby and disgraceful – right beside her. Rooney June grinned at me and shook my hand, and the three of us turned to the crowd, me near blinded in the light what came swooping down from the roof of the building across the street.

And a moment later the next automobile opened its door and out stepped Joe Holder hisself, dressed to the nines and looking swell in his short-brimmed fedora. He handed out Rose Allen, though for all the light and cameras and crowd she was Symphony. Beads was sown into her gloves, them gloves running over her elbows, and as she waved her arms, them gloves shot out more rainbows. So did the beads stuck in her hair, she shooting off rainbows enough to paint the sky with a hundred colors. She took Joe's arm and the two of them strolled along the carpet, Joe wearing a grin what looked to split his face wide open.

When they was close enough Joe hollered out, "How about this, Pooch? Ain't it grand?"

And in that moment, as they neared the steps, it seemed just that. Least it was for him. As grand as the dream he done carried in his heart in all the years since I had known him in Joliet. Only, this wasn't no dream but actual and a fact to be recorded for all time in the flashes of them pictures the newshounds took and in the footage the newsreel camera was shooting.

Now he and Rose Allen mounted the steps and on the last one—

above us now and under the chandelier—they turned and the crowd shouted and shrieked Symphony's name.

And Symphony dropped Joe's arm and stood untouched and complete—like a statue what didn't see nor hear any of this fuss directed at her; like she was alien stone and from another heaven.

And Joe, he gloried in it all.

And as the sound of Symphony's name faded, the last automobile pulled to the curb and out stepped Yancey Dix.

The sound roared up again, and there was whistles and clapping. This was Dix's night, and by god he wasn't going to disappoint nobody, but give them a show to remember, him bowing low before raising his hands to include the sky and moon; and he stood like that while voices rose up to celebrate him.

Now he turned, it a grand turn and full of drama, to ease Astoria—yes, Astoria; and she fair dazzled at the wonder of it—into the flashing lights and sea of sound.

And once she stood, Dix stepped from her, stepping to the edge of the carpet where he shook hands and signed an autograph, with Astoria trailing after, a puppy in his footsteps. When a newshound held up a camera, Dix pulled his puppy alongside him and posed for a flash, only to step from her again and grin at more cameras, him posing by touching the brim of his fedora and keeping his hand there till those cameras flashed.

"What a ham," Minerva muttered in my ear.

She got that right, him carrying on like the king of Japan or some such foolish being. But ham or not, that crowd couldn't get enough of him, it straining at the ropes holding it back, with hands reaching out, grasping at him, till a nervous copper come to Dix's elbow and whispered in his ear; and Dix took Astoria's arm and stepped back. Still, arms and hands reached for him and voices said his name, them voices chanting out, "Yancey, Yancey Dix! Yancey, Yancey Dix!"

After more waving, him cutting a fine figure of a star certain in his triumph, he strutted along the carpet, tiny Astoria lost on his arm, or so it seemed.

When he got to the steps and seen Joe and Symphony, he paused. Ain't that what them stars always do in the flickers? Don't they pause, while the audience gasps? You bet they do.

Now Dix mounted the steps and stuck out his hand to Joe. Only for a second did Joe look fuddled before he took Dix's hand and the two of them shook hands as guys do, shaking firm and without either giving an edge to the other. As if that shake was meant to bury all grudges. It done, Dix took Symphony's hand, and he held it up to the crowd, like the two of them was prizefighters what knocked out the devil hisself.

The crowd shouted out, and that's when it happened. That's when the chandelier over their heads busted and showered down a hard rain of glass.

CHAPTER 44

At first I couldn't make sense of it.

But then one of the fat women shouted out different, shouting out sudden pain, and blood blossomed onto the gray of her coat. She sank, while the other fat women tried to hold up her weight.

Now I heard a crack and a whine as a bullet hit concrete and kicked into the night.

Next a copper on the red carpet grabbed his neck and fell to his knees and gagged before spitting out a ball of blood.

Another shot come, knocking Rooney June's ten-gallon Stetson from his head. Rooney June, unlike the rest of us targets what just stood blinking in all that light, didn't hesitate none but grabbed Astoria and hunched behind her, using her as a shield. As for me, like a damn idiot, I searched the crowd and the buildings across the street but couldn't find who was firing bullets at us.

Three more shots cracked out and an usher near Joe and Symphony groaned and stared in wonder at his arm.

Now there's something you got understand. All this happened in bare seconds, and wasn't none of us on them steps or in that crowd what was ready to do more but gawk, till a woman shrieked. I don't know who nor why, but that shriek broke open the sky, it was that piercing brittle. Mostly like a siren, it was, a siren what stirred the crowd, and it surged on itself, not knowing what direction to take. But most in it was trapped and could only shout to get out of the mass what held them back. Some just ducked and put their hands on their heads, while others looked at the sky, and still others peeled from the edges and started to run off, running while shrieking and screaming.

The coppers wasn't no help, most of them as stunned as the rest of us, though a few took off running down the alley at the side of the building, with guns in their hands. I figured they was looking for a quick way to climb to the roof.

Now all this happened so sudden, we on them steps forgot to move and stood like frozen monkeys, till Dix grabbed Symphony and pulled her down, pulling her into the glass of the chandelier what shone at their feet, while he curled over her, using his own self to protect her from other bullets what come out of black beyond the light.

Searchlights changed their angles and swirled, the light of them crossing and smacking into each other before they settled, aiming themselves across the street at the roof of the white building. And in their beams I seen a guy what stood on the roof, a guy what stood against the black of night with a face too distant to be recognized. A face near hidden while the guy aimed a rifle and fired.

By now coppers fired back, but that didn't stop the guy. Copper bullets chipped into the building and broke windows, and the guy just stood up there in all that white light without ducking or even pretending them bullets coming his way mattered. Course, them coppers only had pistols what don't have the range for high-up shooting, which could be why the guy wasn't scared none. Still, bullets come close to him, kicking at the wall just under his feet. But the guy never broke from his awful mime. That's right; it was a mime, full of the same gestures repeated over and over. But not a mime like Chaplin or Keaton could do, this having no silliness to it—no, this mime was horrible and simple and scary—and it never changed but got stuck in its doing, as if the guy doing it couldn't recall what was supposed to be mimed next and so just did it again. And seeing this mime, seeing him drop one rifle and bend down to take up another to renew his firing, something snagged in my memory and I thought, oh no; oh, Christ, no—

Joe must have seen what I did, and it must have shocked him as much as it did me. I say this cause he knew his duty to a pal, which had to be why he stepped down the stairs and walked down the carpet, him marching straight into the bullets what slapped around him, him marching to the street where people scurried away, bent near double.

Coppers kept shooting at the roof, but people, looking to escape, run into them and tossed them aside, them coppers not authorities no more but caught up in a stampede of scared people what trampled on them.

And still Joe marched down that carpet, marching right at a pal what couldn't hit him, though when he run out of bullets, it took but a moment for him to dip down and come up with a new rifle and start shooting again.

I ran now, running after Joe, me thinking this was no time for him to trust in reason or blind luck, even for a pal. And above, on the roof, I seen Albert's face finally, as he raised up that new rifle to take his aim at Joe. "No!" I yelled at him.

But Albert couldn't hear me, my scream lost in all the other screams.

At the curb now, Joe stopped and stared up at Albert and raised his arms and crossed them. I guess he was signaling Albert, but that signal never got made, cause in that moment, just as I yelled, "He's not—" Dix left unsaid, Albert fired the gun.

And in that same instant, the instant he fired, an instant too late in its recognition, I seen his face cry out a horrified no. As if to call back the bullet he never meant to send Joe's way.

Joe jolted still and stood for raw moments before he turned and looked confused at who I was. He raised his eyes and searched till he seen Rose Allen under Dix's protection, and he reached out a hand for her; reaching, reaching—

Now it wasn't till later when I found out what Minerva did, how she come after me down the carpet to the dead copper and raised up her rifle with the gold buttons, and in that instant Albert shot Joe, she took aim, shooting high, and fired.

Albert straightened and dropped his rifle and teetered, while his face crumpled into itself and wondered at this sudden new pain, until he fell from the roof, falling with the white of that building behind him, to the street. I could hear the wet brutal thunk it made, when he hit cement.

By now I took Joe's hand, the one what reached for Rose Allen, but it wasn't no help. He collapsed and was probly dead before his face smacked into concrete.

Mostly the rest of that night I sat on the curb by Joe. The coppers never bothered me. I guess I was invisible to them. For a time Minerva, fancy rifle propped between us, sat with me and finally said, saying it soft, "I never carry an empty gun."

I said nothing back.

Wasn't long after that the coppers come to ask her to testify or some such thing; and she left and didn't return. Some newshounds come up asking me questions but I told them to fuck off, and they did. After that, Dix and Symphony come up by me and stared at Joe and Albert.

I stood, ready to take on Dix right then and there. But Dix flummoxed me, him saying from a sad face, "I'm damn sorry this had to happen."

And I believed him.

As for Symphony, she didn't cry none. Maybe the grief was too deep in her for tears just then. But she did tremble. She stood there and trembled till even Dix seen her trembling and put an arm over her shoulders and led her off, even as her head turned to watch Joe.

As they walked into the night, a passel of coppers and newshounds surrounded them. I don't know where they went.

In time, after hours, all of the newshounds and the newsreel truck and most of the gawkers had left. So did most of the coppers. Guess they wasn't so interested in the ambulances what arrived. These was new ambulances and not the ones what took away the wounded earlier. These was silent ambulances. The guys in them, the guys in white coats went to each of the dead—there was six of them, Joe and Albert included—and lifted their carcasses on stretchers, and they carried those stretchers to the ambulances and shoved them inside. These ambulances had the same chassis as my Ford touring sedan, only they had tall boxes mounted on the frames, them boxes looking something like two-story coffins.

When they picked up Joe, I walked with them to the ambulance and made sure he got put in there comfortable and secure, and I done the same for Albert. The guys in white coats did what I told them to do. They put a blanket over Joe and another over Albert. So as to keep them warm until morning.

Then them ambulances was gone, none of them screaming into night about their terrible cargo.

After that, a fire truck showed up and a few minutes later, two firemen got a hose spouting out a column of water. They sluiced the blood from the sidewalks, it running into the gutter under my legs and toward a storm drain west of me. Then they sluiced the street itself, sluicing Joe's blood and Albert's blood, till it, that blood, mingled and run under my legs and spilled into the storm drain and headed for the ocean.

CHAPTER 45

The next day I hired a lawyer to get Joe's body and Albert's body released to me. It cost a hundred clams what was jake by me. While he did his lawyer shenanigans, I found a funeral home in Thousand Oaks, knowing Joe and Albert loved riding the outlaw trail in its hills and valleys. And I bought two caskets, both of them polished real warm, like they had tiny suns glowing in the cherry wood they was made from. And I picked out two plots from a cemetery map. But I wouldn't pay for them till I seen those actual plots.

So the funeral guy took me from his office to the cemetery and we walked on a path through graves up a slow-rising hill till we found the plots in the back of the cemetery. Some oak trees squatted off to the side. In the mornings, they'd shade Joe's grave and Albert's grave. And the breezes would cool them in summer. And to the west was a blue smear. It wasn't the ocean, but it looked like it was, and I knew Joe and Albert would appreciate that.

Anyway, we went back to the office and I bought them plots. Then I called the lawyer on the funeral-office phone, with the funeral guy listening, and the lawyer said the coppers was glad to hand over Joe and Albert whenever I wanted. So I give the phone to the funeral guy and the two of them worked out how to get Joe and Albert to the funeral home. After that, he called a minister and we talked of the service, with me saying to keep it simple but classy. I didn't need to hear no sermon, and I know Joe wouldn't want one, neither. Just read something pretty from the bible, I told him. That settled, I didn't let the funeral guy call the news rags. It's customary, he told me, but I wanted to keep this funeral private. That was my duty—to keep it private and not no show for the world to gawk at.

You're probly wondering where I got the dough to pay for their funeral. Well, it come from Minerva. After that night Albert killed Joe, I finally got back to Sunset Haven at dawn, and Minerva showed up an hour later and handed me five hundred smackers, her saying, "This is so we can bury them proper."

I told her I would take care of it.

I don't know why she give me that money. Could be, she was guilty about what she done. Or could be, she just ached like I did and wanted to do something to ease her grief. The reason don't matter none, as long as we buried Joe and Albert proper.

Which was what I done.

The next two days I didn't pay the news rags any attention. A reporter nosed around for a while, but when he couldn't find me, Mrs. Edward Beneke told me he left, giving her a card with a phone number on it for me. I never called him back. Hell, I didn't know anymore than he did, him probly knowing more by now, knowing where Albert got them other rifles what he had on the roof, a fact I didn't know, nor wanted to know. As for the rest, we could never know why Albert mistook Joe for Dix. Maybe it was bad eyesight, or maybe it was how similar they looked in their fedoras, or maybe he seen Dix shielding Rose Allen and figured only Joe would do so a gallant a thing. That's all I could think, and I wasn't sharing that with no reporter. But I never had to cause he never returned.

Not that I'd have seen him if he had. I couldn't, not with me mostly sitting on the beach to stare at where Japan should be. Or I looked for mermaids. But I never did see any.

I suppose you prefer I should ruminate here on the grief of life, but I ain't a guy what searches his heart. I ain't a guy what has a god to turn to. Hell, I don't even got a philosophy to hide behind. All I had was my past with Joe and with Albert.

So, I played it, this history, in my head over and over. It was my way of grieving. I wasn't looking for answers cause I didn't have no questions. And I didn't have no doubts, neither. Back when I started, I told you science and all its facts is a lot of hooey. Same goes for religion. Truth is, I told you at the beginning, we live by our hearts, and these hearts is full of deviances wasn't none of us meant to understand. So, all we can do, is endure.

I did take enough time from my grieving to buy a suit, and on the day of the funeral I put it on, along with a short-brimmed fedora in Joe's honor. I drove early to Thousand Oaks—impatient, I guess.

Only four people showed up in the cemetery's chapel. Two of them was newshounds. I had no idea how they come to know of this funeral, suspecting the funeral guy told them, but I had to give them credit. They lurked in the back and didn't say nothing. I thought it best to leave them alone while they do their sad business. The other two was Minerva and Vanderhoff, me having called them two days before to invite them to sit with me in that chapel.

Which was what we done, sitting on the same bench in front, with me in the middle. The minister, an elderly gent what looked like a vulture—probly cause he was bald and the skin on his face was slipping into his neck—stood at the altar with the flowers I had a boy deliver the day before. He read from the bible and snuck in a bit of a sermon, but I didn't hold that against him. Hell, he meant well by it.

After, the minister leading the way, we trudged on the path up the hill past other graves to where Joe's casket sat by his grave and Albert's by his.

The minister said his words and prayed, though only Minerva prayed with him, Vanderhoff and me staring at each other for a time and then staring at the caskets, waiting until the praying was done. The newshounds wasn't praying, neither, them just standing to the side and scribbling in notebooks.

And then it was over.

The minister shook our hands and took the dough I owed him and left. The newshounds come up and asked us a few questions, but didn't none of us answer them, and they got tired of us and drifted off.

We three just stood and watched while three guys using ropes lowered Joe and Albert's caskets into their graves. And while they did, I said, finally. "She didn't come. I thought she'd be here."

Minerva patted my arm.

I said, "Guess she's busy being Symphony now."

Minerva said, "She's disappeared. Nobody has seen her since the premiere. Not even Dix."

"She should have been here. She owed Joe that much."

Minerva nodded, the knowing of this in her face. She studied me for a moment before I seen her admit to an idea. With that, she opened her purse and took out a notepad and pencil. She writ on the paper and, after, tore out the sheet and handed it to me. "You'll find her there."

I looked to see an address on that paper.

And she said, "When you see her, don't blame her. Please, don't."

"I still got some of your money," I said, getting out my wallet. I handed her forty-three bucks. She give me a curious look, and in that look I seen she knew about my former occupation, so I told her, "I ain't so much a thief as that."

"So it seems," she said and turned to walk back down the path.

But I was some kind of thief cause I didn't give her all of it. I kept the other thirty for me—just so I could get by till I figured what to do next. I don't feel bad about it none, but I can say this—it was the last time I stole from anyone.

You see, I didn't have to steal no more, not after what Vanderhoff did for me.

CHAPTER 46

What she done is; she married me.

Ain't that something? Out of the three of us—Joe and Albert and me—I was the guy what got the girl. Just like in the moving pictures.

This is pretty much how it happened: the night after the funeral she took me to her bed and I ain't been in any other woman's since. The reason she done it was simple. Under her profanity and grit is a gal with a heart shaped for kindness—kindness for an occasional stray animal she nurses to health, and kindness for me what had to be one them strays, I suppose.

I don't know if we love each other. It ain't got the passion to it I thought love was supposed to have. But she's a good woman, and I try to be a good man for her. I really do try. Least we don't argue much, but enjoy each other's company. And maybe that's enough. Maybe that's love, too, though it ain't so loud as Joe's love for Rose Allen.

Anyway, a few months after the funeral, we married and went to Frisco to see the redwoods. I purely did enjoy that honeymoon. Them trees did not disappoint; they was majestic. But that's all they was, just trees what reached up to heaven; reaching, reaching—

And not touching nothing but air.

I didn't see more to them like I expected, so I was glad when we got back to Hollywood. Vanderhoff put me right to work in her next serial, and I been working in them steady since. When sound come into style, Vanderhoff didn't miss a beat, and merged with two other moving-picture companies from Poverty Row, them calling themselves Three-Star Production. They specialize in serials and quickie "B" movies.

And me, I'm one of their salaried actors. On a contract, I am. $450 a week. In these days, what with them soup lines I hear about, that's damn good money. Guess I'm lucky, after all, cause I got a voice for snappy dialogue. I ain't no Cagney, but I get by. Least I ain't no phony but plant myself square and say the words and listen to the other guy before I say my next line. Hell, I've played outlaws and sheriffs and spies and soldiers. Once I was even a Chinaman.

A few years back, me and Vanderhoff bought us a house on the beach in Santa Monica. I like it there. I like watching across the ocean, though I ain't seen no mermaids yet. I like thinking about Japan and them other lands across that water. I read about them Asia places, and someday Vanderhoff and me is going to tour them. I figure Joe would approve.

So there you have it. I got some of what both Joe and Albert hungered after. I got their dreams. And without even trying. Ain't that a hoot, how funny life works?

Well, it's time to finish up Joe's story, ain't it? So, here goes—

A week after the funeral, I got into my Ford touring sedan and went to see Rose Allen. She still hadn't returned from seclusion, or so the news rags reported, but that didn't stop me. I didn't care if it upset her, me knocking on her door. I didn't think of her as Symphony, a figure in private mourning. To me she was just Rose Allen, a dame what should be held to account.

Sure, I know that makes me a hypocrite. I mean, there I was, headed south in my Ford, and while I done so, I judged that dame, me a fella what hates all judges. I convicted her of the cruel crime of not loving Joe back. I know it wasn't fair, but that's how it was, it being one of them anomalies can't nobody explain. Least I can't.

All I wanted to do was tell her of her crime. All I wanted to do was make her suffer in the long nights to come. Suffer for Joe's sake.

As I drove country roads, I come on orchards what run for miles, orchards of orange trees, with the sun pouring gold over them. And I drove past strawberry fields for a time, only to reach more miles of orchard. It looked whole, this place did, and clean. Even the dirt seemed clean. And the trees was planted in rows what ran straight and true, one after the other. I wondered how the growers lined them up like that. Did they have some kind of giant ruler? Did they have to measure things off somehow and use geometry or some such mystery to get them rows so straight and true? Hell, if there ever was a garden for Adam and Eve, this had to be a copy of it.

Then I come to Rose Allen's ranch, it stuck in the middle of its own orchard. I drove up a road past all her trees to a farm house. It wasn't near as big or as fancy as I thought it would be. It was just a farm house—but a fresh-painted one, and well cared for, with a big yard what rambled for near an acre. That yard was fresh mowed, with its flowers and such trimmed recent.

I parked by the mailbox and walked up the walkway what had a scooter on it, one of them wooden kinds made to look like an automobile. The door was open, so I knocked on the screen door and stared through the mesh into a room what didn't look much different from any other farm house. The furniture wasn't no different. How could a moving-picture star live in a place as actual humble as this? I wondered if Minerva had give me the wrong address.

A Mexican gal come to the screen and opened it, but before I could say anything, Rose Allen come from what had to be a kitchen, drying her hands on a towel like she had just been washing dishes. She seen me and stopped herself before she bucked up and said, "Flo, why don't you finish up for me?"

The Mexican gal moved past her, into the kitchen and Rose Allen come to me, her hands still working at the towel, till I knew she wasn't doing this to dry herself but cause she was uncertain of me and what I meant to do. "Minerva said you might come."

"You wasn't there. At the funeral."

She stopped wringing the towel and dropped her hands, looking ashamed, though her eyes didn't drop none, them just watching me and waiting.

"You should have come. Joe deserved that much from you."

A fly come in the door and buzzed past my ear. He tumbled in the space between us. And still Rose didn't say nothing.

When the fly got near, she waved it off with the towel and it wobbled in the air and took off for the kitchen.

I said, "He loved you, Rose Allen. Like no man ever loved a woman, he loved you."

And she said, after the fly came back and buzzed between us more, "When we were kids, in the summer afternoons, the late afternoons, Joe and I, we used to make lemonade together. We'd put in a lot of cracked ice—Joe did that, cracked the ice. He loved his lemonade as cold as it could get. Then we'd go out and pick a couple ears of corn and Joe would build a fire. We'd roast those ears over the fire. That lemonade, the hot corn—I don't think I've ever tasted anything better.

"But that was another time. A dream time, Pooch, and dreams don't last. When Joe left for Chicago, that dream was over. It was time to make a new dream. It's funny, though, since I came to Hollywood, lemonade and corn have never tasted as good."

I took this confession as complete. I couldn't think of what more to say. In her words was a truth can't nobody fix, not even me in my grief. Where Joe held to his dreams and lived by them no matter what, she didn't, she replacing her dreams as circumstance changed. And in that moment I realized, she was no woman meant for one man, but a victim of circumstance. Wasn't no man, not even Joe, much as she could love him, what could stop her from bending to circumstance, and that was the truth.

And I couldn't blame her none, anymore than I can blame my own thieving ways. Hell, she was born to be Symphony, and so—

A boy come from the kitchen now, a boy of six or seven, him walking in the warm dark of the afternoon shadows until he stood at Rose Allen's side and put his hand to her dress.

And in how he stood, with his feet planted like they was, and his hair falling to his forehead like it done, I seen Joe.

"This is Joey," Rose Allen said.

"Hello, Joey."

Joey leaned into his mother.

Rose Allen put a hand to his head and stroked his hair what fell back in place the way Joe's did. "Say hello to Pooch, sweetheart."

Joey raised his head to see me but I guess the looks of me scared him cause he turned and run off, back into the kitchen.

"He's shy, Joey is," she said.

"Not like his father."

"No, not like him."

The fly buzzed between us more.

"I got something for Joey," I said.

I turned and went to my Ford. I got the ball and glove from under the seat and took them to Rose Allen, who stood now on the porch with the towel over her shoulder, watching me.

I handed her the ball and glove and said, "Maybe when things settle down, in a month or so, you can get Minerva to take you the cemetery."

"I'll do that, Pooch. I promise."

"And you can take Joey with you."
"Yes, I will."

So there you have it—my memorial to Joe. He was a damn good egg.

ABOUT THE AUTHOR

California born and bred, Wayne Beauvais in his younger and more hectic years was an actor who fell in love with the movies, particularly those made in Hollywood's heyday. Turning to education—a regular paycheck has its advantages—he taught A.P. English and film studies for more than thirty years. But, still fascinated with the early days of movie making, upon retirement he finally wrote WAIFS OF THE WASTELAND, the first of a series of novels which explores the "flickers" and the people who made them. He is married and lives in Vista, near San Diego. His daughter is also a writer.

13252594R00142

Made in the USA
Lexington, KY
21 January 2012